Praise for Nancy Thayer

## A NANTUCKET CHRISTMAS

"Thayer's Christmas story is as sweet and warm as a fresh-baked cookie . . . heart-twisting moments and a Yuletide miracle will get readers in the holiday mood."

—*RT Book Reviews*

## AN ISLAND CHRISTMAS

"A wonderful contemporary novel with lovable, sweet characters . . . Thayer weaves a magical Christmas story with the description of the island and its history."

—*RT Book Reviews*

*NANTUCKET SISTERS*

"Thayer obviously knows her Nantucket, and the strong sense of place makes this the perfect escapist book for the summer, particularly for fans of Elin Hilderbrand."

—*Booklist*

"Thayer keeps readers on the edge of their seats with her dramatic story spanning the girls' childhood to adulthood. This wonderful beach read packs a punch."

—*Library Journal*

BY NANCY THAYER

*A Very Nantucket Christmas*
*The Guest Cottage*
*An Island Christmas*
*Nantucket Sisters*
*A Nantucket Christmas*
*Island Girls*
*Summer Breeze*
*Heat Wave*
*Beachcombers*
*Summer House*
*Moon Shell Beach*
*The Hot Flash Club Chills Out*
*Hot Flash Holidays*
*The Hot Flash Club Strikes Again*
*The Hot Flash Club*
*Custody*
*Between Husbands and Friends*
*An Act of Love*
*Belonging*
*Family Secrets*
*Everlasting*
*My Dearest Friend*
*Spirit Lost*
*Morning*
*Nell*
*Bodies and Souls*
*Three Women at the Water's Edge*
*Stepping*

# A VERY NANTUCKET CHRISTMAS

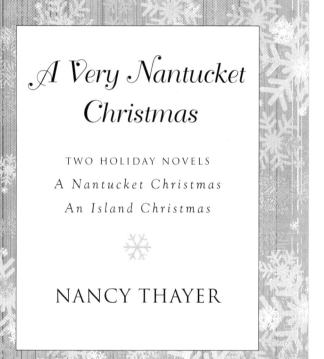

# A Very Nantucket Christmas

TWO HOLIDAY NOVELS

*A Nantucket Christmas*

*An Island Christmas*

## NANCY THAYER

BALLANTINE BOOKS

NEW YORK

2015 Ballantine Books Trade Paperback Edition

Published in the United States by Ballantine Books,
an imprint of Random House, a division of
Penguin Random House LLC, New York.

BALLANTINE and the HOUSE colophon are registered trademarks of
Penguin Random House LLC.

Originally published in hardcover as two separate works
entitled A *Nantucket Christmas* and An *Island Christmas*
in the United States by Ballantine Books, an imprint of
Random House, a division of Penguin Random House LLC,
in 2013 and 2014 respectively.

ISBN 978-1-101-88481-2
eBook ISBN 978-1-101-88514-7

randomhousebooks.com

Book design by Mary A. Wirth
Title-page art: © iStockphoto.com

# A NANTUCKET CHRISTMAS

*For Meg Ruley*

# PROLOGUE

This tale begins, as do many Nantucket tails, with a dog. A Norwich terrier, the runt of the litter—which made him very small indeed—a stubby, sturdy, tan, pint-sized pup with a face like a fox's, ears like a panda's, and the dark passionate eyes of Antonio Banderas.

His name was Snix.

Back in his chubby days, he was adopted by the Collins family visiting from Rhode Island. His plump bumbling made Cota, their teenage daughter, squeal that he was *so cute*. Cota named him Snix because she knew no other dog in the world had ever been named Snix. Cota was at the age when she wanted to be noticed for being the kind of special girl who would have a dog named Snix.

At the beginning of the family's summer vacation, Cota doted on Snix, letting him sleep in her bed, brushing his coarse coat, tickling his fat belly, and taking him for lots of walks up and down Main Street on Nantucket, with Snix tripping fetchingly over his rhinestone leash.

Three months later, Cota was fourteen instead of thirteen. Her hair was two inches longer, her legs were three inches longer, her bosom was three inches fuller, and she didn't need a pet of any kind to get noticed. Meanwhile, Snix had lost his puppy fat and his roly-poly ways. He now wore a mournful and slightly baffled expression, having gone from adored to ignored in three short months.

At the end of the summer, the Collins family did what many vacationers do when they return home from their holiday—they left their adopted pet behind. They drove their black SUV out to the moors in the middle of the island, where dirt roads ranged over low hills and past small ponds, where rabbits, moles, and deer hid in the bushes. They removed Snix's collar, name tag, and leash before Cota opened the door, leaned out, and set the pup on the dry, end-of-summer grass.

"Bye, Snix," the teenager chirped hastily, slamming the door shut.

The family's large black SUV roared off, leaving a cloud of sandy dust floating in the air.

Snix sat with his head cocked, watching. Waiting. Expectant. Then, not so expectant, more hopeful. Then, sad. Snix lay down with his head on his paws, his eyes fixed steadily on the dirt road where his family's car had last been—he could still smell the gas fumes, and Cota's light fragrance.

No other cars passed. It was just after Labor Day. Everyone had left the island. Well, not everyone, of course—twelve thousand people still lived and worked on the island, but none were strolling that hot day on a secluded sandy track through the moors.

September was much like August on the island of Nantucket. The sun beat down on the crackling brown grass and on Snix. Overhead, small planes zipped back and forth, taking people from the island back to the mainland. From time to time a sparrow would tweet and flutter from one tree to another. Snix watched a spider creep across the dirt road and disappear in the bayberry bushes. That was about it for action that afternoon.

Snix was by no means a stupid dog, but he was naturally loyal and he was young and naive. He didn't have the experience even to consider the possibility that the sweet-smelling long-haired girl who hugged him and cuddled him and chucked him under his chinny-chin-chin was never coming back for him.

So he waited. His stomach growled. He got very thirsty. He smelled water, fresh water, nearby, but he didn't want to leave this spot in case the Collins family came back for him. So he lay there, a little brown puppy more gangling than chubby, more dog than baby, more awkward than adorable. He lay there with his head on his paws until the sun set and the world around him turned black and he saw no lights anywhere. He'd never been in a world without lights, and that made him shiver, and that made him whimper, and then he let out such a disconsolate howl that he frightened himself and a few other critters nearby.

He began running very fast down the road, toward the scent of human civilization.

# 1

✳

On Nantucket, the Christmas season is different.

Really.

The island, fifty-two square miles of flat sandy land, lies in windswept isolation almost thirty miles away from the continent and all its institutions and entertainments. In the summer, the sun shines down on golden beaches and a serene blue sea. In the winter, gale force winds lash and howl over the ocean, cutting its residents off from family, friends, and often fresh bread and milk as Nantucket Sound freezes over and no planes fly, no boats sail, to or from the island. When the sun sets early and rises late, deep black water surrounds the land in infinite darkness.

Then Nantucket comes truly alive. Islanders have the leisure to savor the Charles Dickens charm gleaming from the glistening cobblestone streets and historic brick buildings. They relish the coziness of the small town where they know everyone, and everyone's dog. After a hectic summer, they enjoy the tranquil pace. They take time to stop, look, listen, pat the dog, tickle a baby's chin, chat, and laugh. They attend Christmas pageants, holiday fairs, and all manner of cabarets. The town lines the central streets of the village with dozens of small evergreens twinkling with multicolored lights and weatherproof decorations. The islanders pause to gaze up at the forty-foot spruce blazing at the top of Main Street, and they nod in appreciation and gratitude.

They celebrate light, life, and laughter as the winter dark wildness descends.

The Christmas Stroll began as an occasion for merchants to welcome islanders into their shops for hot buttered rum, spiced apple cider, warm gossip, and good cheer. Store windows were artistically decorated with mermaids and Santas, seahorses and fairy-tale scenes. Mr. and Mrs. Santa arrived on a Coast Guard boat and were delivered to the Jared Coffin House by horse and buggy. The aroma of fresh fish chowder and island-brewed beer wafted enticingly from the restaurants. The town crier strode through the streets in tall hat and cape, and Victorian carolers enchanted the salt air with song.

Not surprisingly, and oddly around the same time the one-hour fast ferries started their rounds, news of Nantucket's Christmas Stroll spread to off-island friends and relatives of the townspeople. One sparkling winter day, a Boston television station sent a reporter and cameraman. After that, the annual event was famous.

For children, it was magic. For adults, it was a chance to be childlike.

For Nicole Somerset, the Nantucket Christmas Stroll was close to miraculous.

Four years ago, Nicole was a widow. Her friend Jilly insisted that Nicole travel down from Boston for the weekend to enjoy the Stroll. Nicole came, and fell in love with the charming small town, its festively bedecked windows, its fresh salt air and chiming church bells. She fell in love with a man, as well.

She met Sebastian Somerset at a party. They liked each other a lot, rather quickly, if not immediately, but being older, and possibly wiser, they took time getting to know each other. Nicole was widowed and childless. Sebastian was divorced, with a grown daughter.

Nicole was a nurse. She had just retired at fifty-five, but she missed her patients and colleagues. She missed her work, too. She liked to keep busy. Sebastian, sixty-two, had worked for a Boston law firm. He had also just retired, realizing he'd spent too much of his life working. He wanted to enjoy life.

Slowly, cautiously, they began to date, discovering that *together* they enjoyed life a great deal. Sebastian owned a house on the island, and as the days, weeks, and then months went by, he introduced Nicole to the pleasures the island offered—swimming, sailing, and tennis. In turn, Nicole introduced Sebastian to the delights his first wife had disdained: homemade pie, eaten while watching large-screen television; walking rather than biking through the island moors; stopping to notice the birds and wildflowers rather than jogging to keep his heart rate up; or watching the sun set on the beach rather than attending a cocktail party.

Sebastian's first wife, Katya, was a perfectionist who had kept him on a tight leash and a rigid routine. After a few months of relaxed satisfaction with Nicole, Sebastian worried he would gain weight and develop heart trouble. To his surprise, he gained no weight, and his blood pressure actually dropped. When he asked his doctor about this at his annual check-up, Maury Molson leaned back in his chair and shrewdly raised his hairy eyebrows.

"Sebastian, you've been going through life as if everything is a competition. During this past year, you've stopped to smell the roses, and it's been the best thing you could do for your health."

Sebastian chortled in surprise. "I'm shocked."

"Me, too," Maury told him. "I don't believe I've ever

heard you laugh like that before. And it's true, happiness is the best medicine."

When Sebastian told Nicole about this, she beamed and responded, "You make me happy, too. Although I haven't had my blood pressure checked."

"I wish we could live together for the rest of our lives," Sebastian allowed, looking worried.

"Darling, why can't we?"

Sebastian had furrowed his brow. "I think you should meet my daughter before we go any further."

Sebastian and Katya had a daughter, Kennedy, who was, Sebastian uneasily confessed, emotionally complicated. A carbon copy of her blond, beautiful mother, Kennedy tried to emulate Katya, meaning that she tried to be perfect, still not understanding, after all the years of living with her, that it was so much easier for a woman to be perfect when she focused only on herself.

Because Katya had been a kind but cool mother, Sebastian had, he admitted, cossetted, pampered, and perhaps even spoiled Kennedy a bit. Okay, perhaps a lot. Now married to a perpetually flustered stockbroker named James, Kennedy found herself overwhelmed herself by the responsibilities of grocery shopping, cooking, cleaning, and caring for their son Maddox.

Kennedy was further dismayed by her parents' divorce.

Katya had been thoughtful enough to wait until Kennedy's wedding five years ago to leave Sebastian for her tennis coach, Alonzo. Kennedy couldn't understand why her father, who could always do anything and everything, couldn't win Katya back. When Sebastian had admitted to Kennedy that he didn't *want* Katya back, that he was more contented without her, Kennedy had dissolved into a weeping fit and said she never wanted to see her father again.

Kennedy changed her mind when her baby boy was born. She didn't want her son to grow up without his grandparents, even if they were no longer married. For the past four years, Sebastian's relationship with his daughter had been close and comfortable. Kennedy had even accepted Alonzo's presence in her mother's life, although she told her father it broke her heart every time she saw Katya with that other man.

So naturally, Sebastian worried about telling Kennedy about Nicole.

Sebastian paced the living room of Nicole's Boston apartment as he strategized the first meeting. "I've told Kennedy I've been seeing someone. I'm going to tell her I want to bring you to dinner, to meet her. That should indicate that I'm serious about you."

Nicole had no advice to give. She had not been able to have children. All her nurturing instincts had gone into her nursing profession. She thought Kennedy sounded like a difficult personality, but how bad could she be?

"Tell Kennedy I'd like to bring dessert," Nicole offered.

"Why would you do that?" Sebastian looked genuinely puzzled.

"It's a nice thing to do," Nicole explained gently. She'd begun to see that in Sebastian's former social-climbing world, *niceness* had no place. His life with Katya had been all about ambition. "It will save her from cooking something."

Sebastian thought this over. "I see."

When she stepped into Kennedy's home, it was Nicole who *saw*, and her heart plummeted for the man she'd come to love and for his daughter. Clearly Kennedy had copied her mother's style of décor, best described as "Glacial Chic." Walls, furniture, floors, even wall *art*, were white. The living room coffee table was glass with sharp edges. The dining room chairs and tablecloth were black; the plates white. It was a hot summer evening when she first entered Kennedy's home, and Nicole wished she'd brought a pashmina to ward off the chill.

Kennedy, blond and wire-hanger thin, wore a white sleeveless dress. Her husband, James, wore a starched

white button-down shirt with khakis. Only little Maddox, chubby in his navy blue and white sailor outfit, provided a dash of color.

Everyone shook hands politely, and then Nicole sank
to her knees in front of Maddox.

"Hi, Maddox. I've brought you a present." She held
out a brightly colored gift bag. She'd spent hours considering what to bring for the child, knowing as she did all
the restrictions his mother placed on his life. Maddox was
two then, much too young, Kennedy insisted, to watch
any television. Also, he could not have any candy or anything sweet. Also, he was not to have anything "techno-
logical"—no remote-controlled cars or dump trucks, no
handheld video games.

Wanting to get him something special, Nicole had
bought him a silly-faced, shaggy-haired white goat which,
when a button was pushed, burst into "High on a hill was
a lonely goatherd" and continued singing through the entire song, wagging its head and batting its long black eyelashes.

Maddox clapped his hands and giggled when he saw it.
Kennedy opened her mouth to object, but after a mo-
ment could think of no objection, and managed to say,
"Tell Nicole thank you, Maddox."

"Thank you," Maddox said.

Nicole beamed as she rose to her feet. She had passed the first test. Proudly, she wrapped her arm through Sebastian's arm, giving it a quick smug hug.

"Love-dovey—ick!" Maddox giggled.

Nicole started to pull her arm away.

But Sebastian laughed and with his other arm reached out and pulled his daughter next to him. "Maddox, I like hugs from my women."

Nicole watched emotions flicker over Kennedy's lovely face: surprise at her father's unusual spontaneity; joy at being hugged by her father; consternation at being hugged when her father was with Nicole.

Dinner was a complicated casserole with a French name and a salad of puzzling gourmet lettuce called frisée that felt like sharp bitter hair in Nicole's mouth. Still, she appreciated the trouble Kennedy had gone to.

"This meat is so tender," Nicole complimented Kennedy.

Kennedy actually blushed. "Thank you. It's *daub au poivre*. The meat is marinated with wine and all sorts of herbs. I had to find lard for the recipe. *Lard*. Who uses lard anymore? But I wanted to make it authentic . . ."

She's nervous, Nicole realized, as Kennedy babbled on. Not nervous about Nicole, but about the excellence of her cooking. Kennedy's eyes flitted to her father as she spoke, waiting for him to praise her. Nicole kicked Sebastian in the ankle until he spoke up.

"It's delicious, Kennedy. Never tasted anything better."

Nicole could see Kennedy's shoulders actually relax, dropping a few inches away from her ears. A tender spot blossomed in her heart for the young woman.

But when time came for dessert, Kennedy refused to taste Nicole's deep-dish apple pie.

Putting her hand on her waistline, Kennedy said, "I don't eat desserts. We all know that sugar is bad for us. And I have to watch my weight, like mother does. I don't want to get"—she glanced at Nicole's rounder figure—"pudgy."

Sebastian chuckled around a mouth of delicious pie. "We all gain weight as we grow older, darling."

"Mother hasn't," Kennedy reminded him. "She's got a gorgeous shape and a flat tummy."

She probably doesn't eat *lard*, Nicole wanted to say, but kept her mouth shut.

And that, as far as Nicole was concerned, summed up her relationship with Kennedy. One step forward, one step back.

Nicole and Sebastian married. The January ceremony was attended by only a few intimate friends since they assumed Kennedy would refuse to attend. Katya was bliss-fully redecorating her Boston townhouse and continuing to see Alonzo. Kennedy's husband, James, was doing well with his work, and Maddox was growing out of the tod-dler stage, becoming more manageable. A delicate har-mony existed in Sebastian's inner circle; Nicole and Sebastian did not want to disrupt the peace.

Nicole sold her small apartment and moved to Sebas-tian's Nantucket house to live year-round. She made friends, loved the small town, and began to anticipate the holiday season.

This year Katya and Alonzo were going to a tennis and cleansing spa. That meant that Kennedy, James, and Maddox were coming to the island for Christmas week.

The entire seven-day-long Christmas *week*.

# 2

❄

Why did his parents need another baby? Maddox wondered about this constantly. It was going to be a boy, too,
his mommy had told him. Wasn't Maddox a good enough
boy for his parents?

He tried to be a good boy. He ate his vegetables, even
though they sometimes made him gag. He strained desperately to comprehend the funny squiggles on the page
every day when his mommy tried to teach him to read,
and he had already mastered the art of using the potty.
Most of the time.

But Maddox had seen babies. They couldn't use the
potty at all. So why did his parents want one?

"You'll have someone to play with," his mommy promised. But a kid couldn't play with a *baby*. Babies couldn't
throw a ball. They couldn't even lift their heads.

It was a puzzle.

He'd suggested many times that instead the family

could get a dog. With all his heart, Maddox wanted a dog. He could throw a stick for a dog and play ball with a dog and cuddle in bed with a dog . . . although maybe not. Mommy said they would bring dirt and germs into the house.

Nicole had given Maddox had a stuffed goat and even though Mommy said Nicole was a hag, he loved the animal, which sang—until Mommy removed the battery. Maddox named him Yodel and held him when he went to bed at night, rubbing Yodel's silky tongue between his thumb and finger. It helped him fall asleep.

He knew, of course, that a real goat wouldn't have a satin tongue, and he wouldn't be able to rub the tongue, anyway, that would get drool all over the bed. Anyway, he didn't want a real goat, which was too big. He wanted a small dog, so he could put his arm around it and feel its furry warmth against his body. He would like that.

When he was little, his mommy had held him in her arms a lot. Now that she was all stuffed with the baby, holding Maddox was too hard for her. She didn't have a lap to sit on anymore, and Maddox was always, she said, poking him with his elbows or knees. He tried to be careful, but now Mommy said she was getting breathless since the baby's bum was pushing against her lungs.

"I love you, Maddox, but you're *too much* for Mommy." That's what she said yesterday. He was *too much* when he made a *zoom zoom* noise with his cars. He was *too much* when he wouldn't eat asparagus.

Ugh, asparagus was so gaggy, like a long package of strings that caught in his throat. Maddox shuddered, remembering.

He hoped when they went to Granddad and Nicole's house for Christmas he would get to eat other stuff. Maybe cake or pie. Nicole was nice to Maddox, even if she wasn't a real grandmother. She had sent Maddox his very own Christmas card, and it had a cute puppy on it, sticking out of a Christmas stocking.

"That woman is just trying to make trouble," Maddox's mommy said with a frown when she saw Nicole's card. Maddox didn't understand how a card could cause trouble. He hid it under his mattress so his mommy wouldn't throw it away.

# 3

As they drove home from the firm's Christmas party, Kennedy didn't speak but allowed her frustration to steam out of her body as if she were an overheated pressure cooker, which she was.

"Kennedy," her husband James pleaded. "Talk to me. Did you honestly have such a bad time?"

"I had a *terrible* time. I'm fat, my face is covered with blotches, I can't breathe, and all the secretaries oozed around you with their four-inch heels and cute skimpy dresses, smirking and flaunting their cleavage."

James sighed loudly. "Kennedy, hon. You're almost eight months pregnant. Your hormones are making you crazy. No one flirted with me. Plus, I saw several secretaries and quite a few lawyers stop by to talk to you."

James was right, but that didn't make Kennedy feel any better. "I feel so ugly," she wailed.

"You know you're beautiful," James assured her in a bored tone. He'd been having to say this a lot recently.

Kennedy closed her eyes and let her head fall back against the seat. Why couldn't she be like her mother, who was always perfect?

The last time they had visited her mother, Katya had taken out her photograph albums to show Kennedy what she had looked like during her pregnancy, and of course Katya was glorious and glowing, seeming energetic and fit enough for another set of tennis.

Kennedy looked like Shrek.

Her obstetrician assured Kennedy the expected baby boy was of normal size, but she felt as if she were carrying a full-grown linebacker rigged with shoulderpads and helmet.

"You'll feel better when we're on Nantucket," James said soothingly. "Your father and Nicole will pamper you."

"But I don't like that woman," Kennedy protested.

"You scarcely know Nicole," James reminded her.

Kennedy whimpered. "I want my parents to be together."

James exhaled, losing patience. "That's not going to happen. We've been over this before."

*Fine.* Then Kennedy wanted to be with her mother. But Katya was much too busy playing tennis with her *lover*, Alonzo, and furnishing her new Boston condo. The fact that her mother didn't want Kennedy around made Kennedy hate her father's new wife even more. She knew, somehow, this wasn't logical, but who ever said emotions were logical, especially during pregnancy?

Kennedy glanced over at her husband, seeing his strong profile as the streetlights flashed past. She could tell by the way his jaw was clenched that he was exasperated with her. She couldn't blame him. She might be a pain in his neck, but *she* had pain everywhere! He wanted this second child as much as she did, but she had to do all the heavy lifting. Literally.

James didn't understand the stress of parenting. Choosing the right preschool; keeping her child away from the evils of sugar, fat, and pesticide-spiked protein. Trying to keep the world safe by not buying plastic, while at the same time trying to give her child fun toys to play with. Keeping her four-year-old away from the damages television could inflict on an innocent mind, protecting her son from the sight of monsters, swords, and cannons . . . The list was endless. It was all up to her, because James was so busy supporting the family.

And now it was the Christmas season! Maddox was begging for a puppy, but Kennedy was going to have a baby. How could she cope with puppy poop as well as a new baby?

Sometimes she just wanted to cry and cry.

"Buck up, Kennedy." James clicked the remote that opened their garage door and guided his BMW into its berth. "We're home. You can go to bed."

Right. There was another issue: bed. Bed with James. They hadn't made love in forever. Why *wouldn't* James want to have an affair with one of those sleek young secretaries in those tight-fitting dresses?

Kennedy burst into tears.

# 4

❄

NICOLE'S TO-DO LIST

*Make ten dozen cookies for Stroll.*
*Make Buche du Noel and freeze.*
*Make beef Wellington and freeze.*
*Lose ten pounds.*
*Make gingerbread house; use sugarless candy for*
    *decorations.*
*Find sugarless candy.*
*Christmas tree.*
*Laurel around stair banister?*
*Find freezable breakfast casserole recipes.*
*Start buttock-tightening exercises.*

Early on the morning of the Nantucket Christmas Stroll, glittering crystal sunlight streamed through the mist onto the shops, streets, houses, and harbor, a mirror-like light it seemed you could almost touch with your fingertips.

But then the temperature plummeted and white clouds pillowed the sky, shaking out feather-like snowflakes.

Standing in her Nantucket kitchen, Nicole snapped the Saran Wrap off the roll with such force the sheet flew up in her face.

*Live in the now,* she admonished herself. *Cherish the day.*

*Smell the damned roses.*

She unpeeled the plastic from her nose and carefully covered the last platter of cookies for the library bake sale at the Stroll. She poured herself another cup of coffee, sank into a kitchen chair, and forced herself to appreciate her surroundings.

Honey-warm wide-board floors laid in 1840, a fireplace with a simple Greek Revival mantel, and an antique pine table mingled perfectly with state-of-the-art appliances and slate countertops. It was Nicole's good fortune that Katya chose to keep the Boston house in the divorce and Sebastian decided to live here permanently. The house was a masterpiece—especially, Nicole mused with a satisfied grin, the brand-new bed she'd insisted on having installed in the master bedroom.

Nicole had made other changes in the décor. Though small and inexpensive, they had transformed the house from a museum-like sterility into a welcoming home. She placed plump cushions in jaunty patchwork designs on the chairs around the kitchen table, filled colorful pottery jars with flour, sugar, and other staples to brighten the counter, and hung an oil painting of an oystercatcher by Bobby Frazier on the wall. The comical seabird, with its orange legs and beak, amused anyone who saw it.

Nicole had lightened the rest of the house with similar changes: She'd removed most of the useless antiques sitting around collecting dust—how many brass lanterns, cobbler's lasts, and hard-bottomed old benches did any one house need? She'd added a couple of deeply comfortable chintz-covered armchairs to replace the wooden ladder-back cane-bottomed relics in the living room, plush pillows softened the white sofas, and Claire Murray rugs woven with coastal scenes, Nantucket hydrangeas, or mermaids brought seaside color to the rooms.

Yes, she'd made the house hers. Hers and Sebastian's. And with that thought, her mood flipped into happiness. She picked up the phone and speed-dialed her best friend on the island.

"Jilly," Nicole said, "I've finished the cookies for the Stroll."

"Fab," Jilly said. "Want me to drive over and help you get them to the Atheneum?"

"No, thanks," Nicole said. "Seb can help me tomorrow morning. I'm just calling to vent."

"Vent away," Jilly urged.

"I've got so much to do and I don't think I can accomplish it all," Nicole worried. "Katya was such a Martha Stewart purist. I'm a clodhopper by comparison."

"You're a nurse," Jilly reminded her. "You can save lives. Plus, you've made Sebastian truly happy."

Jilly spoke with authority. She'd known Sebastian when he was married to Katya. She considered Katya lovely but profoundly socially inept. Katya strived to be the best at everything, but her frosty empress façade hid an even frostier heart. Men lusted after her and woman were intimidated by her, but anyone who spent over five minutes with her went away feeling shorter, fatter, and flawed.

"Kennedy phoned Seb last night," Nicole confided. "She says she wants both her mother and her father to be with her during the birth of her second baby."

"When's the due date?"

"January tenth. I know Kennedy hopes her parents will get back together, and what better bonding moment than the birth of their second grandchild?"

"I get the picture. A major family event and you're left out."

"Exactly."

"What can you do?" asked Jilly.

"In reality? Nothing." Nicole looked toward the kitchen window. If today's crisp weather lasted through tomorrow, it would be ideal for the Stroll. "So I should stop obsessing over that and go back to obsessing over Christmas."

"What are you getting Maddox for Christmas?"

"Kennedy insists we buy only wooden toys."

"Oh, please. What does Seb say?"

"Um, let's see: variations on 'don't worry about it' and 'it will be fine.'"

"Perhaps he's right," Jilly said. "After all, this is the season of miracles."

Seb drove Nicole to the library before it opened. He parked on India Street and helped her carry in her platters of cookies decorated like wreaths, trees, snowmen and snowwomen. This allowed him the opportunity to dash down to the used book sale in the basement of the Atheneum a few moments before the crowds arrived.

Nicole stood on the front porch of the library behind a table laden with her cookies, chatting with Jilly, who was manning the hot chocolate urn. Nicole wore her red wool trapeze coat and a red Santa cap with white fake fur trim. Jilly wore a green wool coat, a headband shaped like reindeer antlers, and earrings, one red, one green, fashioned like Christmas tree lights. They flashed off and on.

This was conservative attire for the Stroll, when townspeople and tourists alike descended on Main Street to celebrate the season. Nicole and Jilly served hot chocolate and cookies to elves, polar bears, the puppeteer Joe Vito and his gigantic puppet Grunge, and to the carolers costumed in Victorian garb, with long velvet cloaks, bonnets, and top hats. Posh off-islanders wore fur coats and diamond pins shaped like snowflakes. Even the more staid citizens sported red mittens, green and white striped mufflers, and red wool caps.

At eleven, Seb appeared on the library porch. "Ready?"

"Absolutely. Here comes my replacement." Nicole hugged her friend, took Seb's hand, and they went down the wooden library steps and through the picket fence to the brick sidewalk.

"Which way?" Seb asked.

Nicole linked her hand through her husband's arm. "Let's go see Santa arrive."

They sauntered along, taking it all in, waving at friends. Several of the streets were blocked off for the gathering crowds whose pleasure was reflected back to them by the shining shop windows. Clever wreaths of evergreen or seashells or buoys decorated the doors, and dozens of small Christmas trees twinkled up and down the six major streets of the town. A fiddler strolled through the town playing folk tunes. The town crier strode around in his long black cape, waiting to ring the bell to announce the arrival of Santa.

"Look, Sebastian!" Nicole pointed at a Great Dane in a Santa Claus hat and a cherry-red Rudolph nose.

"Nantucketers love their dogs," Sebastian told her.

Nicole spotted dogs decked out with reindeer ears and red velvet bows, hand-knit sweaters and blinking lights. A corgi wore a jingle bell collar that tinkled as she waddled along. "The dogs seem quite pleased to be in costume," Nicole observed.

The town sheriff, Jim Perelman, waved at Sebastian and Nicole. "The boat's on its way!" he called to them.

Nicole tugged Sebastian's hand. "Hurry."

Straight Wharf was already crowded with families. Daddies held children on their shoulders, older kids worked hard to appear blasé, dogs sniffed the ground in search of dropped cookie crumbs. Everyone looked to the harbor waters, watching for the Coast Guard boat that brought Santa and Mrs. Claus.

"Here it comes," Sebastian told Nicole. He waved. "There's John West, he's the captain."

"The one with the candy-cane-striped muffler?" Nicole asked.

"Right."

The vessel motored steadily through the waves toward the pier, the Coast Guard decked out in red jackets and Santa Claus hats. The American flag with its red and white stripes rippled gaily in the breeze.

The boat docked. The ramp was secured. The crowd applauded as Santa and his wife stepped off the boat and were escorted into a carriage pulled by a handsome black horse. They processed up the cobblestone street toward the historic Jared Coffin House, where Santa would sit children on his knee and listen to their Christmas wishes.

"This certainly puts me in a holiday mood." Nicole squeezed her husband's hand from sheer delight. "Let's stop and listen to the bell ringers."

They paused at the top of Main Street, where a glittering Christmas tree towered in front of the Pacific Bank. The peals of the bells floated like golden bubbles through the frosty air.

"Lunch, I think," Sebastian said, tugging Nicole away from the music.

At 12 Degrees East, they dined on creamy clam chowder and healthy green salads, sipped glasses of sparkling Prosecco, and treated themselves to bread pudding topped with whipped cream.

"I feel a nap coming on," Sebastian confessed.

"I feel the need to shop!" Nicole countered.

"Nicole." Sebastian shook his head fondly. "You mustn't get carried away with this Christmas business."

Nicole swirled milk and sugar into her coffee. "Tell me about your Christmases with Katya."

Sebastian shrugged. "No big deal. When Kennedy was small, we went to either my parents' or Katya's for the holidays. After our parents died and Kennedy was older and more manageable, we took family trips over Christmas. To Fiji, and Paris, and Aruba, that sort of thing."

"Did Katya decorate the house?" Nicole restrained any tone of judgment from her voice.

Sebastian considered her question. "Somewhat. Candles, that sort of thing. She never put up a tree because the needles would fall off, making a mess on the carpet. And after all, the trips were the main event."

Nicole put her hand over Sebastian's. "You know, Gordie and I never had any children. I always loved the Christmas season, but I missed being able to share it with a child. Now that Maddox is coming, I'm eager to get a big tree and do it up right, and buy lots of presents for him. And for the new baby. Maybe something fabulous and sparkly for Kennedy, too, to buoy her up since she's so weighed down with her pregnancy."

As she spoke, Nicole's face brightened. She loved giving gifts.

Sebastian's face lit up, too. "Sweetheart, you're such a dreamer. Sure, let's get a great big evergreen and you can trim the tree to your heart's content." He leaned forward. "What would *you* like for Christmas?"

Less than a year old, their marriage was still new. Nicole blushed. "I have everything I want," she told her husband.

# 5

*※*

On that dreadful September day, Snix had run like a wild thing so fast and so far he'd finally come to the end of the moors. Here on the hilltops, huge mansions overlooked the world around them. Many were in the process of being shut up for the winter and refrigerators were cleaned out, their contents tossed into garbage containers that were easily opened. For a few weeks, Snix sniffed out sufficient food to sustain him.

Wandering this way, he found himself approaching the main cluster of population, where houses gathered closely together along winding lanes. As the days went by and the leaves turned colors and drifted down, some of these houses emptied out also. Still, many houses were lived in. Snix could tell by the smells. Some dogs even possessed homes, great massive structures with yards where entry was forbidden by their urinary territorial postings. He avoided those places.

He could usually find a comfortable wicker chair on a back porch to sleep in for the night. He searched the center of the town for food, hitting the jackpot where the ferries and boats docked. There, the trash barrels were always full.

The trees grew bare. The temperature fell. The lights disappeared from summer homes. Hunger didn't hurt him as much as loneliness. No one petted him, no one held him, no one even ever said hello. He trotted along the streets of town like a ghost dog, unrecognized, unapproached. After a while, he noticed that all the other dogs kept their owners on a leash, and Snix didn't blame them. If he had someone who loved him, he'd want to be permanently connected, too.

During the days, as he hunted through the town for something, anything, to eat, he couldn't help catching sight of what he was pretty sure was himself in the shop windows. He was scrawny, with ribs curving beneath tangled matted hair. It was embarrassing.

No wonder the girl had left him behind.

It encouraged him slightly when locals began to put up lights all over their houses and the town lined the streets with fragrant green trees covered in small glittering bulbs. Frigid air blew over the island, but more visitors kept arriving, gabbing away with their hands clutching hot cups of coffee, munching heavenly-scented sweet rolls, dropping the occasional crumb that Snix tried to get to after the people walked away, before the seagulls swooped in.

He was surviving. It was worse when the blowing rain or snow began. Back porches provided little shelter, so he huddled, shivering, inside bushes or beneath cars. In the daylight, what little there was of it, he ran through the streets, searching for food and a warmer spot.

He was so lonely.

# 6

"Know what, Mommy?" Kennedy grumbled. "I hate this season."

"I never liked it, either," Katya sympathized.

"It's such a *bother*." Kennedy was reclining on her mother's living room sofa, visiting for the afternoon. Alonzo had taken Maddox down to the condo's gym to play, which almost made Kennedy like the man, even if her mother had run off with him. Kennedy could still hope with all her heart that her mother would come to her senses and return to her father.

"All the awful parties," Katya agreed. "It's so hard not to gain weight."

Kennedy cast a skeptical eye at her mother, who hadn't gained an ounce after her twenty-fifth birthday.

Katya had learned to slenderize her body and her life before it became all the rage. She always chose modern furniture with sleek, clean lines. She hated clutter. She disdained "collectibles." Her clothing, too, was classic. No ruffles, no lace, no faux anything. White shirts and khakis in the summer, white cashmere turtleneck sweaters and khakis in the winter. Black dresses for evening wear. Real pearls. Costume jewelry—ugh. Only real, large—but not vulgar—diamond solitaires for her ears. Her blond hair was always cut to fall just to her chin, sweeping from a side part.

"How do you stay so skinny?" Kennedy asked.

"Exercise and willpower," Katya told her. "Your weight has to be your first priority in life. It's extremely hard work. I'll admit I've suffered at times."

"But it's worth it, right, Mom? I mean, just look at you."

Katya preened. "Thank you, darling."

"I'll lose weight after I have the baby."

"Of course you will."

Kennedy made a face. "But we've got to go to Dad's next Sunday for the whole *week*!"

"It will be fine," Katya assured her daughter. "Come on. This way, Nicole has to do all the fussing about Christmas. She'll do all the cooking and cleaning. You won't have to do a thing. Sebastian will take care of Maddox. He and James can go off and do manly things. You'll be able to rest."

"I hope so, because you know Nicole is going to fill

Maddox with candy and icing. He'll be a hyperactive monkey boy."

"What are you getting Nicole for Christmas?" Katya sipped from her mug of unsweetened green tea and settled more comfortably into her chrome and leather chair.

Kennedy shrugged. "I have no idea. I've only met her once. I don't know what that woman likes."

"Get her some chocolates." Katya leered wickedly over the top of her mug.

Kennedy giggled. "You are bad." Nicole wasn't fat, exactly, but she didn't have Katya's lean, lithe lines.

"Why?" Katya widened her eyes innocently. "All women like chocolates."

Kennedy snorted. "Nicole obviously does."

"Don't be mean, Kennedy. My sources tell me Nicole is a very nice woman, and your father seems satisfied enough with her."

"Oh, Mommy!" Kennedy struggled to sit up. "Why'd you have to leave Daddy?"

"Darling, we've been over this before. Your father and I were boring together. You are grown and married. It was right for me to have some ME in my life."

Kennedy flopped back against the pillows. "By ME, you mean Alonzo. Sex."

Katya rolled her eyes and directed the subject back to the holidays. "So. You can order chocolates for Nicole online. Go Godiva, that's always easy and best. Send her the biggest box. They'll gift wrap it. *Done.* For your father, go online and order a few of the newest biographies. You know all the man does is read." Katya yawned. "SO boring."

"Mommy." Kennedy didn't like her parents criticizing each other.

"What did you get James?"

"Nothing yet." Kennedy poked her enormous belly. "Maybe I'll order him a life-size blow-up doll he can have sex with."

Katya ignored this. "Does he need a new golf bag? Tennis whites?"

"For Christmas? In New England? We can't go anywhere, may I remind you, because this baby boy is coming in January. So, no Florida, no Aruba, just snow."

"Now let's be positive. How about cross-country skis for James and for Maddox? They can go out together."

"That's a good idea. I've ordered a sled from L.L. Bean for Maddox." Kennedy gazed around the living room. No tree, no pines on the fireplace mantel, no presents. "What are you doing for Christmas?"

"I told you, Kennedy. Where is your mind these days? Alonzo and I are going to a cleansing spa in Switzerland for ten days. No fats, no alcohol, no sugar. Lots of exercise and fresh air. Indoor tennis, of course."

"You told me you were going to a spa, but you didn't say Switzerland!" Kennedy sat up, alarmed. "Mommy, what about the baby?"

"Kennedy, he's not due until the middle of January. I'll be back on December thirtieth. Plenty of time."

"You've got to be!" Kennedy ran her hands over her belly. "I need you there, and Daddy and James."

"We'll do our best."

"I know you will. Still—"

"Ssh. It's going to be fine." Katya glanced at her watch. "I've got my yoga class in about thirty minutes . . ."

"I know. I should get Maddox home for his dinner, anyway." Kennedy pushed her arms back, trying to extract herself from the sofa.

Katya watched her daughter with an assessing eye. "I promised to give you money for a nanny."

"I know, Mommy, and I'm grateful. But I want to bond with the new baby, even if he is a boy."

"It's a shame about that. Girls' clothes are so much cuter. But never mind, Kennedy, it will be fun for Maddox to have a brother to play with."

Kennedy had achieved a standing position. "I wish James would take a week's vacation and spend it with me and the new baby, and especially with Maddox. It would be wonderful for Maddox to have his father give him special attention when we have a new baby."

"James has an important job with his brokerage firm, Kennedy. You're being far too idealistic with this bonding mumbo-jumbo. Get a nanny, let her care for the baby, and *you* spend time with Maddox. I had a nanny for you, and you turned out all right."

Kennedy lumbered across the room and into the hall. She pressed the intercom and told Alonzo that he should bring Maddox up.

"Maddox wants a puppy," she said over her shoulder to her mother. "I told him no. I can't deal with a puppy and a new baby. Plus, I'm allergic to animals."

"Are you, darling? I never knew that."

Kennedy stared at her mother. "I thought that was why we never had a pet."

"Oh? I must have forgotten." Katya opened the closet door and took out Maddox's little black dress coat and wool cap. She handed them to Kennedy. "I'm sure you're right."

# 7

❄

It was the middle of December. Nicole wore a blue roll-neck cotton pullover with a large white snowflake in the center. She'd opened her holiday jewelry box and selected snowflake earrings to match. They'd cost less than five dollars and were iridescent—she could still remember how pleased she was to discover them at a local pharmacy. She looked pretty cute, even if she did say so herself. Kennedy, of course, would consider her sweater sappy. But Kennedy wasn't here yet.

And today they were going to buy the tree!

They bundled up in puffy down coats and leather gloves and drove out of town to Moors End Farm on Polpis Road.

Snow wasn't falling, but the wind blew fiercely, and overhead the sky hung low and white, as if ready to drop its load of flakes at any moment. Sebastian squeezed the car between two others. He and Nicole slammed their car doors and leaned into the wind, battling toward the trees propped against wooden supports.

Nicole headed toward the tallest trees. After a moment, she noticed Sebastian was no longer beside her. He'd stalked over to the area with the midget trees.

"Sebastian!" she called. "Over here!"

Sebastian waved to her, indicating that she should come over to where he stood.

"No!" Nicole called. "Tall!" She raised her arms high and wide. "BIG!"

Sebastian hurried over to her, looking worried. "Nicole, we don't have the decorations or the lights for such a large tree."

Nicole wriggled cheekily. "*I* do. I brought a couple of boxes when I moved here. Plus, we can buy more lights in a flash!"

Sebastian chuckled at her weak joke. "I'm afraid I'm not much help with all this tree business."

"You'll be all the help I need when you carry it into the house," Nicole assured him.

A burly sales clerk in a red-checked flannel jacket and a fuzzy green hat appeared.

"What about this one?" he suggested, pulling out an eight-foot-tall tree and shaking it so its branches fell away a bit from their tightly twined position.

"Look, Seb, it's *flawless*." Nicole clapped her hands in

delight. She'd never seen such a sublime evergreen. "It's shaped like an A. Each side is bushy, so we won't have to tuck one bad side in a corner to hide it."

Sebastian glanced fondly at his wife, who was practically levitating in her pleasure. "Okay," he surrendered. "This tree."

At the small shed where they paid, Nicole bought a wreath for the front door, too. A *tasteful* wreath with a large red bow and nothing else, no small decorations, no candy canes, no pine cones dusted with faux snow, which she would have preferred. This was her private concession to Sebastian's decorous (lackluster) tastes. While he and Katya had never had a Christmas tree in the house, Nicole couldn't imagine Christmas without one.

With the lumberjack's help, Sebastian easily hefted the tree to the top of his SUV and fastened it with rope and bungee cords.

Getting it into the house was a different matter entirely. The tree was heavy. Sebastian removed the cords and wrestled it to the ground, but once he'd gotten his hands on the trunk, he had trouble lifting it and for a moment stumbled around the car as if dancing with a clumsy drunk in a green fir coat.

Nicole stifled a giggle. "Let me take the top to guide it in." She stuck her hands in between the branches, grabbed the slender trunk, and together they carried it into the living room. They dropped it on the floor, then wrestled it into the stand Nicole had placed in readiness.

Sebastian stood back, staring at the tree. "It's awfully big."

"I know," Nicole agreed smugly. She cocked her head, studying her husband. "Tell you what. If you'll help me put the lights on, I'll do the rest of the decorating."

His posture relaxed. "That's a deal. I was hoping to meet the guys for lunch at Downyflake."

After they strung the lights on the evergreen, Sebastian walked into town to meet his friends. Nicole brought out her beloved old ornaments, set them on the floor, and evaluated them. She was in a new stage of her life, this was the biggest tree she'd ever had, and she wanted it to be the most glorious. She hurried into her car and drove to Marine Home Center.

In the housewares section of the shop, "White Christmas" played softly over the sound system. Christmas baubles filled the shelves, each more adorable than the other. Mothers with children knelt down to discuss which miniature crèche scene to purchase for their houses. Honestly, the ornaments became cleverer every year, Nicole thought, in a frenzy of confusion over how to limit herself to just a few choices. Penguins on ice skates, red-nosed reindeer, trains with wheels like red and white peppermint candy, airplanes with Snoopy waving and his red scarf flying backward, snowflakes, grinning camels, tiny dolls in white velvet coats with red berries in their hair . . . Oh, Nicole *loved* this season!

She bought lots of decorations, and if she thought she might be going just a wee bit overboard, she remembered Maddox. What fun it would be to have a child in the house for Christmas!

Back home, she listened to a holiday CD while she hung the ornaments. As she worked, she discovered she needed to rearrange the furniture, to push the sofas and chairs away from the tall, bushy tree. Standing back, she wondered if it wasn't just a bit overwhelming. Had she made a mistake? Misjudged? Was the tree too big? Was she just a hopeless cornball with no sense of restraint and elegance?

She resisted hanging one last candy cane, plugged in the small multi-colored lights, and collapsed on the sofa to review her handiwork. It was quite an amazing sight, she thought, bright, joyful, playful . . . absentmindedly she chewed on the end of the candy cane. Oh! She was hungry! She'd worked right through lunch. No wonder she had misgivings about the tree. Her blood sugar was low.

Or was the tree *too much*? Would Sebastian's heart sink when he saw it, would he realize with horror that the woman he married lacked all sense of refinement? Nicole worriedly crunched the candy cane.

"I'm home!" Sebastian's voice boomed out as he came in the door, bringing a blast of cold winter air with him.

Nicole glanced up nervously. "Did you have a nice lunch?"

Sebastian strode across the room, pulled her to her feet, and kissed her soundly.

"My," she sighed. "What's that for?"

"That's for the tree," Sebastian told her. "You should come out and see it from the street. It's great. I've never seen anything like it."

She laughed with pleasure. "It's not too big for this room?"

He studied it. "It's big. It's so big it reminds me of the trees my parents used to put up when I was a little boy." His face softened. "So long ago."

"Oh, you've still got a bit of little boy in you," Nicole teased him, nuzzling his neck.

Sebastian grinned. "Don't you mean big boy?" he joked.

"Why, Sebastian." She hugged him, turning her head sideways to gaze at the tree, feeling warm and loved and smug and absolutely brimming with holiday spirit.

# 8

❄

The ferry from Hyannis to Nantucket was like a game of bump-'em cars Maddox once had been on at a friend's birthday party. The big boat raised up, then smashed down, and waves slammed into the giant boat's hull, making it shudder. Maddox thought it was *awesome*.

His mommy didn't like it much, though. She lay on a bench, wrapped in her coat, hands clutching her belly.

"Let's go up top, Mad Man," James said, taking his son by the hand.

This was awesome, too. Maddox rarely got alone time with his daddy, who was always working. Maddox felt secure with his tiny hand tucked inside Daddy's large warm hand. They went up the stairs, taking care because of the heaving boat, and stood by the high windows looking out at the water. His daddy lifted him up into his arms so Maddox could see better, and Maddox inhaled deeply of his daddy's masculine scent, his aftershave lotion, his wool sweater, his cotton turtleneck. Maddox wrapped one arm around his father's neck and leaned against him slightly, so he could feel the raspy skin on his face.

"Maybe we'll see a whale out here," his daddy said.

"How do they stay warm?" Maddox asked.

James explained, "The animals and fish that live in the water have different bodies from human beings. They can breathe in the water, and they never get cold. But they can't breathe in the air like we do, and our air is much too dry for them."

Maddox marveled at this thought. He gazed out into the waves, which were dark blue, crested with frothy white, rolling relentlessly toward the boat to crash into the sides, making the boat shiver and the waves explode into fizzy silver suds.

He tightened his hold on his father. The world was so big, and this view of it on such a cold December day made him feel very small. In preschool, he'd seen a picture book depicting Santa Claus traveling to an island in his sleigh. The sleigh was drawn by porpoises, seals, walruses, and whales, and it skipped over the top of the waves while Santa held the reins.

The book had made Maddox uneasy. Santa was supposed to fly through the air. Maddox had seen pictures of the sleigh in other books. What did Santa do with the reindeer when he used the porpoises? And if he crossed the water with the sea creatures, what happened when he got to the island? If what his father said was right, porpoises couldn't breathe on dry land, so how did Santa get up to the chimneys of the houses? It was hard to understand how the world worked, especially on an island.

A funny *yip* interrupted Maddox's thoughts. Looking down, he saw a yellow puppy tugging the laces of his daddy's sneakers.

A lady with gray hair and earrings shaped like Christmas trees rushed over. "I'm so sorry," she apologized pleasantly. She picked up the puppy and held him in her arms. "This is Chips," she told Maddox and his father. Holding the puppy's paw, she waved it in a hello gesture. "We're taking Chips to give to our granddaughter for Christmas." Seeing Maddox's face, she asked, "Would you like to pet him?"

Maddox nodded solemnly.

"I'll put him on the floor. You can play with him. Be careful, he bites, well, not actually *bites*, he nibbles, he's got his baby teeth, and he's only two months old. He doesn't mean to hurt."

James set Maddox down on the floor next to the puppy. Maddox held out his hand. Chips licked it and wriggled all over. Maddox patted the puppy, then scratched behind his ears. Chips turned circles and flopped over onto his back, exposing his fat white belly. Maddox rubbed it and Chips wiggled in ecstasy, kicking his hind legs as if he were riding a bike. Maddox giggled.

"Here." The lady handed Maddox a short rope. "He loves to tug."

The second Maddox took the rope, Chips snatched the other end in his sharp white puppy teeth and yanked so hard he pulled it right out of Maddox's hand.

"Hey!" Maddox yelled, reaching out to capture the rope, but Chips ran away. Giggling, Maddox chased after him. They went only a few steps when Chips tripped on his own feet and somersaulted head over heels, never once letting go of the rope. But Maddox caught up with him and clutched the rope, and the boy and the puppy began to tug. It was so much fun. Maddox laughed and laughed. The puppy let go of the rope and actually jumped onto Maddox, who was on his knees. Chips sort of latched onto Maddox with his puppy paws and began licking Maddox's face all over, as if Maddox tasted delicious. Maddox fell over on his back, delirious with happiness as the puppy's wet pink tongue slurped his eyelids, his cheeks, and once right up his nose!

"Maddox, darling? Why are you on the floor?" His mommy stood at the top of the stairs, clutching the railing, pale and anxious. "Are you all right?"

The older lady quickly bent down and lifted Chips off Maddox. "Hello," she said to Kennedy. "I'm sorry, I was just letting Chips play with the child. I'm afraid I'm rather boring for the poor puppy."

His mommy smiled. "That's so kind of you. Maddox would love to have a puppy. I'm just not sure I could deal with one now . . ." She put her hand on her belly.

The older lady nodded her head. "Wiser to take your time. You can always get a puppy later."

Maddox glanced back and forth between the older woman and his mommy, who seemed to be communicating without saying all the words.

James hefted Maddox into his arms. "Look," he said, pointing. "We're almost there. I see the lighthouse. Soon we'll be nice and warm, and Nicole will serve us a delicious meal."

"Goodbye," the woman said, waving Chips's paw.

Maddox's daddy said, "Kennedy, let me help you go back down the stairs. You shouldn't have climbed them by yourself, not with the boat rocking so much."

Supporting Maddox with one arm, and Maddox's mommy with the other, his strong daddy carefully escorted them down the steps to the main cabin. They were almost on the island!

# 9

✳

Kennedy was so blissed-out she was miserable.

After their arrival yesterday afternoon, her father had helped James carry in the bags. To Kennedy's surprise, the room at the back of the house behind the kitchen had been transformed into a bedroom. This way, Nicole had pointed out, Kennedy wouldn't have to climb the stairs. The room had been called the birthing room when the house was built back in the eighteen hundreds, because it was near the kitchen and easy to keep warm. When her parents were married, this room was the TV room.

Kennedy had worried that Maddox would be afraid to be on the second floor, so far away from his parents, but Nicole had decorated the spare bedroom in a spaceship theme, with posters of rockets and a bedspread printed with comets. All around the ceiling, small stickers of stars, planets, and meteors glowed gently in the dark. A bookshelf held building blocks, children's books, and tractors, dump trucks, and fire engines. Maddox loved it. He immediately called it *his* room.

Last night, Nicole had served a delicious meal, even though the calorie count was over the moon. Pork loin with apples and onions, roasted squash risotto, broccolini, beets with orange sauce, and fresh, homemade, whole wheat bread with butter. She'd bought the kind of veggie burgers Kennedy had requested and cooked those for Maddox, who ate all of them, as well as his broccolini and beets.

This morning, Nicole and Kennedy's father had taken Maddox out for breakfast in town, allowing Kennedy and James to sleep late and spend time alone in bed snuggling, something they had been unable to do for months.

*Then*, because the day was sunny and surprisingly mild, her father and Nicole had suggested having a picnic way out on Great Point, where Maddox could see the lighthouse and the big fat seals who lounged about on the shore, grunting, lolling, and snorting.

The last thing Kennedy wanted to do was to be bounced around in a four-wheel-drive vehicle along a sandy beach path. Her lower back was twinging with such force she felt like a grunting seal herself.

When she begged off going, to her utter amazement, Nicole had cooed, "Of course you should stay home. Why don't you settle on the sofa? I'll have your father build you a nice fire. I've got a stack of magazines and light reading you might enjoy. Go on, put your feet up. Get comfy."

Kennedy had lowered her bulk onto the sofa and raised her heavy feet up to a pillow. Instant ecstasy. Before she left, Nicole brought in a tray. On it were a plate of sandwiches, a bowl of carrots and red pepper strips, and to Kennedy's childish delight, a selection of homemade Christmas cookies. Gingerbread men and women with white icing faces. Irresistible sugar cookies with snowy icing covered with multicolored sprinkles shaped like reindeer, wreaths, and angels. Finally—in a white pot decorated with green holly and red berries—there was steaming, rich, milky, homemade hot chocolate to pour into a matching mug.

Kennedy's father, James, and Maddox were hefting a picnic basket, several wool blankets, and a couple of thermoses out to the Jeep Grand Cherokee.

"Bye, Mommy," Maddox called.

Nicole came back into the living room, wearing jeans, a green Christmas sweater with a snowman on it, and hiking boots. "All set?" In her hands she held a red and green plaid down blanket trimmed in satin. "I'll just tuck this in around you." She fluttered the cover over Kennedy's legs and nudged it in around Kennedy's feet. She scooted the coffee table close, just within Kennedy's reach. "Anything else?"

"This is great," Kennedy admitted grudgingly. "Thank you."

"Bye, then. See you in a few hours." Nicole fluttered her fingers and left.

A few hours? A few hours alone in the house with cookies, hot chocolate, and peace and quiet? Kennedy almost wept with relief.

Although . . . something about being tucked in with a blanket unsettled her, brought up memories from the far distant past that filled her with a melancholy longing. Now she was the one who made sure her child was covered with a blanket, but there had been times, she could almost remember, like reaching out through a fog, when her own mother had fluttered a blanket down over her.

Katya hadn't ever cared much for the messiness of motherhood. She'd always had babysitters, or nannies, and of course, housekeepers. Kennedy's father was always working. From an early age, Kennedy was encouraged to be a good girl, a "big girl"—meaning no fussing, no running, no whining.

Kennedy worried that she wasn't a natural mother. She never felt the rush of exultation when Maddox was born that she'd read other mothers had. True, she'd had an epidural, which Katya had advised her to have, in order to avoid the pain of labor and birth that, Katya said, would savage Kennedy. Even with an epidural, Kennedy was shattered for days, which stretched into weeks and months. When Maddox was about seven months old, he started sleeping all night, and after that Kennedy very nearly felt like a normal human being. But when he started crawling and toddling, her fears for him, the need for constant vigilance, the shrieks he sent out when he fell, wiped her out all over again.

She loved him more than her life. He was her joy, her angel, her darling boy. After he was a bit more steady, she and Maddox had entered a kind of honeymoon period, when they had such fun together. He was her darling pal.

It was during that spell when she submitted to James's desire for another child. She had prayed for a girl, but the ultrasound tech said it was another boy. Kennedy tried to be content with that. Certainly it made James feel manly, as if every cell in his body was masculine.

This pregnancy had been as difficult as the first. Morning sickness came early and lasted for months, spiraling nausea through her system day and night. Even though she scarcely ate, the baby grew inside her as if her umbilical cord were an enormous beanstalk attached to a giant. She was uncomfortable, awkward, blotchy, waddly, and incontinent. *Cranky*.

Now she had this dreadful week to get through with

her father and his new gushy wife. Nicole had never had children, she probably had no idea of the difficulties of keeping a four-year-old boy amused and under control. Kennedy was terrified that Nicole would feed Maddox so much sugar he'd never sleep. Plus, the environment Nicole had provided—the huge tree, the toy crèche, the stockings hanging from the mantel—they would overstimulate her already active son, causing him to spin out of control.

Kennedy wanted to go home. She wanted this Christmas fuss to be over and done with. She wanted Maddox back in preschool and her days quiet and calm, so she could sleep and rest up for the coming baby.

Although, Kennedy admitted to herself as she poured a cup of hot chocolate and nibbled a sugar cookie, this wasn't so bad. Pretty nice, actually.

So, fine. Nicole was obviously doing her best. That didn't mean that Kennedy had to like her or be glad that her father had gone and *married* her.

Why couldn't her father understand that women had midlife crises just like men? Obviously, Katya had been bored with her husband of thirty years and had just needed some excitement. Perhaps Katya was beginning to feel—not *old*, Katya would never be old—but less alluring than usual. After all, Katya's daughter was grown up and married now, and Katya had become a *grandmother* with its connotations of gray hair in a bun and flapping upper arms. Kennedy totally *knew* her mother had run off with Alonzo to prove to herself that she was still desirable. Instead of divorcing Katya, Kennedy's father should have gone after her, wooed her, and won her back. He still could, if he hadn't married that damned Nicole.

What was so great about Nicole, anyway, that Sebastian had to marry her? She was pretty, but not beautiful like Katya, and she was, okay, not fat, but definitely plump. She wasn't classy, couldn't play tennis or sail, didn't know any of Sebastian's friends. Why couldn't Kennedy's father just have had a frivolous fling with her and then gotten back together with Katya?

Maybe he still could.

Maybe this week could illuminate for Sebastian how awful it was to be without his beautiful, sophisticated, silky ex-wife.

Maybe Kennedy could demonstrate to her father how hard it was for her to be in this house, her mother's house really, with Nicole the Interloper, and Sebastian would be overcome with guilt for marrying Nicole, and divorce her and remarry Katya!

This would take some cunning on Kennedy's part.

Kennedy ate another gingerbread cookie. She finished

her mug of hot chocolate. She reached for a magazine, relaxed back against the cushions, and read about the loves of Hollywood celebrities and pregnancies of princesses until her eyes drifted closed and a soft slumber possessed her.

# 10

❅

Nicole sat in the backseat with Maddox during the long bumpy ride out to Great Point. Seb's Jeep Grand Cherokee easily churned through the deep sand, tossing the passengers up and down, which made Maddox shriek with glee. The day was full of wind and surf and clouds blowing over the sun, sending a glancing, dancing brilliant light across the beach and into their eyes.

Sebastian stopped the Jeep near the lighthouse. Only a few yards away, scores of harbor seals lounged on the sand.

Maddox giggled as they stepped out onto the beach. "I want to pet one," he told his daddy.

"Darling, they bite," Nicole warned. "You can't go near them. They're wild creatures."

They strolled the beach, picking up shells, staying far away from the winter waves crashing on the shore. Nearby, a clan of the larger horsehead seals bobbed in the water like a gang of curious wet gorillas. James lifted Maddox up on his shoulders so the boy could see a fishing boat anchored in the distance, among the white-capped waves.

"I'm hungry!" Maddox declared.

"Then let's eat," Nicole replied easily.

Sitting on a picnic blanket, they munched lunch while watching the seals, who muttered and oinked like sea pigs. At one point, two seals got into a snorting argument, a comic scene that made everyone laugh.

After lunch, they walked through the dunes up to the sixty-foot-high, whitewashed stone lighthouse. They returned to the Jeep and bumped back down the sand to the area called Coskata, where to Maddox's great delight, they spotted a snowy owl, pristine white and immensely arrogant, seated on a scrub oak. They tromped through a wooded glade to find Nicole's favorite tree, an ancient beech with arms stretching out like elephants' trunks. It was perfect for climbing, so Maddox scrambled up onto one of the lower branches, and Sebastian took his photo. They continued on the narrow path until they arrived at a pond where a white heron stalked among the marshy grasses. Maddox helped Nicole fill a bucket with mussels they picked from the shoreline and they scampered about on a fallen tree trunk. Sebastian led them to a midden, a gathering of broken shells left from a long-ago Native American tribe. He told Maddox about how the early

Americans had lived here, eating fish and berries, drinking water from the ponds, covered with goose grease in the summer to protect them from mosquito bites. Maddox's eyes went wide with amazement.

In the late afternoon, when the sun was beginning to set, Sebastian steered the SUV off the sand and onto the paved road leading back to town. He yawned. Beside him, in the passenger seat, James yawned. In the backseat, both Nicole and Maddox caught the contagious reflex and yawned so hard they squeaked.

"Close your eyes," Nicole urged Maddox. "Take a nap."

The boy didn't need to be invited twice. He sagged into his rented car seat and was immediately asleep.

So much fresh air and exercise. Nicole leaned her head back against the seat and closed her own eyes, congratulating herself for having prepared a casserole for their dinner tonight. She'd steam the mussels for a first course with melted butter, but that would take only a few minutes. She hoped Kennedy had had a restful day and would be pleased by Nicole's efforts.

Sebastian brought the Jeep to a stop by the two air pumps stationed by the side of the road just past the Trustees of Reservations cabin. He took the tire pressure gauge out of the glove compartment. Air had to be let out of the tires for easy driving on the sand, and Maddox had been fascinated by the way his grandfather made the air hiss out by pressing a rock on the valve stem. Nicole wasn't surprised when Maddox sprang awake from his light doze.

"Want to help me put the air back in?" Sebastian asked his grandson.

Maddox eagerly unfastened his seat belt and jumped out of the car. James filled the tires on the right side, Sebastian and Maddox took the ones on the left. Then they buckled up and drove away toward town.

Back at the house, Nicole was delighted to discover Kennedy with rosy cheeks and bright eyes.

"Thank you, Daddy." Kennedy waddled up to Sebastian and gave him a hug. "I had the best rest I've had in weeks."

Nicole waited for Kennedy to thank her, too. Instead, Kennedy squatted down, bracing herself with one hand on a wall, to hug Maddox.

"Did you have fun, honey-bunny?"

"Mommy, I saw seals! And a rabbit! And an owl! And I put air in a tire!" Maddox was almost stammering with excitement.

"Tell me all about it in the bath," Kennedy suggested. She held out a hand and her husband hoisted her to her feet. "I'll take Maddox up for a nice long bath. You guys can enjoy drinks before dinner."

With her son yammering away, Kennedy slowly went up the stairs.

Nicole carried the bucket of mussels into the kitchen, trying not to mind that Kennedy had not even bothered to say hello to her. She set the bucket in the sink, washed her hands, and went into the living room to gather up the plate of cookies and the hot chocolate. The cookies, she noticed, had disappeared. The magazines were scattered over the floor. The blanket was balled up, hanging half over the arm of the sofa. Crumbs littered the sofa and the carpet, as well as a used napkin and a few used tissues.

At the sight of the tissues wadded up on the floor, Nicole sat down with a sigh and took a moment to compose herself.

*Really?* she thought. Did Kennedy expect Nicole not only to provide all the meals and snacks, but also to pick up after her like a servant? True, Kennedy was bulky with her pregnancy, but she was standing up when they arrived home. Surely Kennedy could have carried her used tissues into the waste basket in the bathroom. Sebastian had told Nicole what a neat freak Katya was, and Nicole was certain Katya had passed along her tidiness to Kennedy, so this clutter Kennedy had left was more than a mess—it was a message.

*I don't like you, and I never will.* Was that the point of the lumpy tissues, the strewn magazines? What on earth had Nicole done to warrant such animosity? She knew Kennedy wanted her parents to get back together, but Kennedy was not demented, she had to realize her mother had been hooked up with the gorgeous Alonzo for years.

Nicole gathered up the magazines and patted them into a neat pile on the coffee table. With thumb and forefinger, she pinched up the used tissues and napkin and dropped them on the tray next to the empty cookie plate, mug, and pot. Nicole was slow to anger, but she was on her way now. She took a moment to feast her eyes on the Christmas tree, trying to absorb its gleaming serenity into her mood.

She had never had children, but she believed that if Kennedy were her child, she would confront her. She would scold her. At the least, she would force Kennedy to recognize her existence and her attempts to make this a pleasant holiday for everyone.

Sebastian stuck his head into the room. "James and I are going to have a drink. Could I fix you one?"

Nicole relaxed her gritted teeth. "A glass of red wine would be excellent right now," she replied. Perhaps that would calm her down, put her back in the Christmas spirit, and prevent her from doing or saying something she would later regret.

# 11

❄

Maddox woke early, as he always did. He played with the cool toys in his room as quietly as he could, because his mommy needed her sleep for the baby. He looked at the picture books. He stood at the window staring out at Granddad's backyard. It was kind of interesting, with its toolshed and wooden picnic table and benches. If he tipped over the benches, and maybe if he could find a big cardboard box, he could make a fort like his friend Jeremy had. Cool!

He trotted out of his room, down the stairs, through the hall to the kitchen and the mudroom with the back door.

"Going somewhere, sport?" Granddad sat at the kitchen table with a cup of coffee and a newspaper.

Nicole was at the other end of the table, drinking coffee and making a list on a pad of paper. They were both wearing pajamas, robes, and furry slippers.

Maddox requested, politely, "May I please play in the backyard?"

"I don't see why not," Granddad answered.

"Hang on," said Nicole. "You need to get dressed first, Maddox. You'll freeze in your pajamas. Have you been to the bathroom yet?"

Maddox slumped. He'd thought Nicole was different, but she was just like the other adults, full of rules.

Nicole rose from the table and held out her hand. "Let me help you get dressed. I'll pick out your warmest pants."

Maddox stared at the door to the room where his mommy and daddy slept.

"We won't wake your parents," Nicole whispered. "We'll be quiet as two little mice."

She was as good as her word. She tiptoed with Maddox up the stairs. They didn't speak as she helped him dress and use the bathroom. They went like pirates back down the stairs, and no one woke up.

In the kitchen, Nicole asked, "Want some breakfast before you go outside, Maddox?"

"No, thank you. I want to make a fort out of the picnic table and benches." He thought he might as well just come out with the truth in case they didn't like that sort of thing, their yard getting all messed up.

Nicole surprised him. "Good idea. We've got some folding lawn chairs in the shed that will make a good doorway on the ends. I'll get them out for you after I get dressed."

Maddox eyed her skeptically. He wasn't sure about those lawn chairs. He wasn't sure he wanted his idea tampered with.

"Boots," Nicole said. "Coat, cap, and mittens." She retrieved the items from the hooks in the mudroom and put them on Maddox, a cumbersome process he hated. He was never cold and the extra padding made it harder to move. But he allowed himself to be yanked, tugged, and zipped, because he understood the adults were right.

Finally, Nicole unlocked the back door. Maddox stepped onto the back porch.

"Stay in the backyard, now, Maddox," Nicole warned. "Don't go away, promise?"

"I promise."

The back porch was like a room without walls. It had a swing hanging from the ceiling, and a wicker sofa and two wicker armchairs. The wide steps going down had railings on each side. Maddox hung on to them as he went, his slightly-too-big boots hampering him, making him clumsy.

The backyard was bordered by a fence and also by hedges with stubborn green-brown leaves hanging on to the brown twiggy branches. He could see where flowers had been in the summer, because the beds were edged

with shells. A white birdbath stood at the other end of
the yard. He ran through the brown grass to check—it
had water in it, and a black feather. He picked out the
feather and put it in his pocket. Returning to the flower
beds bordering the lawn, he spent some time checking
out the shells. Most were white, with pale purple streaks
on the inside. Some had tips sharp enough to cut, others
were rolled up like burritos. Here and there green or blue
sea glass twinkled, edges smoothed to satin by the ocean
waves.

A hawthorn tree grew at the end of the garden. It had
a few red berries left. Nicole told him the birds liked the
berries, so he liked the tree, even though its thorns made
it impossible to climb.

It *was* cold out. He looked up and up, at the sky. It was
white, heavy, and damp-looking, like a wet pillow. Maybe
it would snow. He hoped so. His mommy said he'd seen
snow before, but he couldn't remember. If it did snow, his
fort would be a perfect place to keep warm, so he stomped
over to the picnic table and benches.

It took him a few tries to wrestle the bench over so it
was lying on its side, legs sticking out, the long flat seat
side acting like a wall. He stomped around to the other
side and struggled to tip the other bench over. Finally he
succeeded. He went to one end of the table and crawled
under.

It wasn't much of a fort. The seats of the benches didn't come all the way up to the table top, so a long space was exposed on each side. The dry grass was crackly. He sat for a moment, considering what kind of fort it should be. Pirate? Spaceship? Indian?

A door opened. Nicole stepped out onto the porch, wearing a navy blue sweater with ice-skating penguins slipping and twirling all over it. The sweater made him laugh.

"Penguins don't ice-skate!" he called.

Nicole came down the steps. "Oh, I wouldn't be so sure." She headed toward the shed at the back of the garden and yanked the door open. "Let's see what we've got for you."

Maddox raced over to peer inside the dark enclosure. Reaching up, Nicole pulled a chain, and a light came on, a single bulb hanging from the ceiling. The building was wonderful, with a slate floor, high work benches along two walls, shelves along the third, and yard implements leaning on the fourth. He saw rakes, a lawn mower, shovels, saws. Coiled onto a special rack was a green garden hose. Pots, paint cans, and other containers sat on the shelves. Above them, outlined in white chalk, were the tools: hammers, pliers, wrenches, screwdrivers. He wanted to get them down and *do* something.

Nicole said, "Look, here: the folding lawn chairs I told

you about. See?" Picking up an aluminum chair with
webbed seat and back, she opened it, and turned it sideways, to display how it could be used as a wall.

Maddox nodded. "Cool."

"Shall we take them out?"

Maddox nodded again.

Nicole hoisted two chairs, one under each arm. Maddox took a third chair, which was surprisingly lightweight,
holding it as well as he could in front of him, following
Nicole back to the picnic table. Returning to the shed,
Nicole reached up to lift a couple of fat vinyl cushions
from a shelf.

"These might be good as seats in your fort," she told
him.

Maddox grinned. "Oh, yeah."

She tossed him one and carried two out herself. She
dropped them outside the fort, seeming to understand
how private the enterprise was to him. He wanted to arrange things himself, even if it took him time and struggle.

Back in the shed, Nicole stood with her hands on her
hips and scanned the walls. "Let's see. What else?" Cock-
ing her head, she suggested, "What about these?"

She handed him a pair of field glasses. Puzzled, he
turned them around in his hands. Nicole knelt down and

demonstrated how to use them. She helped him turn the round knob until the view went clear.

Maddox was speechless. This was the most excellent fort toy he had ever seen. He raced away, binoculars in hand, ready to enter his fantasy world.

# 12

❄

Nicole returned to the kitchen, shivering slightly. She'd gone out to the shed without a coat or hat and the day was frosty.

Sebastian rose from the table. "I'll get shaved and dressed and bring in more firewood." He smacked a kiss on her lips.

Nicole poured her second cup of coffee and stood at the window, keeping an eye on Maddox as he dragged a floral cushion from the shed to his fort. Hearing a shuffling noise, she turned to see Kennedy coming into the kitchen, wrapped in a puffy pink robe that couldn't quite close over her belly.

"Good morning, Kennedy," Nicole said brightly.

Kennedy collapsed in a chair. "I hope you've got bacon and eggs for breakfast. I'm starved."

Nicole stared. She counted to ten. She recalled her years on the wards as a nurse, when patients were too ill to be polite, unable to do more than mumble. Kennedy was only pregnant, not sick, but still, this was a state Nicole had never endured, so she decided to be kind.

"I'll be glad to make you some, Kennedy," Nicole offered.

Kennedy buried her face in her hands.

Alarmed, Nicole came closer to the table. "Kennedy, do you feel all right?"

Kennedy didn't raise her head. "I told you. I'm hungry."

Without another word, Nicole set about microwaving bacon and scrambling eggs. She shaved slivers of cheddar into the eggs and added a pinch of basil. She squeezed oranges and set a fresh glass of juice in front of Kennedy. She placed a napkin and utensils near Kennedy's place.

She had to admit, Kennedy had stamina. Nicole could never sit in steaming silence while another woman cooked for her.

Gosh. Maybe Kennedy was truly ill. Worry spurted into Nicole's chest.

"Good morning, gorgeous!" James came out of the guest bedroom, smelling of soap and aftershave. "Morning, Nicole."

"Hi, James. Would you like some eggs and bacon? I'm fixing some for Kennedy."

To Nicole's delighted surprise, James gave her a quick

one-armed hug. "The answer is yes." He poured himself a cup of coffee. "Where's Wonder Boy?"

"Look out the window."

"Ha! A fort! I remember building one like that as a boy. Is it okay with you that he's creating havoc in your yard?"

"Of course. He's having fun."

"Where's Sebastian?" asked James.

"Right here." Sebastian came into the kitchen, fully dressed. "Hi, James. Hey, Kabey." He used his old pet name for his daughter.

Kennedy lifted a beaming face to her father. "Hi, Daddy."

"How do you feel?"

"Like a wheelbarrow full of potatoes," Kennedy told her father.

"You don't look it," Sebastian lied, sitting down next to her.

Nicole placed the plate of eggs and bacon in front of Kennedy.

Kennedy stared ruefully down at the food. "Mommy always used to serve such *healthy* meals," she said mournfully. "Fruit for breakfast, with granola and raisins and dried cranberries."

Nicole stood very still. Her mind raced. Why was Kennedy so obviously setting her up? Kennedy had asked for bacon and eggs, and now that she had them, she wanted fruit and granola? Food was not the issue here, clearly. Nicole would not rise to the bait.

Forcing a smile, Nicole asked, "Kennedy, would you prefer fruit and granola? We have both."

"I don't want to be any trouble," Kennedy pouted.

"No trouble at all," Nicole purred. Reaching out, she moved the plate of bacon and eggs from Kennedy's spot to James's. "Here, James, why don't you have these?"

"Great, thanks." James picked up his knife and fork.

Smoothly but quickly, like Martha Stewart on ice skates, Nicole took out a bowl, a box of granola, and a spoon. She set them before Kennedy. She poured skim milk into a pitcher and set it next to the bowl.

Plucking a banana from the fruit bowl in the middle of the table, Nicole extended it to Kennedy. "Would you like to slice this onto your granola?" *Round one to me*, Nicole thought.

Kennedy nearly quivered with stifled indignation. Her eyes slid over to her husband, happily stuffing the rich creamy eggs into his mouth.

"Oh," Kennedy bleated, pressing her belly. "I feel so awful."

"Maybe you should go lie down," Sebastian suggested.

"Try to eat a little," Nicole urged in honeyed tones. "Your blood sugar is low in the morning."

With a heavy sigh, Kennedy poured the milk, sliced the banana, and ate the granola.

"Feel better?" Nicole inquired sweetly.

Kennedy ignored her. "Daddy, would you take me shopping like you did when I was young?"

"Sure, honey, but I don't think there are any maternity shops on the island."

"I don't need maternity clothes, silly daddy," Kennedy laughed. "I'm thinking some nice winter boots, maybe a purse . . . and I can always use jewelry, of course."

"Kennedy, you little minx," James teased, "why don't you wait and see what you get for Christmas?"

"Because I want to be with my daddy," Kennedy cooed.

"Get some clothes on, princess," Sebastian said. "I'll take you wherever you want to go."

Kennedy threw her arms around Sebastian. "Oh, thank you, Daddy. And will you take me out to lunch, too? Just you and me?"

Sebastian gave his winsome daughter a doting glance. "Of course. Where do you want to eat?"

"Oh, I don't care," Kennedy told him. "Any place where the food is hot and plentiful." Clumsily, she rose from her chair and shuffled into her bedroom to dress.

In a low voice, Sebastian asked James, "Do you mind that I'm going off for a private lunch with Kennedy?"

"Are you kidding? This will give me a chance to spend some time alone with Maddox. Besides," James winked, "I'm kind of *persona non grata* with Kennedy right now."

"You are? Why?"

"Because she's pregnant and I'm not."

The two men shared a conspiratorial chuckle.

Nicole busied herself at the sink, forcing back a gulp of self-pity. Everyone in the house had intimate knowledge of pregnancy and birth. James had, and was sharing it with Kennedy. Sebastian had shared it with Katya. Nicole had never been pregnant. As a nurse, she'd seen babies come into the world, but she'd never had her own.

"Thanks, Nicole." James brought his empty plate and silverware to the sink. "That was a treat."

His friendliness flashed over her like warmth. He headed through the mudroom to the back door. "Maddox!" he called. "Hey, Mad Man! Guess what?"

Nicole watched out the window as James squatted down to peer inside the fort. A moment later, Sebastian's arms circled her waist. His breath stirred her hair.

"You don't mind, do you?" he whispered. "I think Kennedy will be more receptive to you once she sees you haven't come between us."

"Of course I don't mind," Nicole lied. She wanted to burst into tears. She wanted to stamp her food like a child, crying, *Everyone's leaving me out!* Turning in his arms, she snuggled against him, soaking in the steadiness of his love.

"Daddy, I'm ready!" Kennedy entered the kitchen, chic in her camel-hair coat and tasseled wool hat.

"I'll get my coat," Sebastian said, going into the front hall.

"I'll go out back and tell Maddox and James goodbye," Kennedy said. "Meet you outside."

Kennedy walked right past Nicole and out the door without saying a word, as if Nicole didn't even exist.

# 13

Kennedy linked her arm through her father's as they strolled down India Street toward town. Her heart swelled with triumph. A light snow was just beginning to fall, its flakes as white and soft as down, making the day even more magical.

"I love being here with you, Daddy." She leaned her head against his arm for a moment.

"I'm glad, Kabey."

"Let's look at the windows on Main Street," Kennedy suggested. "The merchants are always so clever." She was subtly steering her father toward lower Main Street and the Jewel of the Isle. Truly, she deserved a diamond for Christmas, and she knew she wasn't getting one from James because she'd had a secret shuffle through his desk and discovered he was giving her a new Mercedes SUV. Nice, but of course he was being more practical than romantic. He wanted his precious children to ride in safety.

"Oh." Kennedy gripped her father's arm. "Stop a minute."

Concerned, Sebastian inquired, "Are you having a contraction?"

"Yes. Don't worry. They're just Braxton Hicks. I went into the hospital three times with Maddox, thinking I was starting labor."

The Nantucket Pharmacy had an ice-skating scene in the window. Fluffy white fleece surrounded a pond made from an oval mirror. Elves, Santa, and a couple of reindeer pirouetted over the shimmering "ice." Snow people made of cotton balls with candy eyes, noses, and mouths stood next to Christmas trees adorned with tiny blinking lights. Mrs. Santa bent over an open box of chocolates, as if deciding which to choose first.

"Cute," Sebastian said.

"Adorable. Lucky Mrs. Santa. She can eat all the chocolate she wants."

"Why can't you?" her father asked.

"Daddy! I'm already a whale." Kennedy tugged on his arm. "I'm okay now. Let's walk some more."

A fabulous Icelandic sweater in the window of Peach Tree's caught her eye, but she bypassed it, determined to get her diamond.

"Shall we walk down to Straight Wharf and buy a few

wooden toys for Maddox at the Toy Boat?" Sebastian suggested.

Her father was heading them in the perfect direction.
She squeezed his arm. "Good idea."

In the small fisherman's cottage housing the Toy Boat,
Sebastian strode around gleefully, seeming like a kid himself. "Lighthouses, ferries, sailboats—so much to choose
from. What do you think, Kennedy?"

Kennedy started to warn her father not to spoil Maddox, but bit her tongue. What she thought was that she
wanted her father to spoil *her*. Why did children get all
the goodies? The mommies did all the work. Sure, James
had Maddox today, but most days of the year, her husband
escaped their chaotic house wearing suit and tie, heading
to the sophisticated adult world while Kennedy wrestled
Maddox into the car for preschool then returned to the
grocery shopping, laundry, and dishes.

She could understand now why her mother had em-
ployed a live-in nanny. Kennedy did have several good
babysitters, and a cleaning service that came in twice a
week. The laundry did James's shirts. They ate out or
brought in takeout several times a week, especially since
this second pregnancy. Compared to many others, she
was spoiled, but she certainly didn't *feel* spoiled.

Kennedy loved Maddox with all her heart. He was the

light of her life. But nothing had prepared her for the noise, the mess, the constant, relentless neediness of a child.

Thank goodness Maddox enjoyed the preschool he attended in the morning. In the afternoon she tried to coax him into napping, but he was a living typhoon. In a month, she'd be saddled with two children, a baby who wouldn't sleep at night and a boy who tore around all day.

And yet . . . something deep within her cherished all this. Kennedy admired her mother intensely and wanted to be just like her, except perhaps a bit less perfect, which heaven knew was easy to achieve. Kennedy remembered the messes—real and emotional—she'd made as a child and how her nanny had consoled her and helped Kennedy clean them up. There'd been something so warm, so real, so *bonding* about those times. She wanted to provide that for her own children, even if she did it imperfectly, and oh boy, did she do it imperfectly.

If only someone would understand. No one ever praised mothers for the tedious work of child caring. No one ever gave a mother an award for not losing her temper ten times a day or for cajoling a kid to eat his vegetables. James tried to sympathize, but he was preoccupied with his work.

Perhaps that was why Kennedy wanted her father to give her something, a spontaneous surprise to show her that *she* was the light of *his* life. Something like—a diamond?

Returning along Main Street, they passed Jewel of the Isle.

"Oh," Kennedy gasped. "Isn't that pretty!"

Sebastian paused, grateful for an opportunity to set the bags full of toys down and relax his hands. "What, sweetheart?"

"That diamond Christmas tree brooch. So sweet."

Sebastian peered in the window. "It's nice." Suddenly an idea struck him. "Let's go in, Kennedy."

Inside, the shop sparkled with gemstones, silver, and gold. Kelli Trainor approached them. "Hello, Mr. Somerset. Merry Christmas."

"Merry Christmas, Kelli. Could you tell me, how much is that Christmas tree brooch in the window?"

Kellie lifted the pin out and set it, in its black velvet box, on the glass counter. She named a price.

Sebastian asked Kennedy, "I think that's reasonable, don't you? The diamonds are quite clear."

"It's gorgeous, Daddy," Kennedy gushed. She was almost fainting. It was a Christmas fairy tale. Her father had sensed her wish without a word, almost as if they had ESP!

"I'll take it." Sebastian removed his wallet from his pocket and slid out a credit card.

"Would you like that wrapped?" Kelli asked.

Kennedy opened her mouth to suggest they pin it on her coat instead, but before she could speak, her father nodded.

"Yes, please, Kelli." He beamed when he looked over at Kennedy. "Thanks for suggesting it, Kennedy. Nicole will be so surprised. I never think to buy her romantic presents. She's been working so hard trying to make this a perfect holiday for everyone. I can't wait to see her face when she opens the package on Christmas morning."

Kennedy's mouth fell open. Her throat closed tight with dismay.

"That's so sweet," Kelli said, filling the awkward silence.

"Next—" Sebastian's chest swelled with satisfaction as he tucked the wrapped package in with the others.

"Yes, Daddy?" Kennedy widened her eyes innocently.

"Where shall we have lunch? Someplace cozy. The wind's whipping the snow around."

Kennedy trudged next to her father in silence as they headed to the Brotherhood of Thieves. She was blind to the holiday-bright windows. Her father hummed "White Christmas," totally unaware of the disappointment steaming off her. She wanted to stop right there on the brick sidewalk next to the damned Christmas tree, throw her head back, and bawl. Everything was wrong. This holiday sucked. She was a warthog of a woman with a belly that weighed down her every move. She couldn't look sexy for her husband, she couldn't even look pretty, and when she tried to look winsome for her own father, what did he do? He bought diamonds not for his own daughter who was carrying his second grandchild, but for his new wife, who wouldn't even care about them. Who certainly wouldn't know how to wear them! Nicole was so more a rhinestone person, she didn't have the elegance to appreciate diamonds. What a waste. While Kennedy, at a time in her life when she could use some affection and pampering and *gratitude* didn't even get a stupid silver bracelet!

Did Nicole have some kind of psychological hold over her father? Did Nicole plant drugs in his coffee? She was way less attractive than Katya, she had no sense of style, she was like a cleaning woman who got to sit with the family, and Sebastian had bought her diamonds? Kennedy wanted to shriek.

"Here we are." Sebastian ushered his daughter into the brick-walled bistro. "After we eat, maybe you'll have the energy to look at boots."

"Boots," Kennedy muttered.

The hostess appeared and seated them in the front room next to the heartening warmth of the fireplace.

They removed their coats, settled in, and ordered. Sebastian remarked, "You seem upset."

Kennedy bit her lower lip. "I guess . . . I didn't realize you were so . . . enamored of Nicole."

Her father threw back his head and laughed. "Honey, Nicole is my wife. I would certainly hope I'd be enamored of her." He gave Kennedy a concentrated gaze. "But you're not pleased about this?"

She lowered her eyes and played with her napkin, folding it in different shapes as she talked. "I want you and Mom to get back together."

"Oh, Kabey, that's not going to happen. Be realistic, Kennedy. Your mother left me for Alonzo—"

"But they're not married!" Kennedy protested.

Sebastian shrugged. "Katya probably won't marry again. Your mother likes to have things her own way. As you are now aware, marriage is full of compromises. Come on, Kennedy, you've seen Katya. She's completely fine without me. She's got her own apartment where Alonzo can visit, but it's her place, and she doesn't want it messed up. She's almost sixty, after all. She deserves to spoil herself for a while. So do I, for that matter. I worked hard, providing for my family. Your mother worked hard, raising you and keeping house. Now we want to enjoy life, be free, even a bit silly, before we end up in our rocking chairs."

Kennedy gripped her father's hand. "Daddy, you're not *old*!"

"I'm not young, either. I'm healthy. And now, thanks to Nicole, I'm happy. That's a lot."

Kennedy wanted to appeal prettily, "Don't *I* make you happy?" but at that moment the waiter arrived with their meals.

"It means the world to me that James is such a nice man," Sebastian said as he picked up his fork. "He loves you and Maddox. That's obvious. That's the best gift any father can have, a good, trustworthy, loving son-in-law."

Kennedy conceded reluctantly, "Yes. James's great."

"I wish you could learn to like Nicole," Sebastian continued. "She's a wonderful person, and she would love to be part of your life."

"But she's not my mom," Kennedy reminded him.

"True. Nicole is completely different from Katya. She's not as concerned about style, she's a bit more into politics, she's a nurse, and she likes being part of the community. You know your mother, Kennedy. Katya always wanted to be seen as being *above* the community. Better than."

This was true, but Kennedy protested, "Please don't say negative things about my mother. It hurts my feelings."

"I'm sorry, Kennedy. Let's change the subject. What did you get James for Christmas?"

"Just some outdoor gear ordered from catalogs," she replied. "After all, I'm about to give him another son."

"I'm glad you brought that up. I feel kind of lousy, joining your mother and James at the hospital and leaving out Nicole."

This conversation was SO not going the way she'd planned! "She can hang out in the waiting room with Alonzo," Kennedy suggested.

Sebastian patted her hand. "I think you need a nap."

Kennedy wanted to say she needed a diamond brooch, but she kept her silence and focused on her food. If only she weren't so tired with this pregnancy, she'd have better ideas about how to get her parents back together, or at least how to get rid of Nicole. But her father was right. She was tired. She'd think more clearly after a nap.

Because she wasn't finished yet.

Whatever happened, Kennedy suddenly wondered, to Cinderella's father and the wicked stepmother after Cinderella married the prince?

# 14

❄

The snow was coming down quickly now, coating the lawn with a layer of pristine white. Snix was cold, and he was hungry.

He was also curious. This morning he'd hidden in a hedge to watch a boy build a peculiar house, a kind of cave, perfectly dog-sized. His father had come out to help him reinforce it with layers from cardboard boxes, covered with some old blankets, then wrapped around and around the outside with duct tape.

Now the boy and his father had gone. It seemed all the humans had gone.

Snix trotted to the funny makeshift house. Easing his way between two lawn chairs tilted on their sides, he entered.

It was warm. Cushions covered the floor. No snow got in. It would be the best place to sleep at night!

But as hard as he sniffed, he could find no food in here.

Reluctantly, he left the warm cave for the cold snowy outer world. Time for another food quest. Before he ventured away, he peed on a bush, the side of the garage, and the side of the house, so he'd be sure to know where to return.

He headed toward town. Many of the narrower streets were still and empty, the owners of the houses away in their winter homes, the windows dark, the trash barrels scentless. He found his way to Centre Street, where the aroma of bacon drifted from the Jared Coffin House like a love song, but the trash barrels had special locks on them, probably against marauding cats.

Across the street, Le Lanquedoc was shut tight. He trotted past the brick town buildings and the Whaling Museum until he came to the most likely place to find food.

Broad Street. Steamboat Wharf. Dog heaven. Taco Taco. Walters gourmet sandwiches to go. A pizza place. A coffee shop. The trash barrels lids were not so tightly fit, and being this close to the water, the ravaging gulls often did the work of breaking and entering for Snix.

Sure enough, in an alley he found a barrel on its side, papers and cups spilling out. A group of sky rats were pecking away at the contents.

He hesitated. Gulls were mean. They were almost bigger than Snix. Those beaks were as sharp as knives. His only hope was to fake it, so he charged toward them, barking savagely, showing his white pointed teeth. To his relief, with much irate screeching, the birds flew away.

He'd gotten there in time. Nosing away the papers, he hunted out buns, taco shells, hamburger, and cold fries. His belly swelled. He felt so much better. So much stronger. So much more hopeful.

He ate until he couldn't squeeze another morsel into his body. Replete, his body begged for sleep.

He retraced his steps to the house with the warm cave. People were out on the streets, calling out gleefully about the snow, elated that it was going to be a white Christmas. Snix wasn't so pleased. He was scared. Still, it swelled his heart to see so many people smiling, chatting, waving, dressed in red, white, and green, their arms full of packages. It made the world seem like a friendlier place.

Near Nantucket Bookworks, a teenage boy noticed Snix. "Hi, guy," the kid said, reaching down to scratch Snix between the ears. "Aren't you a cute little pooch."

Snix cocked his head, trying to send a message: *Take me home with you.*

A girl came out of the shop, a book bag in her hand. "Okay," she said, "now let's go to Murray's Toggery. I'll get Dad a sweater." She linked her arm through the boy's and led him away, not even aware of Snix sitting there wagging his tail. The boy walked off.

But the friendly warmth of his touch remained, all through Snix's body.

He continued on his way, back through the maze of narrow lanes, until he found his own scent on a bush. The house had lights on inside, but he heard no sounds of people, so he took a chance and dashed straight into the backyard and through the lawn chairs into the cave.

Oh, it was warm. The cushions were soft. The wind howled but no snow made its way inside. His belly was full. His neck had been scratched. A human had told him he was cute. Curling up in comfort, Snix fell asleep.

# 15

After breakfast, Nicole cleaned the kitchen. Upstairs, she made all the beds. She considered picking up the clothes littering her stepdaughter-in-law's floor and putting them in the laundry basket, because it had to be difficult for Kennedy to bend over. On the other hand, Princess Kennedy might object to Nicole touching her things, so she let them lie. She did a quick run through the house with the vacuum.

As she worked, she longed to wallow in the delicious self-indulgent behavior she once treated herself with as a widow. She could no longer curl up on the sofa shoveling popcorn into her mouth while watching *Terms of Endearment* and weeping so hard she choked on her popcorn. Sebastian was too elegant to imagine she could behave in such a churlish manner, so she restrained herself. Frankly, she missed it.

She phoned Jilly. "I'm a pariah in my own house."

"Poor thing. Come to Mama."

"I've got too much to do."

"Nonsense. If they can go out to lunch, so can we. It's snowing, Nicole. Look out the window! We can take a long walk on the beach and let the wind blow away our troubles, then have clam chowder at Met on Main."

Nicole hesitated.

"Oh, you'd rather stay home and sulk?" Jilly teased.

"I'll meet you at the Hub in ten minutes."

Putting on her snow boots immediately lifted Nicole's mood. Brown suede with thick rubbery soles, they were lined with white fleece and had red and green tartan laces. She pulled on her puffy red down coat and a red wool hat adorned with a knit green holly leaf, complete with red berry, shouldered her purse, slid on her red mittens and hurried out into the invigorating air.

Jilly was already at the Hub, festive in green wool coat and hand-knit creamy white cap and muffler. She greeted Nicole with a big hug and kiss. "Let's walk down to Straight Wharf and then over to the town beach."

"Good idea." Nicole glanced around. "People are out shopping."

"I've done all mine. I've got two duffel bags full of presents to take to Boston when we go for Christmas with the grandchildren."

"You leave tomorrow?" They passed Peach Tree's. "Great sweater."

"I know. Don't tempt me." They walked on toward the water. "First thing."

"I'll miss you," Nicole said.

"You'll be fine. Christmas is in two days. They leave on the twenty-seventh. You can survive that long."

Buoyed by her friend's companionship, Nicole thought just maybe she could. "Maddox is an adorable child, and James is nice. He tries hard to be pleasant to everyone. But I swear Kennedy is on some kind of campaign to make me lose my cool. She's absolutely devious, Jilly." As they ambled along through the falling snow, Nicole described the morning's breakfast psychodrama with the bacon and eggs.

"You're attributing too much premeditation to her," Jilly insisted. "Kennedy's a nice enough girl, as I recall. She's pregnant, remember? Pregnancy makes you irrational. Give her a break."

"You're right," Nicole conceded reluctantly. "I just wish Sebastian would stick up for me more. He always seems to think his daughter is flawless."

"Typical father," Jilly said knowingly. "I can't tell you the times Bob and I have argued over something Stacey's done or wants to do. He always takes her side. I'm always the disciplinarian. But in a few days, Kennedy will go home and you'll have Seb back for yourself."

Nicole's sigh of satisfaction was cut short. Across the street and down a block, she saw Sebastian and Kennedy leaving the Jewel of the Isle. Sebastian had a small dark green bag in his hand. He linked his arm through his daughter's and carefully escorted her around the corner onto Easy Street.

"Look." She nudged Jilly with her elbow. "Sebastian just bought Kennedy some jewelry."

Jilly spotted the retreating pair. "It's Christmas, Nicole."

"Oh, I know! I hate the way I feel, like a sniveling jealous fairy-tale witch. Let's change the subject. Tell me what you're reading."

Both women were voracious readers. Books kept them talking for the rest of their walk and most of their lunch at Fog Island. When they parted to go their separate ways, Nicole was back in her usual optimistic, level-headed mindset.

In the early afternoon, Maddox and Kennedy took naps while the others lounged in bed or the den, reading and watching television. Kennedy was still sleeping when Maddox woke, so Nicole, who was in the kitchen, gave him permission to go in the backyard and build a snowman.

"I'm making pumpkin lasagna for tonight," she told the boy. "Just as soon as I put it in the oven, I'll come out and join you."

She helped him don his outdoor gear and watched as the child ran joyfully out into the snowy late afternoon. She sprinkled fresh Parmesan on the lasagna and slid it into the oven. As she rinsed and checked the fresh cranberries she would make for the duck sauce that evening, Sebastian came into the kitchen.

"Something smells appetizing."

"Good." Rinsing her hands, Nicole murmured, "I wish we had two ovens. I have to sort of stagger what I'm cooking with only one."

Sebastian snorted. "Sorry, Nicole. Cooking was never one of Katya's passions. One oven was more than enough for her."

Nicole bit her lip. She didn't enjoy hearing the words Katya and passion come out of her husband's mouth.

As if he'd guessed her thoughts, Sebastian drew Nicole into his arms. "I hope you realize how grateful I am for all you're doing. Not just the decorating and the cooking, but making the house feel so warm. You've got a gift for perking up people, Nicole."

For half a second, Nicole considered pointing out that

she certainly didn't please Kennedy. But that would have been churlish, especially with her husband's arms around her. "I hope I perk you up, Sebastian."

"Let's go upstairs and I'll show you," Sebastian murmured into her neck.

Nicole drew away in pretend horror. "In the daytime? With your family here?" Secretly, she was tickled.

James chose that moment to come into the kitchen from the birthing room. "Time for a drink yet?" he asked. "Kennedy's sound asleep."

"Maddox is out trying to build a snowman," Nicole told him. "I promised I'd go help him, but I got delayed with cooking and um, everything."

James looked out the window. "Is Mad in the backyard or the front?"

"The backyard, of course." Nicole checked her watch. With a playful glance at Sebastian, she said, "Dinner's ready in about an hour."

"I'll play with him until then." James went out the door.

"Alone at last," Nicole's husband said, pulling her close once more.

# 16

Maddox stood in the backyard with his tongue protruding, trying to catch the flakes of snow that the wind flung into his eyes and up his nose. When his tongue got cold, he decided to go into his fort.

Snow had settled on top of his hideaway. On one side, snow drifted up into a wall. Maddox dropped to his knees and crawled between the lawn chairs into the warm security of his cave.

It was dark inside. He blinked, thinking about this, trying to understand. Back in the real world, the sun had almost set, but some pale rays still illuminated the sky and the brightness of the snow reflected back the shine. In here—with cardboard walls secured by duct tape wrappings and a ceiling of picnic table wood—no snow entered, and not much light.

After a moment, his eyes adjusted to the dim interior. It was nice and warm compared to the chill outside. Maddox crawled farther in and closed the cardboard flap that served as a door. Now it was supercozy.

Except . . .

Something was in the corner. Something as big as Maddox. Something dark, at least it looked dark, and as Maddox watched, it moved.

Too paralyzed with terror even to squeak, Maddox stared at the lump. A wolf? No, wolves were bigger. A rat? No, rats were smaller. A rabbit? That would be okay, but it wasn't rabbit shaped.

An eye gleamed through the darkness.

Maddox didn't know what to do. Should he pretend to be something not alive, a big rock, for example? Should he try to be friendly? How fast could he exit the cave before whatever it was leapt at him, catching him by his shoe?

The creature stirred. Two eyes shone. It appeared to be in no hurry to eat Maddox. He knew it wasn't a lion or a bear; Daddy said those didn't exist on the island. Perhaps it was a baby deer? But the thing shuffled into a standing position, and its legs were not nearly long enough to be a deer's. Was it a cat?

"Hello?" Maddox whispered. "Kitty kitty?"

Encouraged by his voice, the animal slowly, cautiously, moved toward Maddox, stumbling slightly on the uneven cushions, until Maddox could see that the creature was a furry brown dog with black button eyes like his toy animals and a pink tongue peeking between small white teeth.

"Hi, guy." Maddox held out his hand the way his mommy had taught him, so the dog could sniff him, so the dog wouldn't feel threatened.

The dog sniffed Maddox. Its dark eyes raised expectantly to meet Maddox's eyes, and its tail wagged hopefully.

"Who are you?" Maddox asked. "Are you lost?"

The dog dropped to its belly and crept closer to Maddox, still wagging its tail. Maddox reached out and patted the dog's head. The dog responded by scooting even nearer, keeping his yearning black eyes on Maddox's face.

"You're a nice doggy, aren't you?" Maddox said. "What's your name? Where's your collar?" He felt around the dog's neck but no leather or metal met his fingers.

The dog, encouraged by the touching, moved closer to Maddox and licked his fingers.

A wonderful thought suddenly appeared in Maddox's mind. Could Santa have brought him this dog for Christmas?

But Christmas wasn't for two more days. And his mom didn't want a dog.

Running his fingers over the animal, he felt its ribs. Even as a small boy, he understood that the dog hadn't had much to eat recently. This dog was lost. And hungry. Maybe this dog was hiding from a mean owner. Maddox had once seen a man kick a dog. Maybe this dog had run away. Maddox knew what it felt like to want to run away.

"Maddox!" His father's voice boomed out into the yard, making Maddox jump with surprise.

"Just a minute, boy," Maddox whispered. He crawled out the lawn chair entrance, stuck his head up, and called, "I'm here, Daddy, in my fort."

"Let's build a snowman. We've got time before dinner."

"Okay, Daddy. I'll be right there."

Back in the fort, the dog sat very obediently, his eyes searching Maddox's face.

"You're hungry," Maddox whispered, "but I can't bring you into the house because Mommy wouldn't like that. I'll sneak food out after dinner, I promise. Lots of good food, okay?"

The dog wagged his tail.

Delight flashed through Maddox as he realized he had a secret friend, his own private buddy. He could have adventures with this dog!

The dog needed a name. Maddox thought of famous best friends. Frog and Toad. Well, he couldn't call a dog Frog or Toad, that would be silly. He giggled to himself and the dog caught his mood, wiggling all over and climbing into Maddox's arms, licking his chin, wagging his tail. Christopher Robin and Winnie the Pooh! Maddox fell over backward, snickering.

"Pooh!" he gurgled as the dog licked his face. "I'll name you Pooh." Pooh was one of Maddox's favorite words because it had two meanings, one that could make his grandmother Katya raise her eyebrows. He hugged Pooh, who was cuddling as close as he could get.

"Maddox?" His father's voice sounded again.

"Coming!" Maddox answered. He sat up and put his hands on the dog's face. "Now listen. I have to go in. You stay here. I'll bring you some food as soon as I can, okay? You'll be nice and warm here. I'll be back pretty soon."

Pooh cocked his head, his dark eyes deep with intelligence, as if he understood every word.

Daddy decided they should build the snowman in the front yard so people could see him. He showed Maddox how to squeeze the snow tight to pack it. Together they rolled up three balls, stacking them up before adding fallen sticks for arms. Daddy opened the front door, calling in to ask Nicole for a carrot for the nose while Maddox looked beneath the bushes until he found two rocks for the eyes. The rocks were different sizes, so the snowman looked kind of funny but still cute.

When they stepped inside, the house seemed hot and bright. As his father helped him strip off his snow boots, mittens, coat, and hat, Maddox realized how dark it looked outside if you were inside a building, even though a pearly sheen of light lingered in the air from streetlights and moonlight falling on the snow.

"Let's wash your hands and face," Daddy said, taking Maddox's hand and leading him to the bathroom.

Mommy was up, sitting in the living room talking to Granddad. Nicole was trotting back and forth between the kitchen and the dining room. Maddox loved washing his hands and playing with the water. He could make lines of water run one way or the other and splash pools in the sink.

"Enough," his father said. "You're getting your sweater wet. Come on, Maddox."

Reluctantly, Maddox slowly turned off the faucets and dried his hands. Here came the boring part of his day, sitting at the dining room table with adults. They took so long to eat their food! He could gobble his down and be ready to play in a jiffy, but his parents wanted him to sit there like a statue, not rocking back and forth on his chair or tapping his fingers on the table or swinging his feet or even making fart noises with his mouth. This was one of the many things he couldn't understand about adults.

The food smelled good, though. His mommy insisted he eat some of the yucky lettuce salad, and he forced himself to swallow a few bites of the cranberry sauce, but the dark meat on his plate that his mommy said was duck made him cringe. Maddox preferred meat in tiny ground pieces, not hunks. Fortunately, the pumpkin lasagna had lots of creamy cheese, so he had two helpings of it, and all the adults praised him.

He had an awesome thought. Pooh would like the duck! He had to think of a way to smuggle it to the dog. He considered various options while the adults blabbed away, their cheeks growing rosy as they ate the warm food and drank their wine. The table was pretty with glowing candles making the silver shine. It was nice, seeing his parents having a good time with Granddad and Nicole. When Granddad got up to pour Daddy more wine, he blocked Maddox from his mother's vision for a few seconds, just enough time for Maddox to sneak a chunk of duck into his trouser pocket. Then he got the cool idea of putting the meat in his mouth, pretending to chew, then wiping his mouth with his napkin and spitting the meat into the napkin. Pretty soon he had a nice glob of meat to take to Pooh.

Maddox was proud. This must be how it felt to be a superhero.

# 17

After dinner, everyone but Kennedy helped Nicole carry the plates, glasses, and platters into the kitchen. Even Maddox willingly skipped back and forth with his utensils and napkin. Kennedy sat at the table, grounded like a blimp, listening to all the others chatter as they loaded the dishwasher and put away leftovers. How peppy they sounded. She put her elbows on the table and dropped her head in her hands.

She heard James yell, "Maddox, where are you going?"

Maddox called back, "I left something in my fort."

The back door slammed.

"You need a coat!" James cautioned, noting in a lower voice, "That kid. Where does he get his energy?" James flicked on the back outdoor light.

The back door slammed again as Maddox returned.

"Don't go out again without a coat," his father ordered

him. "And stamp your feet on the mudroom rug. Don't track snow through the house."

Kennedy's father clapped his hands in the front hall. "Okay, everyone. Time to see Christmasland!"

"What's that, Granddad?"

"You'll see. Put on your coat. We won't be leaving the car, so you don't have to bundle up too much." Sebastian came into the dining room. "You're coming with us, aren't you, Kabey?" Lowering his voice, he added enticingly, "Over by Surfside Road, it looks like the North Pole. Several of the streets have houses with every kind of lighted holiday spectacle you can imagine. Santa and his reindeer and sleigh on the roof. Frosty the Snowman. Beautiful life-size crèches."

Kennedy placed her hands on her belly. "I'd love to go but I'm not feeling very good. I'm not sure the food agreed with me. Duck is so rich."

"Would you like some bicarb of soda in water?"

"That would be great, Daddy, thanks."

Her father went off to the kitchen. Kennedy hauled herself up from the table and slowly lumbered into the living room, where she collapsed on a sofa.

"Mommy, aren't you coming?" Maddox asked.

"Not tonight, sweetie." Kennedy smoothed her son's ruffled hair. "You go with Daddy and Granddad."

"Nicole, too." Maddox's eyes were shining with excitement, his cheeks rosy from his run out into the cold.

"My big boy." Kennedy hugged him to her as well as she could. "I love you, Mad Man."

The others congregated in the front hall, pulling on gloves and coats while Nicole did her St. Martyr of the Household bit again, bringing Kennedy a pile of magazines and tucking a blanket over her feet. Maddox was jumping up and down with anticipation. Kennedy's father helped Nicole into her down coat. Kennedy felt childishly miffed at herself. Everyone else was giddy and good-natured. She was like a fat female Scrooge.

As soon as she saw the Grand Cherokee's lights fade into the distance, she levered herself off the sofa. Trundling up the stairs to the second floor, she headed down the long hall to the last small room, used as a storage room. Turning on the light, she was pleased to see that nothing had changed. Her grandmother's wedding gown was still zipped in a dress bag, hanging from the back of the closet. Her ice skates, skis, and rollerblades were in the closet, along with a few of her more memorable Halloween costumes and her father's high school letter jacket. One wall was lined with shelves filled with books. Her favorite books from childhood had been pillaged to take to her home to read to Maddox. Her high school and college yearbooks were still here.

The family photo albums were here, too. Ha.

Kennedy had been a child before digital cameras hit the scene, so her parents had devotedly snapped shots, had them printed off, and slipped the best photos into handsome leather-bound albums. Getting to them now was difficult, because they lined the lowest shelves, requiring Kennedy to squat—not her easiest posture—to wrench them out of the tightly packed shelf. They were heavy, fat, and bulky. Still, she persevered, tugging them off the shelf until she had them in a pile. Then, two by two, she carried them downstairs to the living room coffee table. It was a time-consuming process. She could heft only two at a time, and she had to hold those against her body with one arm so she could grasp the stair banister with her free hand. Fourteen unwieldy albums, compressing so many years of her family's life. Huffing, puffing, gasping, wheezing, Kennedy climbed down and back up, down and back up, her lower back cramping with protest at the weight.

Finally they were gathered on the coffee table. Excellent. Nicole's prissy Christmas room with its tree, stockings, and small wooden crèche was overwhelmed by the stack of albums. Kennedy dropped like a stone onto the sofa and caught her breath. Her back was a red hot coal of tongs squeezing her spinal cord, but she wasn't ready to rest yet. She spread as many of the albums as she could, open, photos gleaming, on the coffee table. The others she stacked on the floor in small towers of memory.

After resting, she scanned the albums until she found the one filled with pictures of herself at three, chubby and grinning from her father's arms, her mother next to them. Oh, she had been such a darling baby. Her three-year-old self sat smiling on Christmas morning, holding a baby doll in her arms. Katya wore a red and green silk robe; she was astonishingly lovely as she sat on the sofa with Sebastian's arm wrapped around her, both of them flushed with pleasure. Kennedy left that album open on the table so Nicole wouldn't fail to notice it.

Leaning back against the sofa, Kennedy allowed herself a great big helping of self-pity. Why did everything change?

A few photos of her nanny, Patty, had been included in the album. Kennedy happily remembered the woman, who smelled of sugar, flour, and baby powder. Here Kennedy was, taking her first brave steps toward Patty. Here Kennedy was with Patty at the ocean. The reality of being so young floated just out of the grasp of Kennedy's memory, but as she opened more albums, she began to warp back into some of the scenes.

The Halloween when she was four, dressed as a princess. She'd never wanted to take those sparkling clothes off. In fact, she recalled having a fight about it with Patty because she wanted to wear the princess gown and tiara to school.

The Christmas she was ten, memorable because Patty had been let go because Kennedy was considered too old to need a nanny. The family had gone to Aruba for Christmas. Such shimmering turquoise blue water, the palm trees, the cottage that had no television set.

Changing years, changing holiday islands. Rain forests, thatched cottages without walls, hotel rooms with television sets, her mother lying on a beach lounge, eyes covered with sunglasses, turning deep brown in the sun, then dressing for dinner and dancing with Sebastian and their friends. Kennedy got to order room service and watch videos.

Katya's clothes. Swirling silks, a sleek black bikini, skin-sleek satin. Kennedy appreciated even more as an adult how beautiful Katya was and how hard she had worked in the service of that beauty. Not only the strict dieting and exercising, but the hours spent at the beauty salon, having her hair colored and styled, having her legs and eyebrows waxed—and Katya abhorred pain as much as Kennedy. All Kennedy's friends had Brazilian waxes, but Kennedy couldn't bring herself to do it. She could hardly bear to have her legs waxed.

In all the photos, Katya's nails were perfectly shaped and painted. Discreet but expensive gems gleamed on her fingers and in her earlobes, around her neck and arms. Her mother had not been completely self-absorbed, though. She had taught Kennedy well, and Kennedy was grateful. Katya had shown Kennedy how to eat healthily if lightly, so that Kennedy didn't get caught up in the anorexia and bulimia of so many girls at her boarding school. That was a real victory.

Katya must have loved Sebastian passionately to have sacrificed the glory that was her body to the degradations of pregnancy and birth. How Katya had gotten her figure back after her pregnancy, Kennedy did not understand. She was sure she would resemble an exploded water balloon for the rest of her life.

"Mommy!" The front door burst open. Maddox ran into the room, forgetting in his excitement to be gentle with Kennedy, throwing himself onto her before even taking off his coat and mittens. "We saw Santa on his sleigh! We saw Rudolph! We saw Charlie Brown, and Snoopy on his doghouse! One house had lights ALL over!"

James stalked into the room. "Hey, kid, remember to be careful with Mommy and the baby."

Kennedy kissed Maddox's forehead. "Did Rudolph have a red nose?"

"He did, Mommy!"

Squirming slightly to shift her son's weight, Kennedy asked, "Was there a snowman?"

"Yeah! One house had a whole snow family!" In his excitement, he kneed Kennedy in the belly.

Kennedy couldn't help going "Oof!"

James noticed. Swinging his son up in his arms, he said, "Let's take your coat off, Maddox. It's time to calm down now and get ready for bed."

Kennedy sensed her husband's gaze resting on her, giving her a moment to offer to help put their son to bed, to ask about the outing, to send him a look of gratitude. She ignored him, staring intently at the album. She took care of Maddox ninety-nine percent of the time. It was James's turn. Besides, she had a scheme to put into action.

Sebastian and Nicole entered the living room, bringing a rush of fresh cold air with them. Kennedy shivered.

"How are you, Kabey?" her father asked.

"All right."

"Maybe tomorrow night you'll feel like driving over to see the lights," Nicole suggested. "They're amazing—"

Sebastian interrupted. "Kennedy, what's all this? Good Lord, you didn't haul all these albums down the stairs by yourself, did you?"

Elated by her father's concern, Kennedy ducked her head and peered up at her father from beneath her eyelashes. "I wanted to look at them. I wanted to remember all the wonderful times our family had during the holidays."

"But honey, you could have hurt yourself. You should have waited for us to come home and bring them down."

Nicole knelt by the coffee table, focusing on the album Kennedy had left open where Katya was at her most young and staggeringly gorgeous.

"Katya is such a true beauty," Nicole said, touching the photo with her forefinger. "But you know, Sebastian, I think your daughter is even more beautiful."

What? Kennedy wanted to totally *throw up*. Was Nicole demented? Was she some kind of frontal lobe victim? No, she was a genius at pretense, she wasn't going to let Kennedy get to her, she was acting like someone without a stick of jealousy, all gooiness.

"Nicole's right," Sebastian said. "You are more lovely than your mother, Kennedy."

Kennedy's lower lip trembled. "Thanks, Daddy." Bracing herself, she began the awkward effort of elevating her bulging body from the sofa. "I think I'll go to bed now. I did get tired, carrying all those albums. But they cheered me up, so it was worth it."

# 18

Christmas Eve day, a storm was predicted by the Weather Channel, with rising winds toward evening, so after breakfast Nicole and Sebastian headed off to the grocery store. They needed to stock the house with perishables and last-minute goodies and pick up the fresh, twenty-one-pound turkey. Tonight Nicole was serving beef Wellington with lots of veggies and a pumpkin pie for dessert.

First Nicole and Sebastian dropped James and Maddox at the wharves to watch the ferries come home. The wind-driven current was so strong it slammed the great behemoth car ferry the *Eagle* into the side of the dock, crashing like thunder. Fishing boats were tied up to the piers, bobbing like bathtub toys in the churning harbor.

At Stop & Shop, Nicole and Sebastian loaded up the cart, lugging armfuls of bags out to the car.

"We bought fresh cream?" Nicole wondered aloud as they left the parking lot.

"We did. I checked it off the list. We're set," Sebastian assured her. "We have enough food to feed us for the next week."

"I hope so. If the storm is as bad as they say, the boats may not be able to make it over with fresh supplies for days."

Sebastian reached over and held her hand. "The storm might miss us and blow out to sea. If it does hit, we're in a house that's stood for over a hundred years. Twenty-five years ago, we had trouble with power going out, but the electric company installed an underwater cable, so we'll be just fine."

"Oh, heavens, I hadn't even thought about losing electricity."

"You worry too much," Sebastian said.

*You don't have five people to feed three meals a day,* Nicole wanted to remind him, but she didn't want to seem to be complaining. And she wasn't. She loved cooking. She loved the holiday season. She adored Maddox, liked James just fine . . . and she was proud of the way she was keeping her cool with Kennedy. She was unaccountably nervous, though, she was on edge, as if her women's intuition was warning her of trouble ahead. No doubt this was caused by the falling barometer, the increasing wind, and the frenzied ions or protons or whatever was invisibly frothing in the air.

They picked up a windblown James and Maddox and returned home. James helped Sebastian and Nicole carry in the multitude of bags.

Maddox ran straight to his mother. Kennedy was sitting in a chair by the fire in the living room.

"It was awesome, Mommy!" Maddox squealed, throwing himself into her lap.

"Ouch." Kennedy recoiled as her son literally knocked the breath out of her. Seeing Maddox's face flicker with anxiety, she reached out and pulled him up onto her knees, hugging him tightly. "I'm okay, sweetie. Now tell me all about the ocean. How high were the waves?"

"This high!" Maddox proudly raised his arm as far as it would go above his head.

"Wow." Kennedy widened her eyes in appreciative astonishment. "I hope you held Daddy's hand."

"I did, Mommy, I did. And the big ferry boat went *crash* into the—" He frowned, unsure of the right word.

"The dock?" Kennedy suggested, lovingly smoothing her son's hair.

"Yeah! And—" Maddox wiggled with excitement, describing the adventure.

Nicole hummed as she stripped off her coat and unpacked the groceries. It was good to see Kennedy happy. She put on Christmas music in her kitchen, and the sparkling arms of her holiday sweater brightened her mood as she worked. This was her favorite sweater, with Santa on his sleigh in the front, the reindeer prancing around the side so that Rudolph with his cherry-red nose glittered on her back.

She prepared an easy lunch of tomato soup and grilled cheese sandwiches (on whole wheat bread, of course).

Maddox was still overexcited from his outing, almost jumping up and down in his chair.

"Sit still, Maddox," Kennedy told her son. "You'll spill your soup." She looked tired. "James, would you help him with the soup? It's so difficult for a four-year-old to eat."

Nicole's heart cringed. "Tell you what." Quickly she rose from the table, easing Maddox's bowl away from him. "I'll pour your soup into a mug, and then you can drink it."

"Good idea," James affirmed.

Kennedy was silent as Nicole got down a Christmas mug.

"The snow's accumulating," Sebastian reported, turning the conversation to the view out the windows. "We don't usually have snow this soon," he explained to James. "Thirty miles out at sea, we're caught in the Gulf Stream, which keeps us warmer than the mainland."

"It's ideal for Christmas." Nicole set the mug in front of Maddox and resumed her seat. "It makes everything so pretty."

Kennedy rolled her eyes and sighed.

James, with an impatient thinning of his mouth, shot his wife a glance. "Are you okay, Kennedy?"

"As a matter of fact, no," Kennedy puffed. "I think I'm coming down with some kind of flu. Or something I ate last night didn't agree with me."

Sebastian leaned forward, concerned. "Perhaps you should go back to bed."

"It's Christmas Eve," Kennedy protested. "I don't want to lie in bed today."

Nicole took a deep breath. She kept her mouth shut. Let the men sort Kennedy out, she decided. Nothing Nicole could do or say would help.

"Want to read to Maddox by the fire?" Sebastian suggested.

"Good idea," James quickly agreed. "He's had a good outing this morning—"

James's words were interrupted by a loud pounding at the front door.

Nicole jumped up. "I'll get it. It might be presents from someone!" Hurrying optimistically down the hall, she threw open the front door, letting in a blast of cold air and snow.

A woman in a mink coat and hat strode past Nicole, slamming the door behind her, shaking flakes off her shoulders, stamping her leather high-heeled boots on the rug. She acted as if she were entering her own house.

Well, in a way, she was.

Nicole had never fainted but at this moment she had an excellent sense of how it might feel.

"Katya?" She had seen photos of Katya before, but she'd never laid eyes on the woman in person, in her glorious Technicolor glamour.

"Damn, it's wicked out there," Katya said. She stripped her leather gloves off her long hands and dropped them on the front hall table. "You've moved the front hall chair," she said to Nicole. "Where am I going to sit down to take off my boots?"

Nicole was speechless.

"Mommy?" Kennedy hurried into the hall, eyes wide. "Mommy! What are you doing here?"

"Oh, Kennedy." Katya turned her back on Nicole and held her arms out to her daughter. "Sweetie, thank heavens." She hugged Kennedy tightly.

Sebastian entered the hall, a perplexed expression on his face. "Katya?"

"Sebby." Reaching out, Katya put her hand on her ex-husband's chest. "I apologize for arriving like this, but I just *had* to be here with my family. Alonzo and I had a terrible fight." Katya's head drooped elegantly, like a tulip. "We're finished."

Kennedy's face lit up like a beacon. "You and Alonzo

broke up?" Her eyes fluttered back and forth between her father and mother.

Nicole allowed herself to tilt backward slightly, in order to be supported by the wall. She forced herself to breathe.

Sebastian stepped away from his ex-wife's touch. "Why did you come here?" he asked. His voice was cool, and for that Nicole was grateful.

Katya simpered. "I've spent practically every Christmas of my life in this house. Kennedy's here. My grandson is here. Where else could I turn for comfort?"

"You did the absolutely right thing, Mommy," Kennedy assured her mother.

Sebastian's face darkened. "Don't you think you're being rather insensitive?" he demanded.

Katya gazed innocently, widening her crystal-blue eyes. "What do you mean?"

Nicole's heart fluttered so rapidly she was afraid she was going to hyperventilate, pass out, and slide down the wall to the floor.

In three strides, Sebastian was next to Nicole. He put his arms around her shoulders. "This is Nicole's house now, not yours."

"Daddy!" Kennedy cried.

"Oh, surely—" Katya began to object.

"Grandmama!" Maddox ran into the hall and stared up at Katya, mouth open in wonder.

"Katya," James said, following his son. "What are you doing here?"

"James, darling. And precious Maddox, my own grandson." Katya knelt to embrace the boy. "Grandmama's here to spend Christmas with you, Maddox. Isn't that wonderful?"

# 19

Her mother was here! Kennedy was breathless with amazement, and her heart seemed to be expanding alarmingly as emotions jostled within her.

*Rapture* at seeing her mother, actually here in this house.

*Dismay* at having her mother see her, Kennedy, who had allowed herself to relax. She hadn't put on her makeup yet, and it was already after lunch. She'd been lying down in front of the fire and hadn't brushed her hair since—well, she couldn't remember. Compared to Katya in her camel-hair trousers and cashmere sweater, her heavy gold necklace and earrings, Kennedy was absolutely frumpy in her red maternity tent.

*Hope* at the possibility of her parents getting back together, because here they both were in the same house, and Alonzo was in the past!

*Despair* at seeing her father move away from Katya to put his arm around Nicole.

"I need to sit down," she murmured.

"Of course you do, sweetheart." Katya handed her mink to James. Over her shoulder, she said to Sebastian, "My suitcase is on the front stoop. Could you bring it in, please?" With an arm around her daughter, she cooed, "Let's go into the living room and get you comfy."

They settled on the sofa. Kennedy angled her bulk to allow herself to study her mother's face. Katya's eyes were slightly pink and swollen. Obviously she had been crying, something she seldom allowed herself to do, and Kennedy's heart broke for her mother.

"Are you okay, Mommy?"

Katya bristled. "Don't I look okay?"

"Of course. You're as beautiful as always. But you must be sad without Alonzo."

Katya stared down at her hands. "Devastated." A shadow passed over her face.

In that moment, Kennedy saw the slight sag of flesh around her mother's lovely jawline and the pouch beneath her eyes that had not been quite disguised by concealer.

"Oh, Mommy."

Katya stiffened at the compassion in Kennedy's voice. "It happened only last night. I haven't slept. I know I look dreadful, but I'm extremely tired. Shattered, really, with the packing and the trip. It was a horrendous flight, very bumpy, the wind *shook* the plane. What I'd *adore* is a hot bath and a good nap."

"Of course," Kennedy began, just as her father walked into the room. Kennedy's spirits lifted. "Daddy, Mommy wants—"

"Katya." Sebastian's voice was terse. He remained standing. "You've got to realize how inappropriate it is for you to be here."

"Daddy!" Kennedy burst out.

"I'm sorry if you and Alonzo broke it off, but the fact is that is *your* matter to deal with, not mine. You and I were divorced years ago. You're a grown woman, you have plenty of financial resources—I've seen to that. You need to make other plans."

Katya slanted her head submissively. Fluttering her lashes, she pleaded, "I have no place else to go."

"You must have friends on the mainland," Sebastian pointed out.

Katya shrugged. "No one I could go to for the holiday."

"Fine. Then a hotel. You've always been fond of first-class hotels."

Kennedy's mood rose at this sign of her father remembering what her mother preferred.

"A hotel? On Christmas?"

"We've often stayed in hotels on Christmas," Sebastian reminded her as he stalked to the fire, stirred it with the poker, then shot Katya a sober stare. "I suggest you try to get a room at the Ritz or the Taj in Boston."

Katya lifted her shoulder coyly to her cheek. "I'm not sure I can leave the island. With this storm . . ."

Sebastian's face darkened with annoyance. Straightening, he decreed, "Then go to one of the hotels on Nantucket. The Jared Coffin House."

"The expense—" Katya started to object.

"I'll pay for it." Sebastian folded his arms over his chest, a sign that he was not going to yield.

Katya tossed her lovely blond hair. "Fine. But Sebastian, be kind. I'm so awfully tired. I was just telling Kennedy that I didn't sleep a wink last night. Couldn't I take a brief lie-down here before I go back out into the storm?"

"Please, Daddy," Kennedy begged. "Mommy can rest on my bed, and while she rests, I'll phone the Nantucket hotels and see who has a room."

Sebastian did not look pleased.

"Sebby." Katya stood up, stepping close to her ex-husband, putting her hand on his arm. "I'm sorry about all of this. I know I've made so many many terrible mistakes. If I could only turn back the clock . . ."

Kennedy watched her mother and father with hope springing up in her heart.

"You can't turn back time, Katya." Sebastian didn't sound angry or bitter or punitive, but adamant. Quietly, he walked away from her to the door into the front hall. "And I'm glad about that. Now please have some consideration and take yourself to a hotel."

Her father left the room.

Katya turned away so that Kennedy couldn't see her face. Kennedy's stomach cramped with regret and despair. It was not going to happen. Her parents were never going to get back together. That damned Nicole had bewitched her father, although how anyone so plain could bewitch anyone was past Kennedy's comprehension.

She heard Nicole in the kitchen, chatting quietly with James and Maddox. "Well, Maddox," Nicole said, "if you eat every bite of your sandwich, you may have a candy cane, but only if your daddy says so."

Who was Nicole to control what Kennedy's child ate? Annoyance propelled Kennedy ungracefully off the sofa.

"Mommy. Let me take you to my room so you can rest."

In the hall, Katya started to climb the stairs.

"No, wait. We're in the birthing room behind the

kitchen," Kennedy informed her mother. "So I don't have to climb the stairs all the time."

"Good idea," Katya replied. She hesitated, understandably reluctant to enter the kitchen.

Kennedy took her mother's hand and pulled her along. Nicole was at the sink, rinsing dishes before stacking them in the dishwasher. James was covering a platter of fresh veggie strips with cling wrap. Maddox sat on a chair, swinging his legs, sucking a candy cane.

"Mommy's going to take a brief nap," Kennedy proclaimed, her tone of voice leaving no room for discussion.

"I'm going to take a nap, too, Grandmama," Maddox told her.

Katya crouched down to kiss her grandson. "Have a good sleep, my angel. I'll see you later." Rising, she followed Kennedy into the birthing room.

"The bathroom's through here," Kennedy began, then stopped, blushing. "Of course you know that."

Katya looked around the room. "So Nicole changed the den into a bedroom." With a sigh, she sat down on the wide bed that, Kennedy realized with a blip of relief, she had actually made this morning. Unzipping her boots, Katya kicked them off, raised her shapely legs onto the bed, and reclined onto a pillow. "Oh, my. This feels divine."

Kennedy unfolded a patchwork quilt and spread it over Katya. She kissed her mother's forehead. "Have a good rest."

"Thank you, dear." Katya closed her eyes.

Kennedy left the room, quietly shutting the door, thinking how odd it felt to do something so maternal to her own mother.

# 20

The boy's fort was better than nothing, but the temperature was falling while the wind rose. It was late afternoon and the boy who called him Pooh hadn't brought him anything to eat since last night when he brought out that piece of excellent meat.

He worried the boy had forgotten him. The light that came with morning was already fading. This was good for when Snix needed to sneak out of his fort and scurry over behind a bush to pee. It made him less visible to the people inside the brightly lighted house. But it was bad for finding food. So was the snow pelting down everywhere. Already it was piled so high that Snix had trouble lifting his short legs in and out of it. Once or twice he got stuck, which made him even colder. He jumped his way back into the fort, his coat covered with flakes.

He licked the icy white off his legs and shoulders and rolled on the cushions. He tried nosing a cushion up against another one to make a notch where he could wriggle down into for warmth. It didn't work very well. The wind was so strong it rattled the lawn chairs and lifted the edges of the cardboard and blankets.

He couldn't understand why the boy hadn't come back. Perhaps this was the way humans were, hugging and feeding you one day, completely forgetting you the next.

Or maybe it was that Snix was unlovable. He wasn't much to look at, he knew. He was too small to guard a house. He was too small even to make it through the increasing piles of snow to search for food. No one needed a dog like him.

His stomach growled as hunger clawed at it. He whimpered pathetically.

Wait! He heard a noise. The back door was opening. He crawled to the edge of the lawn chair tunnel and peeked out between the slats.

It wasn't the boy. Snix's heart sank.

But it was a woman carrying a heavy clear bag of garbage, and even through the blowing snow Snix could smell the layers of cooked and raw food. These people had a heavy plastic garbage can with a tight-fitting lid that clamped shut so decidedly that Snix had never been able to open it.

But he'd never been this desperate before. He would wait until the woman went back inside, then attack the garbage can with all his might.

# 21

At preschool, everyone talked about Christmas as full of excitement, presents, good food, and fun. But Christmas was tomorrow and everyone in the house was grumpy. Maddox could *feel* the heaviness. He knew he was only a kid, he couldn't understand everything, but he knew when people bustled or whistled or sang, and right now the house was silent except for the sound of Nicole clashing pots and pans in the kitchen.

That was wrong. Nicole always fluttered around in the kitchen like a butterfly, humming to herself. Now her expression was grim. Grandmama had disappeared into the bedroom. Mommy and Daddy were in the living room, talking in low voices. Granddad sat in the kitchen nook, phoning hotels.

The windows rattled, battered by the storm. *Pooh!*, Maddox thought. Maddox hadn't been able to get outside to take him food since yesterday, because he always had a grown-up taking him here and there. The poor dog must be cold and hungry.

This might be the perfect time to sneak outside with some food. Maddox had eaten all of his grilled cheese sandwich, but the grown-ups hadn't. Nicole was piling the crusts into the trash bag now, where they joined bits of bacon, eggs, toast, and other breakfast goodies that had been left over from this morning. It would be a feast for his puppy pal!

How could he steal the bag away from Nicole? Already it looked too heavy for Maddox to carry it, but he could drag it, but not in front of the grown-ups . . . While he deliberated, Nicole swiftly twisted and tied the opening, hefted it up, and headed to the mudroom and the back door.

Disappointment flooded Maddox. He knew he wasn't strong enough to unclamp the garbage cans. But he had to be inventive, he had to be strong, he had to feed Pooh. Quickly scanning the kitchen, he discovered a box of Cheerios left on the counter. Okay, maybe dogs didn't eat Cheerios, but it was better than nothing.

Like a spy, Maddox slipped out to the mudroom, pulled on his boots, then dove beneath the bench where people sat to take off their boots or put them on. The door opened, snow gusted in on an invisible carpet of cold air, and Nicole's feet strode past, stamping snow onto the floor. She went into the kitchen.

Maddox sneaked out from under the bench. Reaching up, he turned the knob and pulled the back door open. Sliding through the smallest possible opening, he stepped out onto the back porch and pulled the door shut tight.

Light from the kitchen fell onto the porch and backyard. From here he could see how the wind buffeted the fort, clattering the cardboard against the wood and making the edges of the blankets lift and drop. Still, it stood. So Pooh was warm inside.

Maddox hurried down the steps toward the fort. Wind spun through his hair and dotted his face with snowflakes, but he was warm enough in the wool Christmas sweater Nicole had knit especially for him.

Kneeling down, he crawled through the lawn chair entrance into the fort.

"Pooh!" he called. "I'm here. I'm here, Pooh. I've brought you something to eat."

Pooh wasn't there.

# 22

As Nicole carried out the garbage, she wondered why Sebastian was making phone calls on his ex-wife's behalf. This garbage bag was heavy, but Sebastian was too busy on the phone, helping Princess Katya. For heaven's sake, couldn't James or Kennedy or Katya herself made the calls? Were Katya's filed, French-tipped fingernails too delicate to punch numbers into a phone?

*Bah, humbug,* Nicole thought as she tromped up the back steps. All her visions of a lollipop Noel had fled before the nightmare of gorgeous, vulnerable Katya arriving to take over the house and the holiday.

Back in the house, she saw James secluded in the living room whispering with Kennedy. Sebastian was in the kitchen, grim-faced.

"Most of the hotels and B&Bs are closed for the season. The few that are open are booked. No rooms available." Seeing Nicole's frustration, he tried to lighten the moment. "No room at the inn."

Nicole was aware that her hair had been stirred by the wind into all kinds of crazy. She had tried to ignore the fact that her middle-aged bottom had grown bigger and rounder as she'd spent the month cooking delicacies for the holiday, but with Katya here, so slim and toned, Nicole admitted to herself that she looked like a peasant compared to a queen. No, not a peasant, a servant. The mild, self-effacing worker bee who cooked the meals, did the dishes, made the beds, and dusted and cleaned so the family, Sebastian's family, could flutter through life like the aristocrats Katya assumed they were.

Nicole lifted her hand to smooth down her hair. "Right now, at this particular moment, I'm not in the mood to be benevolent."

Sebastian swayed back, surprised. Nicole seldom spoke in this way. He apologized, "I'm sorry I didn't carry out the garbage. I know the bag was heavy."

"I'm bushed," Nicole told him, and it was true. She was at the end of her rope, which allowed all sorts of demonic phrases to pepper her mind, filling her with dark thoughts.

*I'll leave. I'll go to Jilly's and let you have your perfect wife and family all back together again.* Those words were on the tip of her tongue, but she knew they weren't rational, she was simply overemotional and overwhelmed. Sebastian had not done anything to make her doubt his love for her. He had stepped away when Katya tried to paw him. He had put his arm around Nicole. She had to tamp down her temper.

"I'm going upstairs to lie down," Nicole said. "I need a rest."

Her heart lightened when Sebastian said, "I'll come with you."

They lay side by side on their backs on the bed. Nicole stared at the ceiling.

Sebastian reached for Nicole's hand. "I'm sorry Katya showed up like this. She's never been considerate of other people."

"She wants you back," Nicole stated bluntly.

Sebastian rolled over and put an arm around Nicole, pulling her close to him. "I am married to you. I am in love with you." He nibbled her ear. "You and I are a team, Nicole. In a couple of days, everyone else will be gone, and you and I will have our house and our lives back to ourselves."

"Yes, but when Kennedy has her baby, you and Katya and James will be with her and I'll be exiled."

Sebastian took a deep breath. "Exiled is putting it a bit strong."

Nicole didn't speak.

"What can I do?" Sebastian asked. "It's what my daughter requested. And Katya and I are the biological grandparents." After a moment, he continued, "Give Kennedy a break. She's a good person, deep down. She's not thinking clearly. I think she's pretty overwhelmed by pregnancy hormones."

Nicole turned on her side, away from Sebastian. Truly, she was fed up with shopping, cooking, cleaning, decorating, not to mention pretending that Kennedy's little act with the photo albums hadn't wounded her. And the worst was yet to come. If Katya stayed for Christmas, how would that work? Everyone was aligned to Kennedy except Nicole, who was left out. And what about the cooking and cleaning up? If Katya didn't help, Nicole would feel like her maid. If Katya *did* help, Nicole would be painfully aware that Katya had cooked in the kitchen for years.

Tears were pressing against her chest and her eyes. "I w-wanted this to be a wonderful Christmas," she managed to stutter.

"What can I do to help?" Sebastian repeated. "There must be something."

Why couldn't Sebastian just *know*? Nicole struggled for an answer. "Be with me," she told him. "Don't let Katya touch you. Don't respond to her flirting. Make it clear that this is *our* house now, your house and mine."

Sebastian cuddled her against him. "I'll do that. And remember, Nicole, Katya and I were estranged even before the divorce. She pretty much lived in the Boston house while I preferred to live here. I was relieved when she ran off with Alonzo—but I've told you all this before."

Reassured by the warmth of his arms and his words, Nicole agreed, "Okay. I can do this. If you're by my side."

"Don't worry, I'm right here." Sebastian hugged her tightly.

Yet Nicole knew that, for her, Christmas was ruined.

# 23

Kennedy could not get comfortable on the living room sofa. She had eaten too much of Nicole's amazingly delicious food. Rubbing her hands over her swollen belly, she closed her eyes and tried to relax, but thoughts of her mother stirred through her emotions. As much as Kennedy had hated it when her mother divorced her father, she had been glad for Katya whenever Katya was with Alonzo, because this new love had made Katya glitter in ways Kennedy had never seen before. Katya had acted silly, hugging and smooching Kennedy with a carefree, spontaneous enthusiasm that was entirely new.

Now Alonzo and Katya were over. Kennedy could tell her mother was hurting more than she let others see. The fact that Katya wanted to take a nap? *Whoa.* Katya had never taken naps before.

James was outside, shoveling the walk and the drive.

The sound of the blade hitting the bricks made Kennedy grit her teeth. Couldn't he wait?

If only Nicole would just *leave*. Then Kennedy's father wouldn't have to behave so dutifully to his new wife. Sebastian would be free to gaze upon Katya with clear eyes, he would see that they belonged together, he would take her in his arms, and everyone in the house would belong.

# 24

"Pooh!" Maddox struggled through the back yard, following the bumpy path through the snow toward the garage. "Pooh! Where are you?"

The snow reached the top of his boots. The wind pushed at him, and snow swirled up his nose. Fear burned his heart, shame sliced his belly. He should have brought the puppy some food this morning. If Pooh had run away because he thought Maddox had abandoned him . . . Maddox sobbed aloud. The sound flew away in the storm.

It wasn't quite dark yet. Lights from the house fell over the yard, and as Maddox went around the side of the garage, his heart exploded with gladness. There he was! The little terrier was standing on his hind legs, trying to push over the heavy garbage container, which rocked but did not fall.

"Pooh!"

The dog turned, saw Maddox, and, yelping jubilantly,

bounded through the few feet between them, throwing himself at Maddox with delirium. Maddox put his arms around the animal. Pooh was shivering. Pooh whined with ecstasy, licking Maddox's face with an icy tongue.

"You're going inside with me," Maddox told the animal.

He tried to pick Pooh up in his arms, and he did manage it, but the dog's weight made Maddox almost fall over backward. Heroically, Maddox toiled forward, one step at a time, through the mountains of white. The dog rested his head on Maddox's shoulder. It was the most wonderful feeling. Keeping to the jagged path he had broken through on his way out, he managed to labor his way right up to the steps to the back porch. Here, he collapsed, out of breath.

"Pooh," he gasped, setting the dog down next to him.

Pooh squeezed as close to Maddox as he could. They were both quaking with cold.

Maddox stood up. His snowboots were warm, but they were heavy. He'd be glad to get them off. Resolutely, he climbed the wooden steps.

"Come on, Pooh," he called. The dog leapt up the steps, right alongside Maddox.

Maddox reached way up to turn the doorknob. He shoved the door open. Warmth flooded out from the mudroom.

"Come on, Pooh," he called again.

Pooh didn't hesitate. He bounced across the porch and into the house. Maddox pulled the door shut. In the bright light, he saw how each individual hair on Pooh's body was crusted with snow. It frosted poor Pooh's nose and the tips of his ears. Maddox seized his own navy blue coat with the red plaid lining and wrapped it over the dog, holding him tightly.

"Maddox!" Suddenly Grandmama Katya loomed in the doorway, looking cross and even kind of mean. "What is *that*?"

# 25

Snix nestled his head on the boy's shoulder, savoring this surprising moment of belonging. He was wanted. He was *chosen*. He was very nearly warm.

And he'd bet the little boy would feed him any minute now. His stomach rumbled hungrily. He hoped the boy could feel it.

The boy's arms tightened around Snix when the thin blond woman came into the mudroom. Snix felt him tense up. He could smell the woman's scent, much like cat pee, and the boy's anxiety. Snix stayed still, sensing it was a good time to be invisible.

The woman kept saying *Maddox*. Maddox must be the boy's name. Good to know.

"Santa brought him to me," Maddox told the woman.

She laughed, but the sound wasn't lighthearted. "Maddox, Christmas isn't until tomorrow, *darling*. Besides, dogs aren't allowed in the house."

Maddox's arms were trembling from supporting Snix's weight. Squatting down, he put Snix on the floor. He removed his coat from Snix's body. "He's just a *little* dog," Maddox pointed out.

Snix tried to squeeze himself small. He lay down on the floor—the soft rag rug felt good against his belly—and put his head between his paws.

"I don't care what size the animal is. Dogs are not allowed in this house."

"*Excuse me?*" Another woman entered the mudroom. This one didn't smell like cat pee. She smelled wonderful. She smelled like food. "Oh, Maddox, who is this?"

Food Woman knelt next to Snix. Snix lifted his head hopefully. Food Woman slowly reached out to let Snix smell her hand, a true courtesy, then gently scratched him behind his ears.

"Hello, cutie-pie. What's your name?"

In reply, Snix licked her wrist, perhaps a bit too enthusiastically, but it was ringed with the slight aroma of melted cheese.

"Pooh," Maddox told Food Woman. "I've named him Pooh."

"Well, Pooh, you appear just a tad bedraggled. I'll bet you'd like something to eat. Perhaps a nice bowl of warm milk and a bit of—"

"Don't tell me you intend to feed that creature!" Blond

Woman was indignant. "If you do that, you'll never get rid of him."

"Santa brought him!" Maddox protested, getting to his feet. "He did, Nicole!"

"Dogs are not allowed in this house," Blond Woman said, her voice as cold as the wind outside.

Food Woman spoke, her voice low, vibrating with indignation. "May I remind you, you do not make the rules here. This is not your house any longer."

"Mommy!" shouted Maddox as another woman squeezed her bulk into the room. She was young and pretty and hugely fat.

"What's wrong? Maddox, what have you done?"

"Mommy." Maddox babbled, suddenly crouching over Snix. "Santa left me this dog. I want to keep him. His name is Pooh. He won't eat much."

*Actually* . . . Snix thought, almost dizzy with hunger and the enticing bouquet of beef, cheese, and oatmeal . . .

His thoughts were interrupted. "I've told you, Maddox, you can't have a pet. I'm sorry, but we're going to have a new baby soon."

"But, Mommy—" Maddox argued, stamping his foot.

"MADDOX, you are being a very BAD boy!" his mother yelled.

"Then *I'll* keep him," Food Woman announced.

"You will *not!*" Blond Woman bristled with outrage.

"An animal will ruin this house! The floors will be scratched, the furniture ripped to shreds—"

"As I said," Food Woman replied calmly, "this is not your house."

Maddox's mommy turned bright red and stuck her face into Food Woman's face. "How dare you be rude to my mother!"

"What's going on?" An older man came into the room, which made the mudroom crowded.

"Daddy!" the fat lady with the bulging tummy cried.

"Sebastian," Blond Woman said and at the same time, Food Woman said, "Sebastian."

Everyone talked at once, which made it possible for Maddox to pick his coat off the floor, toss it over Snix, clutch Snix to his chest, push open the back door, and run back out into the cold.

# 26

❆

"Tell her, Daddy, *tell* her!" Kennedy threw herself into her father's arms. Tears flew from her eyes. "Tell Nicole she is not allowed to make rules for *my* son!"

"I didn't—" Nicole began.

"Kennedy?" James came into the room. He'd finished shoveling the front walk, and snow topped his wool hat and the shoulders of his coat. "What's going on?"

Kennedy could hardly remain standing. She was out of breath, overwhelmed by the situation, bent in half by her emotions.

Katya spoke, her voice laced with contempt for Nicole. "Nicole thinks she can tell Kennedy how to run her life."

"No, I do not," Nicole disagreed, almost spitting each word.

Kennedy shuddered. "Daddy, make her stop being mean to Mommy."

"Kennedy." James stepped forward and put his hand on her shoulder. "Honey, what's gotten into you? You sound like a whining adolescent."

Nicole folded her arms in the most *satisfied* way. Kennedy wanted to *slap* her.

"Don't you speak to my daughter that way!" Katya snapped.

"Why don't we all calm down," Sebastian suggested. "Let's get out of the mudroom and discuss this reasonably."

"Discuss *what?*" James asked.

"Nicole wants to let Maddox keep the dog," Kennedy told him.

"What dog?" James asked.

Kennedy shrieked. "WHERE'S MADDOX?"

Silence suddenly filled the mudroom as everyone turned to stare at the place where the boy and dog had been standing. Now there was only a wet spot on the rug and a small pile of melting snow.

Sebastian strode across the empty space, yanked open the back door, and yelled out into the dark night: "Maddox? Maddox!"

Nicole hurried to his side. Stepping out onto the back porch, she called, "Maddox, honey, it's okay. The dog can come in, too."

"How dare she," Katya muttered.

Sebastian took a flashlight from the shelf above the coat hooks and hurried out into the yard. "Maddox? Maddox!"

"Maybe he's in his fort." Nicole trotted down the back steps and through the snowdrifts, fell to her knees, and crawled inside the lawn chair tunnel. After a moment, she backed out. "They're not in there."

Kennedy's heart seemed to explode with anguish. "What have I done?" Snatching the first coat her hand found, she pulled it over her shoulders.

As Kennedy wobbled out onto the porch and down the steps, her mother shouted, "Kennedy! You can't go out in this weather. Not in your shape. You'll fall! Kennedy, get back in here."

James brushed past his mother-in-law, rushed out the back door, and caught Kennedy as she reached the bottom step. "Kennedy," he crooned. "It's okay." Taking a moment, he stroked the side of her face with his hand.

James's caring touch, his concerned gaze, soothed Kennedy. For a second, in the midst of the swirling snow, the world made sense.

"James," she sobbed. "I was mean to Maddox. He wants to keep a puppy he found and I said he couldn't. He said Santa brought it to him. I said . . ." She couldn't finish. She hated herself at that moment. She was the worst mother in the world. "I told Maddox he was *bad*. On

Christmas Eve. So he ran away." She bent over double with pain.

James wrapped his arms around her tight. He was so strong. His love for her was a healing balm. "Let's get you back inside. You need to take care of yourself. I'll go find Maddox. He can't have gone far."

Sebastian and Nicole approached, ghostly in their snow-covered clothing.

"He's not in the yard or garage or at the front of the house," Sebastian announced.

Kennedy choked back a sob.

# 27

❄

Nicole had a sudden thought. "Maybe he went up to his room. I'll check." She raced out of the mudroom, through the front hall, and up the stairs. The door to Maddox's room was open. The room was empty.

"He's not there," she called as she hurried back down the stairs.

"We're going to look for him," Sebastian yelled.

"We'll find him!" James promised desperately. The two men hurried out.

The front door slammed. Nicole hesitated in the hallway, wondering whether she should join the search party, too.

Just then, to her great surprise, there came from the mudroom an extended, anguished, guttural bellow. It was a sound Nicole knew well from her days as a nurse. She closed her eyes and took a deep breath.

Katya was helping Kennedy into the front hall.

Katya looked exasperated. "For heaven's sake, Kennedy, enough with the melodrama. They'll find him."

Nicole said, "It's not melodrama, Katya. Your daughter's in labor."

"Don't be ridiculous," Katya countered.

Kennedy was almost crouching, hands on the wall for support.

Nicole went to the young woman. "Let's go into the living room. It's the warmest room in the house. I'll check your contractions."

Unable to speak, Kennedy allowed Nicole to support her as they slowly made their way into the living room. A fire flickered brightly in the fireplace, and the Christmas tree glittered in the window.

"Put your hands on the back of the chair," Nicole told Kennedy.

Kennedy leaned on the armchair with Nicole standing behind her. Suddenly, a gush of blood-tinged water flooded from her body.

"Kennedy! What are you doing? The rug is Turkish!" Katya cried.

Nicole ignored the other woman, her hands on Kennedy's belly.

"Katya, the baby is coming. Call 911."

"The baby isn't due for three more weeks," Katya argued, adding, "Maddox was ten days late."

Kennedy was growling constantly now. Digging her hands into the back of the chair for support, she gasped, "Mommy. *Call 911.*"

With a sniff, Katya took her cellphone out of the pocket of her cashmere skirt and punched in the numbers. She punched them in again. She looked at the phone, mystified. "It's dead. My cell is dead."

"Try the landline," Nicole told her. "In the kitchen."

"Ooooooooooh." Kennedy's legs were shaking. "Nicole, I think I'm having the baby."

"Yes. I think you are, too. Don't worry, Kennedy. You'll be fine."

Kennedy lifted her face to the ceiling, straining. A long wail tore from her body.

Katya ran in from the kitchen. "That line's dead, too."

"Must be the storm," Nicole murmured, preoccupied.

"Kennedy, are you okay?" Katya's splendid forehead wrinkled in concern.

Nicole calmly informed her: "Katya, she's having the baby. Now."

Katya opened her mouth to object, but her daughter's moans drove the reality past her doubts. "Dear Lord. What can we do?"

Nicole guided Katya's hands onto Kennedy's waist. "Hold Kennedy. Support her from behind. It's good that she's standing. Gravity will help the baby come down the birth canal."

"Where are you going?" Katya shrieked, her voice shrill with fear.

"To scrub up. I'll get some scissors, twine, and towels."

Katya went white. "I'm going to faint."

"Not now you're not," Nicole said in a tone that brooked no disagreement. She hurried from the room.

In the kitchen, she quickly, knowledgeably, gathered the things she needed. She dashed into the guest room to collect a pile of towels and pillows. She scrubbed her hands with hot water and soap, then raced back into the living room, where Kennedy was roaring in pain while Katya held her daughter up. It was impossible to guess which woman was trembling the most.

Nicole knelt behind Kennedy and lifted the skirt of her red dress, tucking it into the neck. She sliced off Kennedy's sodden maternity panties.

"Kennedy. I'm going to check how far down your baby has come."

"I can't do this!" Kennedy howled. "Give me something for the pain! Please!"

"Whiskey? Brandy?" Katya offered helpfully. "I have some Advil in my travel kit."

With expert gentleness, Nicole put one hand on Kennedy's hip, and with the other hand, she slowly explored the birth canal, delicately moving her hand up. She felt the head. As always, this first touch filled her with wonder and gratitude.

"Kennedy. Your baby's almost here."

Kennedy screamed. "Please! It hurts too much! I can't!"

Katya was weeping. "Help her, Nicole. Do something."

"Do you think you can move to the coffee table?" Nicole asked.

"Are you mad?" Katya asked. "The coffee table isn't long enough for her to—"

"I don't want her to lie down on it. I want her to lean her arms on it. I don't think she can stand up much longer."

Gasping, crimson-faced, Kennedy managed the few awkward steps, supported by her mother and Nicole.

Nicole swept the bronze bowl of nuts off onto the floor and tossed a pillow in its place. She helped Kennedy lower herself so that each knee was on a pillow and her arms and upper body were supported by the table. She put another pillow between Kennedy's legs.

"Oh, God!" Kennedy shrieked. "The baby's coming! The baby's coming! I can feel him coming!"

"Kennedy, listen to me. I want you to take a deep breath. When I say, I want you to push."

"What can *I* do?" Katya wrung her hands with worry.

"Go around to the other side of the table. Hold Kennedy's shoulders. Hold her tight when she pushes."

Katya did as Nicole said, kneeling on the floor among the flung walnuts, putting her hands on Kennedy's shoulders.

"Now, Kennedy, *push*," Nicole said.

Kennedy gripped her mother's arms and pushed down so fiercely her body shuddered with the effort. When she stopped, she collapsed against the pillow on the coffee table, gasping for breath, too drained to speak.

# 28

"Okay, Kennedy. Again. *Push.*"

Kennedy pushed. She felt a force helping her. Her mother was helping her, holding on to her shoulders with a strength Kennedy never knew Katya had. Nicole was helping her. Nicole was a calm blur of movement and words, a serious, capable, confident strength. Something else possessed Kennedy now, a formidable, irresistible power that filled Kennedy's body like water rushing into a vessel.

She pushed, lowing like a beast.

Pain tore through her. Something ripped inside her. She bellowed.

"Your baby's crowned," Nicole said. "One more push and he's here."

Shuddering, lost to the world, surrendering to what she could not evade, Kennedy yowled and pushed. The pain was unbearable—and then it diminished. She sagged against the coffee table, broken, mute, and helpless.

Behind her, Nicole was moving rapidly. "Come over here, Katya," she directed. "Give me the twine. Cut it here. Tie it here. Okay, now cut."

"Oh, God," Katya wept. "Oh, God, oh, God, oh God. Kennedy, you have a baby!"

Kennedy could only keen as she felt the placenta move through her, carrying more pain along with it.

"Kennedy, we're going to help you lie down now," Nicole said. "Katya, pile those pillows on the floor. Kennedy, you're going to rest against the pillows so we can put your daughter in your arms."

Through the fog of shimmering fatigue, one word stood out, in startling, terrifying bluntness. When the ultrasound was done months ago, the technician had told them the baby was a boy.

"Something's wrong with the baby," Kennedy sobbed.

Katya and Nicole laughed together.

"Nothing's wrong with your baby," Nicole insisted. "Now I'm going to help you lie down. Come on, lean on me, I can take your weight, we're going to turn a bit . . . there. More comfortable?"

Kennedy's eyes cleared as her weight was supported by the cushions behind her. She saw her mother kneeling next to her, holding a naked baby in her arms.

"Kennedy, she's a little girl." Katya lowered the baby into Kennedy's eager arms.

The baby was magenta-pink, covered with white wax, peeping like a bird, waving its arms and legs. Kennedy checked: yes, she was absolutely a little girl. The most beautiful little girl in the world.

"Oh, my baby darling," Kennedy cooed softly.

The baby turned her face toward Kennedy, instinctively settling into Kennedy's arms, against her breasts.

Kennedy looked up at Nicole. "Is she healthy? Does she have everything?"

Nicole was weeping and laughing at the same time. "She's perfect. She has everything. She doesn't even seem underweight. And she's long. Look how long her legs are. She's got her all her toes, fingernails, eyebrows—she's absolutely complete."

"She's beautiful," Kennedy whispered.

"She is. As soon as we can get hold of a doctor, or get over to the hospital, we'll get some antibiotic ointment to put in her eyes." Nicole held up her hand. "It's state law. It's done for all babies at birth, to prevent infection, but it doesn't have to be done immediately, it can wait, don't worry."

Kennedy couldn't stop staring at the tiny creature in her arms, so strange, so unknown, so entirely, absolutely belonging to her.

"Katya," Nicole said, "could you please get something

clean and warm for Kennedy? Something soft, that opens in the front? Perhaps a cotton robe?"

"I don't want to leave the baby," Katya confessed with tears in her eyes.

Nicole laughed. "She'll be here when you get back. Go to my room. My softest old robe is tossed over a chair." Nicole bent over Kennedy. "I want to wrap your baby in this towel for warmth, then I'll give her back to you."

Kennedy was vaguely aware of her mother leaving the room. When Nicole lifted the baby away from her, Kennedy realized how uncomfortable she was, and how soggy the towels were beneath her bum.

"Am I okay?" she asked. She realized she was shaking.

"You're fine. Childbirth is a messy business." As she spoke, Nicole wrapped the baby and placed her back in Kennedy's arms. "You're trembling because you've just had a baby. It's normal."

Katya returned with the white terry cloth robe.

"Help your daughter put it on," Nicole said. Once again, she took the baby.

Kennedy groaned as she struggled to sit up. Her mother knelt behind her, unzipping her red dress and pulling it up over her head. She unsnapped the maternity bra, which was wet with sweat, and swiftly patted Kennedy's neck and back with a towel before helping her slip her arms

into the downy robe. Katya's delicate ministrations released memories of her long-ago childhood, when her
mother had helped her dress. As her mind cleared of pain,
a kind of bliss replaced it at the thought of such care, such
tenderness.

"Do you think you could stand up?" Nicole asked.
"You'd be more comfortable on the sofa."

Kennedy nodded. With her mother's help, she shoved
herself into a standing position. Fluids ran down her legs.
"Sorry," Kennedy said. "Gross."

Nicole chuckled. "Natural." With another towel, she
dried Kennedy's legs.

Katya supported Kennedy as she limped toward the
sofa. "Don't fall on the nuts."

"Now why do I find that statement humorous?" Nicole
wondered aloud with a grin. She was layering the sofa
with more towels and plumping up pillows, working with
ease and efficiency with the baby tucked in one arm.

"I need a pad between my legs," Kennedy said.

Nicole paused. "I don't have any."

"I haven't had any for some time," Katya said.

The two women looked at each other and a comradely
expression of relief mixed with regret passed between
them.

"Well, I certainly haven't needed any for months,"
Kennedy told them.

"A towel will work," Nicole decided.

Kennedy lowered herself onto the sofa, which took her weight like a mound of clouds. Her mother arranged the robe over her legs. Nicole laid the baby in her arms. Kennedy gazed down at the pink, serene, wondering face, a face completely radiant with trust. Someone, her mother or Nicole, tucked a warm blanket around her, and Kennedy thought what a blessing it was to have that, just that, a person who covers you with a blanket and tucks it around you with care. Right now, it seemed a good reason to be born.

# 29

❄

Maddox ran and ran. He ran down the block and around the corner before he had to stop to catch his breath. Setting Pooh down, he huffed, "Don't run away."

The little dog cocked his head, wagged his tail, and scooted next to Maddox's leg.

At the other end of the street, a group of people were coming out of a restaurant, guffawing, hugging, patting one another on the shoulders. The sight and sounds encouraged Maddox, drew him toward them.

It was cold. Maddox glanced at Pooh. "You have fur," he reasoned. "I don't. I'll hold you if you get cold, okay?"

Pooh wagged his tail, so Maddox took his coat off the puppy and slipped his own arms into it. The warmth was immediate and wonderful.

"Come on, Pooh," Maddox said, lifting his chin and setting out optimistically, kicking his way through the snow. "Maybe we'll find some nice people with a cellphone. They can call Daddy and Mommy and then . . ."

His imagination took him no further. He would get there and see what happened next. They would be sorry, his parents, especially his mommy, who had screamed at him in the most terrible voice he had ever heard, as if she hated him, as if she had turned into one of those monsters on the games big boys played. At the memory, his eyes welled with tears. He had *not* been such a bad boy. He'd done worse things before. He'd spilled stuff and been sassy, and he wasn't good at sharing.

Maybe his mommy would be glad he had left.

Pooh slipped and slid along next to Maddox as he walked down the middle of the street. Plows and sanders had come through, so this road was clear, although snow continued to fall, turning to ice as it landed.

Still, Maddox was walking toward the center of town, which blazed with lights, providing a sort of warmth in his heart. By the time he got to the restaurant, the group of people were getting into cars and driving away, so he kept on walking, hands in his pocket, twisting his mouth around as he pondered what to do.

The bookstore was open. He saw people moving around inside.

"Come on, Pooh," he said, reaching way up for the handle on the door.

They stepped into a pool of summer. Merriment, chatter, and delicious warm air. Maddox stood by the door a moment, just savoring the heat, aware of his dog leaning on his ankle.

"We're closing!" someone called out.

Adults, all of them very tall, crowded and jostled to get to the counter with their last-minute purchases. One of them trod on Pooh's foot. Pooh yipped in surprise. The tall man glowered down at Maddox.

"Does that animal bite?"

"No," Maddox began. "We need—"

But the man turned away, moving up in line. A woman with boots like his mommy wore, with long pointed dagger-like heels, stepped near Pooh, who cowered closer to Maddox.

Dismayed, Maddox picked Pooh up in his arms, pushed the door open, and went back outside. He didn't want Pooh to get stabbed in the foot. He plodded down the street, lugging Pooh in his arms.

A sudden melancholy fell over him. By now his daddy should be running down the street, yelling for him, calling, "Come back, Maddox! We'll let you keep the dog!"

His stomach growled. His arms hurt. He set Pooh down on the icy sidewalk. Pooh tilted his head questioningly.

"I'm hungry, Pooh, and I'll bet you are, too." Maddox sniffed the air. No smells lured him forward.

He didn't know where to go or what to do. He'd run away full of pride and courage and filled with a sense of adventure. Now he knew he was only a cold, hungry, helpless boy.

# 30

His boy paused on the corner. Not the smartest thing to do, Pooh thought, because the wind howled so fiercely it almost knocked Maddox over. When they were walking, their momentum carried them forward into the wind, or the wind pushed them along, but standing made Pooh shudder with cold.

He was so hungry he wanted to whimper with misery. Yet he was so overjoyed that Maddox had taken him that his misery was offset. Mostly. His belly still rumbled and complained, as if it hadn't yet received the news of his good luck.

He peered up at the boy's face, searching for a clue to his mood. Where would they go next? The boy, although young and small, was a human, with access to doors in many warm places. He was smart and resourceful, too. After all, he'd built that warm fort.

Pooh allowed himself a moment—since Maddox was

still standing there like a lump—to puzzle over the mysterious ways of humans. He knew they couldn't be trusted; Cota Collins and her family had taught him that. He had been so sure that she loved him that he hadn't even known she could *stop* loving him. Perhaps, somehow, the fault was his.

But he believed Maddox loved him. Maddox had taken him. Maddox was with him now. And Maddox was certainly lovable, such a smart, valiant boy whose plump fingers were magnificent at scratching behind Pooh's ears.

The mystery was: Why were all those humans so terrible to each other? In the midst of this black, frightening night, they were inside a warm, bright house with the swooningly good aromas of delicious food all around them. They had a *family*, and for a moment a memory flickered in Pooh's mind, of a time when he was new, snuggling with a bunch of other squirming puppies, being licked by his mother, who looked just like him and smelled of warm milk. He remembered how his eyes opened more every day, how he wobbled around the cardboard box, learning his legs, clumsily stumbling into the other puppies—he remembered his brothers' and sisters' sharp tiny teeth! How they had rough-and-tumbled with one another, play-growling and snapping and pouncing.

He remembered how they were released out into the

yard one spring morning when the grass was fragrant and the sun fell benevolently on his back. The world surprised him, it was so enormous and bright. He would run back to his mother, to be sure she was still there, then trot back to play with his siblings.

One day, Cota came. She had picked him up, hugged him to her chest, stroked his fur, whispered lovingly into his ear.

He'd never seen his siblings or his mommy again. He'd entirely lost the trail of their odor.

Would Maddox leave him, too?

His boy's words broke into his thoughts. "Look, Pooh. We can get warm." Maddox marched bravely forward, slipping on the occasional icy patch, lifting his feet high over drifts that had avoided the shopkeepers' shovels.

Pooh struggled along behind, leaping, sliding, trotting, limping—ice had frozen between his toes, slicing the pads of his paws.

They progressed up the sidewalk, their way lighted by the small twinkling Christmas trees, toward the giant tree at the top of Main, the one in front of the brick building. Even this mammoth evergreen swayed from the force of the wind.

"Here!" Maddox shouted.

Snow blew into his eyes. Pooh blinked, then saw it. In

front of the wide white Methodist church, on the snow-covered front lawn, stood a funny structure: a three-sided shed golden with light. A spotlight was aimed at it, making the interior blaze, and on top of the shed was another light in the shape of a star.

Inside were people and a donkey. Pooh lifted his lip to growl a warning, but as they got nearer, he realized something was off about the other creatures. They weren't the right size. They didn't smell. Ah, they were statues. A father, a mother, a baby in a cradle, and the donkey.

But on the floor of the shed was real straw. Thick, golden straw.

Pooh felt himself lifted up into Maddox's arms. The boy shoved through the snow and into the shed. They were warmer immediately, from the spotlight.

"We'll stay here," Maddox told Pooh. The boy wriggled down at the back of the shed, holding Pooh close to his stomach, and used his hand to rake straw over their legs and torsos.

Warmer and warmer. The wind buffeted the sides of the shed, but it stood firm.

"We'll be safe here," Maddox assured Pooh.

Pooh yipped once, lightly, in agreement. He arched his head so he could lick Maddox's hands, which were red with cold.

"We'll rest and keep warm while I think what to do next," Maddox decided.

Pooh snuggled as close to the boy as he could. The wonderful warmth made him drowsy. But the hunger cramping his belly kept him awake.

# 31

The living room was toasty. Nicole added logs to the fire and stirred it with the poker. The Christmas tree lights threw off a bit of heat, and of course the furnace was on.

Kennedy and her baby girl were ensconced on the sofa, covered and wrapped with blankets. Katya was performing the unthinkable: Down on her hands and knees, she crawled around the floor, picking up walnuts and replacing them in the bronze bowl.

Nicole gathered up the pile of bloodstained towels. "I'll get these into the washing machine."

"Oh, thank you, Nicole," Kennedy said. "I don't want Maddox to be frightened when he comes in and sees so much blood."

Katya frowned. "The carpet is still stained. Plus, it reeks." Suddenly, her legs buckled and she sat down, hard, on the floor. Her face was white. Her eyes were wide, her pupils dilated.

"Mommy?" Kennedy asked. "Are you okay?"

Katya said, "You had a baby." Tilting her face up toward Nicole, she gasped, "My God. What would we have done if you hadn't been here? Nicole, how can I ever thank you? I'm so grateful." She raised her hands to her face. Her shoulders shook. She made a noise that in any other woman would be considered blubbering.

Nicole bent over and wrapped her arms around Katya. "You're in shock. Let's get you in a chair. Come on, right here, where you can see Kennedy and the baby. You would have been fine without me," she assured Katya. "It's all very dramatic, isn't it?" She helped Katya stand on her shaking legs and stagger into a chair.

"Thank you, Nicole." Katya gripped Nicole's arm. "Truly. Thank you. I am full of admiration."

"You're welcome. I'm glad to be part of it all." She could tell that this was getting to be a bit more sentimental than Katya could easily deal with. "I'll be right back."

She left the room, lugging the heavy soggy towels. Even after a washing, they would be pretty much shot for normal use. She'd keep them in the mudroom for people to wipe off their shoes. She dumped them into the washing machine, added detergent, and turned the dial.

Then she leaned against the quietly humming machine, relaxed, and prayed. She prayed with gratitude for this new healthy baby, for Kennedy's quick and relatively painless labor and birthing, and she sent selfish words of thankfulness that everything had gone so well with Nicole at the receiving end. If anything had gone wrong, and things could have, Nicole would have been blamed. She would have blamed herself. She was always filled with both anticipation and anxiety when a mother gave birth, but this had been an extraordinary situation. Now she was completely out of gas. She could lie down right there on the mudroom floor and take a snooze.

Instead, she went into the kitchen to brew fresh pots of coffee and hot chocolate.

# 32

❄

First, Maddox just lay there, catching his breath, allowing the warmth to sink into his body like melted butter on toast. (Cinnamon toast would be excellent right now.)

He'd never been so cold before, and the cold had made him frightened and confused. Standing on the street corner with the wind shoving him in the back like a giant saying Go *away, you're not wanted here,* he'd wished with all his heart to hear his father call him, to hear running footsteps, to be swept up into loving arms. He'd stood there, waiting, listening, hoping . . . and no one came.

His mother had warned him. "Don't leave my side," she always said when they were in a store. "Don't leave the yard on your own. It's easy to get lost."

He had disobeyed her. His mommy often said, "*Now* look what happened!" when he'd done something wrong.

*Now* look what happened.

Out in the freezing dark, he'd been scared, shaking

with cold and fright. Here, nestled in the sweet-smelling straw with Pooh's tiny body snuggled next to him, Maddox's spirits lifted. Even though there was no wall in front, it was still like being in a house. There was light from the spotlight. There were other people, too, kind of. Even if they were only statues, he felt less alone.

One problem: no food. Of course there wasn't any food, the statues of Mary, Joseph, and baby Jesus didn't require food.

He scrabbled in his pants pockets to see if he had any candy canes left, even a broken piece. But no. He'd eaten every bite. Hugging Pooh to him, he realized the dog was probably hungry, too. Pooh was so skinny. But what a good, loyal, friend! Maddox would *never* throw Pooh out into the cold night.

So he couldn't go home. Could he? If he went back, would they allow him to keep Pooh in the house just for a while?

If he tried, could he find his way back? He thought so. Granddad's house was right up the street from the big brick Jared Coffin House, and that wasn't far away, was it?

Next to him, Pooh began to snore, a sweet rumbling sound that made Maddox grin. Relaxing into the straw, he realized he was awfully tired from all that running and carrying Pooh. Being warm made him drowsy.

A stick of straw poked his ear. He moved his head, trying to get comfortable, and sort of sat up, and sort of scanned the streets outside in case his daddy was out there looking for him.

The street was empty, except for the blowing snow.

His lower lip quivered. Tears filled his eyes. Sadness filled his heart. Snot filled his nose—unattractive, his mommy usually told him. He couldn't help it, though. He was scared.

# 33

❄

The baby slept, but Kennedy was a bubbling emotional geyser threatening to erupt momentarily.

She had a daughter. Joy!

Then terror blasted through her. *Maddox*. Her little boy.

Maddox had run away because she had been horrid to him. Shame, anguish, mommy guilt of the most torturous kind.

She'd given birth without James present. Heartbreak, disappointment, more guilt—couldn't she have waited?

Her mother had been present. Nicole had been helpful. Okay, more than helpful. Nicole had taken charge and conducted the entire chaotic mess with as much expertise as anyone could wish for. She had been an angel of kindness. More guilt, because Kennedy had been such a beast to Nicole.

Her mother was on the floor again with more towels,

soaking up the natural but still rather gruesome muck of childbirth. That in itself—her mother performing manual labor—filled Kennedy with incredulity. Katya did not enjoy housework. Never had. But Katya was humming a Christmas carol, and she looked exultant. Kennedy was confused.

Most of all, where was Maddox? Shouldn't her father and James have found her child and brought him back? She didn't want her son to believe that she'd blithely forgotten about him, or worse, tossed him away—"You're a bad boy!"—then lay down and gotten herself another child. Her heart wrung with worry. She was glad to have a daughter, but so frightened for Maddox.

Was this family life at its most basic? A cauldron of constantly changing sensations? Kennedy was stunned to realize that she'd been in labor all day without realizing it because she'd been so overwhelmed with intense and often ungenerous emotions. How had her own mother maneuvered through family life so serenely, like a sailboat on a windless sea? How would Kennedy survive her own family life, especially if she was as self-centered and myopic as she'd been with little Maddox?

Her sweet little boy, her darling child, with his giggle, his innocence, his wide-eyed trust in his mommy. Her heart broke when she thought of the radiant confidence on his face when he watched her. She knew she'd been cranky with him lately, restless and uncomfortable in her own body. She'd tried to explain that to him, but how could a four-year-old possibly comprehend the discomfort of a pregnant woman? She'd been mad to think he could. She'd been awful to call him a bad boy. She'd been so out of her mind she hadn't even realized she was in labor.

Kennedy was mortified. Here she was, tucked up with her new baby in her arms, warm and well-cared-for, and her precious son was out there in the bitter stormy night. She should search for him. She struggled to sit up. Not a good idea.

"Mommy?" she quavered.

Katya responded instantly. "Yes, sweetie?"

"Would you help James and Daddy search for Maddox? I'm so afraid. They should be back with him by now."

Katya hesitated. "Of course I'll go. But someone should stay with you. Would you rather Nicole searched and I stayed?"

Her mother's words appeared to be free of judgment.

"I suppose since Nicole's a nurse, and the baby is so new, and I'm still a bit of a mess . . ." Kennedy let her voice trail off.

"You're right." Katya rose to her feet. "I'll put on my coat and help look for Maddox. Don't worry, darling. We'll find him."

"Thank you, Mommy." Kennedy began to cry. What if

they didn't find him? What if he was hiding in the dark garage of a summer family who had gone away? What if he developed pneumonia or hypothermia?

What if Maddox thought no one was looking for him? What if he thought that because she'd told him he was bad, she no longer loved him? She imagined her son cold, lost, and frightened, and sobs broke out, startling her newborn babe. But she couldn't stop crying.

# 34

❄

Nicole entered the living room to find Katya with her own arms full of stained cloths and towels.

"I got it as dry as I could." Katya stared ruefully at the stained rug.

"It's fine," Nicole told her. "The heat of the fire will dry it, and we'll toss a throw rug over it. In fact, I know just the one. It's a Christmas rug my grandmother hooked for me, with snowmen and decorations on it."

Katya, who had obviously recovered from her sentimental moment, looked horrified.

"Maddox will like it," Nicole reminded her. "He'll think it's a decoration and won't know what it's hiding."

"Mommy's going to go look for Maddox," Kennedy said from the sofa. She was weeping steadily. "They should be back by now."

Nicole set the tray of warm drinks on the coffee table.

Squeezing onto the sofa next to Kennedy, she lifted the young woman's arm and put her fingers on her wrist, taking her pulse.

"You're fine, Kennedy. I'm sure Maddox is fine, too. He can't have gone far. The three of us need to take a moment to settle down. We've all been part of a momentous occasion. Let's have some coffee—hot chocolate for you, Kennedy. If they're still not back by the time we've finished our drinks, Katya or I can go out and look, too." She handed the drinks around.

Katya was content to let Nicole take charge. She sipped her coffee, so rich and fragrant, with the kick of Bailey's in it. "Alcohol?"

Nicole nodded. "For medicinal purposes," she said, not quite joking. She took a restoring sip of her own coffee.

Katya peered over at her granddaughter, tucked securely in Kennedy's arms. "What is she doing?"

"She's sleeping," Kennedy said. Glancing at Nicole, she asked, "That's okay, right?"

"That's absolutely okay. She's probably tired, too. She's just been born. She's warm, she can smell her mommy, you're holding her next to your heart so she can hear it beating, she's exactly where she should be."

"If only Maddox were here," Kennedy wept. "Today's been such a *jumble*. I feel like I've done everything wrong.

I can't even love this new baby as much as I should because I'm so frightened for Maddox."

Katya chuckled. "Mommy fear. It's the worst. I used to be terrified when you took gymnastics. I often had to leave the meet to throw up."

"I never knew that," Kennedy said.

Katya shrugged. "I thought it would be unhealthy for you to be aware of my emotional turmoil."

Kennedy gawped. "You had emotional turmoil?"

Nicole hid her smile by drinking more coffee.

Katya rolled her eyes. Obviously the coffee had helped her regain her composure. "Thank you for this most reviving drink, Nicole." She emitted the most elegant, subtle of sighs. "It will help. I promised Kennedy I'd help search for Maddox."

"I'll go." Nicole stood up. "You should stay with your daughter."

"But you're the nurse," Katya reasoned. "You should stay, in case something goes wrong."

"Nothing will go wrong," Nicole promised Katya. At the same time, a warmth flushed through her, not entirely caused by the Bailey's and coffee. Katya trusted her with her daughter and the new baby. Katya had stepped down from her pedestal. Perhaps they could never be friends, but possibly she and Kennedy's mother, Sebastian's former wife, could be allies.

Katya glanced toward the window, almost completely iced over by blowing snow. She shivered delicately. "Perhaps I will stay here . . . with my daughter."

Nicole didn't hesitate. "Of course," she agreed, heading to the hall and her coat.

# 35

✳

Snix snored so enormously he woke himself. It took him a moment to realize where he was—he'd slept in so many different places during his young life.

He was lying in straw inside a shed, warm as warm could be, cuddled next to his boy Maddox.

But Maddox was *crying*.

Snix sat up and licked Maddox's cheeks. The tears tasted salty and made Snix even hungrier.

"Oh, Pooh," Maddox sniffled. "I don't know what to do. I want my mommy and daddy. I want to go home."

Snix sat up straight, attempting to look large and confident. For one thing, he knew he had to think of himself as *Pooh* if he wanted to stay with the boy, and oh boy, did he want to stay with this boy. For another thing . . . well, what? What could he do?

He wagged his tail, hopefully. He gave a yip of encouragement. He tried to look bright-eyed.

His stomach growled.

Maddox's stomach growled.

Perhaps . . . Pooh chewed a stick of straw. Nope, didn't work. He spit it out.

Snow whirled into the shed, glittering in the glow from the spotlight.

"We've got to go back out there, Pooh." Maddox stood up. "We've got to go home."

Pooh yapped once.

Maddox frowned. He thought out loud: "I'm sure they'll take me back." Looking down at Pooh, he clenched his fists. "But I won't let them take you away from me, Pooh. I'll protect you. Even if we have to run away again."

Pooh's heart sank. He wasn't sure he could survive much longer without food.

"MADDOX? MADDOX!"

Running footsteps came toward them. Snow exploded as four booted feet stomped through the drifts in front of the shed. Two huge figures fell on their knees.

"Maddox." The boy's father reached out and clutched the boy to him. "Maddox, hey guy, I'm so glad I found you. What a smart kid you are to discover such a warm place to stay. Aren't you hungry? Don't you want to go home? Your mommy and grandmommy and Nicole are so worried about you. Granddad and I have been looking everywhere for you."

Pooh watched as the boy's father ran his hands over the boy's head and body, as if checking to be certain he was still all there.

"I'm sorry, Daddy, don't be mad at me—"

"I'm not mad, Maddox. Granddad and I are so glad to find you—"

"Maddox, you need a hat. Take mine." Granddad pulled his wool cap over the boy's head.

Pooh trembled as he heard the humans babble, everyone talking at once. The great big men had tears in their eyes. They hugged and touched Maddox as if he were the most precious thing in the world.

"Come on, Mad Man. We're going home. It's Christmas Eve." The daddy lifted Maddox up in his arms and held him tight.

Pooh whimpered, just a tiny whimper that kind of slipped out . . .

"I want Pooh!" Maddox wriggled in his father's arms. "I won't go without Pooh."

Pooh shivered with hope and terror.

Two huge arms reached in and picked Pooh up. "I've got Pooh," the grandfather said. "He's coming home with us, too."

*"In the house,"* Maddox stipulated.

"Of course in the house," said the daddy. "We wouldn't leave a puppy out in the cold on a night like this."

The granddaddy wrapped the outside of his coat around Pooh. "We need to give this dog some food. I can feel his ribs."

The men set off tramping through the falling snow. They passed Sweet Inspirations with its windows full of candy. They passed Zero Main with its bright Christmas wreath. They passed Petticoat Row Bakery with its windows full of gingersnaps and cookies shaped like stars. They zigzagged around the tall brick Jared Coffin House, which had been standing since 1845 and still stood undaunted in the ferocious blizzard.

Pooh could feel the granddaddy's heart beating. The man's arms were big and held him much more securely than Maddox's thin arms had done—not that Pooh was complaining about Maddox, who was his true champion and best friend.

They went up Centre Street, past the Congregational Church. They forked left onto Westchester. Most of the houses were dark and closed, but one house glowed with light.

"Back door," the granddaddy yelled. "We're covered with snow. We can kick off our boots in the mudroom."

Pooh sagged. His memories of the mudroom were not good ones. The woman who didn't like dogs, the yelling . . .

He had no choice. He could struggle out and run away, but where would he go? Surely this time they would allow him to stay.

Doors opened and closed. Pooh was set on the floor. Boots were kicked off, scattering snow onto the already wet throw rug.

Pooh saw a pair of men's feet in red socks leave the room. Then a man's feet in brown socks left.

"We found him!" the daddy yelled.

"Oh, thank heavens!" Voices poured from the front of the house.

"Good Lord!" one of the men cried.

Shouts of jubilation rose and what sounded like dozens of voices intertwined. A thin baby's wail sirened through the noise and the voices softened.

Pooh sat in the mudroom, dripping, probably smelling of wet dog hair, *alone.*

"This calls for champagne," a man announced.

Footsteps grew closer to the kitchen. Pooh peered around the door. Only his nose and eyes . . .

"Hey, you." The granddaddy saw Pooh looking.

Pooh flinched and went small.

"We didn't forget you." The granddaddy lifted Pooh up, carried him a few feet, and set him down again. "But we've got a new baby in the house, the prettiest little girl you've ever seen. My goodness, there is no end to the wonders that can happen. Leave the house for thirty minutes and come home to a granddaughter!" He poured milk into a bowl and set the bowl in the microwave. The man opened the freezer and scrabbled around, all the while singing "Jingle Bells."

Pooh reflected silently, but not unhappily, that human beings were odd.

"Here," said the granddaddy. "I warmed the milk in the microwave. Drink up while I thaw some meatloaf for you, little fellow. Don't tell Nicole. She won't miss it anyway, with all the food in the house. Now where's the champagne?"

Pooh lapped up the warm milk as fast as his pink tongue could go while the man gathered glasses and popped a cork and set them on a tray.

"Dinner is served, your majesty." The man set a plate in front of Pooh. Suddenly, while Pooh watched, he pulled his sweater off over his head and piled it on the floor next to the vent. "Here. When you're through eating, you can rest on this. I'm too damned hot with all this excitement." He picked up the tray and started to leave the room. Stopping, he said to Pooh with a serious tone, "No accidents now, okay?"

Pooh sat down, lifted his head into its most noble pose

and remained still, doing the best he could to signal his comprehension and agreement.

The man chortled. "You're a smart one, aren't you?" He hurried away.

Pooh dove into the plate of warm delicious meatloaf.

# 36

❋

The living room was crowded with people all talking at once. Nicole took off the coat she'd just put on and settled into a chair in the corner to watch the grand reunion. Kennedy handed the baby to Katya and opened her arms to Maddox who threw himself into her embrace. James stood swaying in front of the baby, looking so green Nicole thought he might vomit.

James fell on his knees in front of his wife and took her face in his hands.

"How did you do this?" he asked, his face shining with tears. "We weren't gone more than half an hour, and you had the baby? Are you okay? Do you need to go to the hospital? It's a girl? How can it be a girl? Kennedy, I love you."

Katya sank gracefully into another armchair, both arms supporting her tiny granddaughter. "When I had Kennedy," she mused aloud, "I didn't *comprehend* her at first. I was sort of dozy on painkillers of some sort. Look at this splendid infant. She seems so peaceful."

Maddox squirmed away from his mother and ran to Katya. "Let me see her, Grandmama."

Katya held the bundle out for Maddox to see. "Careful," she warned. "The baby is brand-new and fragile."

As she viewed the lucky family—James with Kennedy, Katya with Maddox and the baby, Nicole allowed herself a moment of self-indulgence. She was spent. The adrenaline and calm ecstasy of practiced, knowledgeable, focused skill that had flooded her when Kennedy began to give birth drained away now, leaving her limp. She was not as young as she used to be. She'd done all the kneeling and bracing and assisting and cleaning with the swift ease of a ballerina, but right now her joints and muscles informed her they needed a nice hot bath with Epsom salts.

Her emotions were in upheaval, too. The birth of a baby was always—to use a terribly overused word—an *awesome* event. She hadn't recovered yet from the anxiety, like background music in her mind, that something was wrong with Kennedy or the baby, or could go wrong during the delivery, or, she hardly dared think it, that *she* could have done something wrong. If she hadn't been a trained nurse and a mature adult, she would have shrieked and screamed right along with Kennedy all through the delivery. The effort of pretending to be calm had taken its toil on her strength.

She could scarcely summon up the energy to keep the proper expression on her face, a smile that asserted "I'm so happy for you all," instead of a childish pout declaring "Doesn't anyone care about *me*?" and she felt wearily guilty about that.

Sebastian entered the living room with a tray of flutes and an opened bottle of champagne. He set it on the side table by the window. "Champagne for everyone."

"Even me?" Maddox asked.

Sebastian and the other adults laughed indulgently.

"It's a special day, so you may have a sip of mine," James told his son.

Sebastian couldn't stop smiling. He stepped away from the table for a moment, drawn inexorably to the sight of his granddaughter. He leaned over the back of the chair where Katya sat holding the baby while Maddox raised himself up on tiptoes to peek at the blanketed bundle.

There they were, Nicole thought. Everyone together who belongs together. By the window, the tall Christmas tree she'd decorated twinkled like love made visible. In the fireplace the logs burned low, crackling with sparks as the bark snapped. Stockings hung from the mantel. The crèche sat in perfection on the table. Nicole didn't belong in this intimate, elementary family group. She had learned in harder times how to steel her heart, and now she did her best to remember. She took deep breaths. She tried to count her blessings.

The phone rang.

"The phones are working again," Nicole noted to no one in particular.

Sebastian answered. His tense shoulders softened. "Katya? It's for you."

Katya hesitated, briefly, before laying the baby in James's arms. She reached for the phone.

"Hello?" Katya's voice was wary.

While the others watched, Katya's face began to glow. "Yes, I miss you, too. Wait a moment." Putting her hand over the receiver, she said, "It's Alonzo. I'll take this into the other room." She left, head high, triumphant.

*Father Christmas, I owe you one,* Nicole thought. Exchanging glances with Sebastian, she could see he was thinking the same thing.

Suddenly, Maddox flew across the room and pitched himself at Nicole. Hauling himself up onto her lap, the little boy leaned against her. "Nicole, Pooh is in the kitchen," he whispered.

Maddox's sweet breath in her ear, his easy confidence in her being his friend, expanded Nicole's heart into confetti and fireworks. For a moment, she couldn't speak.

She cleared her throat. "That's wonderful, Maddox. Is he okay?"

"Yes. I kept him warm all through the storm."

"Maybe he needs something to eat," Nicole suggested.

"Oh, yes!"

Sebastian was pouring the champagne and handing it around.

"I'll be right back for mine," Nicole told him.

Maddox took her hand and pulled her from the room, down the hall to the kitchen, where Pooh lay curled up on Sebastian's sweater, snoring, deeply asleep. An empty bowl and plate were on the floor.

"It looks like Granddad has already fed Pooh," Nicole said. Dropping down to Maddox's level, she put her hands on his shoulders. "You must be hungry, too, after your adventures. Can I fix you something?"

Maddox's eyes sparkled. "You make the best grilled cheeses, Nicole."

"Then I'll make you one right now," she said, and set to work, while Maddox sat next to Pooh, scratching him softly just behind the ears.

# 37

Christmas Eve passed in a blur for Kennedy.

While her father drove off in the blizzard to fetch a friend of his who was a physician, James helped her into their bedroom so she could shower and slip on her maternity nightgown. Dr. Morris turned out to be an older woman, even calmer than Nicole, with gentle hands and a way of humming when she examined Kennedy. Not only did she pronounce Kennedy in A-plus condition, she presented her with a box of pads she'd brought from the hospital, a great relief for Kennedy on this night when every drugstore in town was shut tight. Overloaded with emotion and the drama of the evening, Kennedy thought that this humble, ordinary gift meant more than silver and gold.

Dr. Morris checked the baby, proclaiming her perfectly healthy. She put the necessary antibiotic ointment on her eyes, before, obviously pleased to be so useful, presenting Kennedy with a bag she'd prepared at the hospital. It held disposable diapers, tiny cotton shirts and several sleep rompers with infinitely small cotton cuffs that folded over the baby's hands to prevent her from scratching her face.

After Sebastian drove Dr. Morris home, Nicole set out a buffet on the dining room table: the beef Wellington sliced into pieces, vegetables, warm bread. No one sat at the table, but wandered here and there with a plate and a glass, perching on the edge of a chair, saying over and over again, "Isn't it amazing? Can you believe she's here? And on Christmas Eve!" Everyone was still animated and vaguely flustered, constantly peeking at the baby as if to be certain she really existed.

After some discussion, James helped Maddox rouse the sleepy little dog and take him out into the backyard where the animal performed his physical duties with alacrity, then raced back into the house. Tonight, James and Kennedy agreed, during a private conference, Pooh could sleep on the floor in Maddox's bedroom. After all, Kennedy thought with a private, slightly guilty smugness, if the dog did something on the rug, it wouldn't be her job to deal with it.

Because Pooh was allowed to sleep in his room, Maddox went to bed easily, and after his adventurous evening, he fell asleep at once. The dog, James told Kennedy, curled up on the rug next to the bed as if he considered himself Maddox's protector.

Kennedy was thankful that Maddox had the animal at least for a few nights. It would keep him from feeling excluded in the commotion over the new baby. Perhaps she'd even let him keep the dog.

Kennedy was utterly drained. Her head swam with the buzz of her family's conversation. People loomed up at her like boats through the fog.

"How is she?" Sebastian asked, or James, or Katya.

"Is she still sleeping?" Katya inquired, or Sebastian, or James.

"Would you like me to hold her while you eat?" offered James, or Katya, or Sebastian.

Nicole came to her rescue. "Kennedy, you shouldn't overexert yourself. It's time for you to get in bed and go to sleep."

"But the baby, where will she sleep?" Kennedy worried.

"In a dresser drawer, just as infants have throughout the centuries."

Kennedy recoiled with dismay. "The wood will be so hard."

Nicole shook her head. "I've lined it with quilts. Besides, she'll probably end up in bed with you and James."

Nicole showed Kennedy how to wrap the baby "like a

burrito"—so snugly the baby felt as contently secure as she had been Kennedy's belly.

"Now go to bed and get some sleep. We're not as wiped out as you are. In fact, we're all rather overexcited. So until we all go to bed," Nicole told Kennedy, "someone out here in the living room will hold your baby."

"I want to hold her," Kennedy confessed. "I don't want to let her go."

"The best thing you can do for her now," Nicole assured her, "is sleep."

"I'll see you in the morning, darling." Katya kissed Kennedy's forehead. "Before I leave for Boston."

Nothing had ever felt as soft as the plump mattress Kennedy lay on. Clouds, or perhaps it was a down comforter, warmed her weary body. Sleep came at once.

And good thing, for when the baby's thin cry from the drawer woke her at four in the morning, everyone else was asleep. Next to her on the bed, James snored loudly, a chainsaw noise that drowned out his daughter's cries.

Kennedy lifted her daughter from the dresser drawer and carried her into the living room. She changed her diaper and wrapped her snugly again. She decided to rest on the sofa, holding the infant in her arms.

The windows were black with deep night. The blizzard had passed. The wind was gone. It was silent throughout the house and over the island. The fire had burned out in the fireplace, but the room was still warm. Kennedy turned on the lights of the Christmas tree to keep her company as she rested with her babe in her arms.

She couldn't believe her good fortune. Now she had a son and a daughter, and a husband who loved them. Her mother was leaving in the morning to meet Alonzo in Boston. And now she could finally admit it: Kennedy had never seen her father look so happy as when he was with Nicole.

As for Nicole—all Kennedy's animosity had vanished, replaced by the cheering assurance that she would have her father's new, steady-handed and knowledgeable wife in her life as she went forward as a mother. She wished she had some way to thank Nicole, to express her inexpressible appreciation for all she'd done. What could she possibly do to articulate her gratitude?

In the morning, Kennedy decided sleepily, she'd tell James what she'd like to name their new daughter.

Nicole Katya Noel.

# AN ISLAND CHRISTMAS

To Deborah and Mark Beale

*With love & more memories to come*

# 1

The Friday of Thanksgiving weekend was unusually cold, with a strong salty breeze blowing off Nantucket Sound, but the hundreds of islanders clustered on the corner of Main Street and Orange didn't mind the weather. As twilight fell at four o'clock, friends, neighbors, and visiting relatives chatted together, rubbing their hands for warmth and discussing Christmas plans. Children jumped up and down, all of them antsy with anticipation. Dogs strained at their leashes, trying to sniff other dogs.

On the top step of the Pacific National Bank, a man dressed like an old-time town crier stood in his black cape, red muffler, and glossy top hat, like a conjurer about to perform magic. And wasn't electricity a kind of magic, especially when carried in a cable along the watery floor of Nantucket Sound, thirty miles from the mainland to the island? The town crier offered a hearty greeting, flicked a switch, and suddenly all the way to the harbor, on both sides of the long cobblestone street, short plump festive evergreens burst into twinkling radiance like a chorus line of flamboyant elves. In front of the bank, a thirty-foot-tall fat Norwegian spruce suddenly blazed with white lights and crimson bows. The holidays had officially arrived, the shops were adorned, and the boisterous crowd, led by the town's beloved music teacher, sang the season's first carols.

The exuberant voices of the singers carried a few blocks down to a charming, painstakingly restored 1840s Greek Revival house on Chestnut Street. Jilly Gordon, who in past years had always attended the festivities, now sat in her peach cashmere sweater set, curled up on a down-filled sofa in front of a crackling fire. She was sobbing.

Jilly was on the phone with her best friend, Nicole Somerset. "Oh, Nicole, I really don't know if my heart can take this. I don't understand why Felicia wants to live so far away."

"Of course you know exactly why, Jilly. Felicia wants to live with the man she's going to marry and the man she's going to marry lives in Utah."

"Utah . . ." Jilly moaned. "Why doesn't she just move to the moon?"

"Jilly, you're taking this too personally. Felicia is not trying to get away from you. Not everyone appreciates this funny isolated island the way we do. She'll be happier in Utah, where she can do all that hiking, skiing, and rafting she's always enjoyed."

"It's all so dangerous! Why can't she be more like Lauren? More sensible, more prudent? Plus, if she *has* to climb mountains, why can't she climb them in New Hampshire or Massachusetts? We have perfectly fine mountains in the east!"

"Felicia prefers the desert. You know that. She enjoys the hot sun on her skin. But more than that, and most important, Felicia loves Archie. She sounds very happy with him. He seems to be the perfect guy for her. You can't change that, Jilly, and you can't change your daughter. She's twenty-nine years old."

Jilly frowned. "I will never understand why these girls are so different. Lauren was always such a girly girl while Felicia even thinks her name is too prim! It was my grandmother's name! But I thought she treasured Nantucket. When she's here, she's always swimming or walking on the moors or out in the harbor sailing or in her kayak or on that—that, that new way to drown yourself, what do you call it?"

"Paddleboard. It's fun, Jilly."

"Fine," Jilly sniffed. "Paddleboard. For the elegant woman."

Nicole laughed. "You're just all wound up because she's getting married. Come on, Jilly, give the girl some credit for trying to make you happy. She's agreed—no, *she suggested* holding her wedding on Nantucket on Christmas Day. Isn't that proof enough she wants to please you?"

Jilly blew her nose on a tissue. She could do this on the telephone with Nicole because they were best friends. "I know you're right, Nicole. The irony is, I don't want her to get married here this Christmas. Steven Hardy has just

218NANCY THAYER

bought the house next door to us right here on Chestnut Street."

"Wait. Whiplash. What?"

"Miles and Elaine Hardy were our first close friends when we moved here to Nantucket. Their son Steven is just Felicia's age, and they were best friends and maybe more than that. He's knockout handsome and really sweet."

"You've told me about him. Wasn't he Felicia's prom date in high school?"

"Yes, they made the most stunning couple. They lost touch when they went off to college, and then Miles and Elaine moved to Arizona so we lost touch with them. Now I've just found out that Steven is moving back here. He's a fabulously successful stockbroker, and he's bought the house next door because he wants to live year-round on the island! Just think, Nicole, if Felicia married him—"

"Hang on. How do you know he isn't married?"

"The realtor told me."

"I'm speechless."

"*I'm* desperate! Remember when George and I flew out to see Felicia in Utah last year, we met Archie? He was muddy, bruised, unshaven, and he had blood on his T-shirt!"

"Jilly. Get a grip. You told me he'd just returned from leading a white-water rafting tour. You showed me photos of him. I think Archie's handsome."

"Fine, he's handsome, but in a Gerard Butler, hairy

swashbuckler way. Steven is much more elegant, all very Pierce Brosnan, suit and tie and briefcase. He's been over for dinner since he moved back to the island. I'd like to invite him for Christmas dinner."

"Maybe you should rethink that."

"Well, I didn't know Felicia was going to call me up and drop this wedding on me. I thought she'd come home for Christmas . . ."

Jilly stopped talking as her mind, leaping ahead of her mouth, exploded with such a brilliant idea she almost laughed aloud. Felicia was bringing Archie to the island two weeks before Christmas, so she'd have some time to show her fiancé all her favorite spots. Two weeks might be just enough time for Jilly to throw Felicia and Steven together . . . surely once they saw each other again, and spent time with each other, and . . .

"Jilly? Are you still there?"

"Um. Sorry. My mind wandered. I guess I'm overwhelmed with Felicia's news, plus the responsibility of turning this house into a magic Christmas scene plus a house for a perfect wedding reception."

"Jilly, you've got to slow down. You always set your standards way too high. You'll drive yourself crazy this way. Your house doesn't have to look *perfect*, although I've got to say you are starting with perfection. I've never seen a house so beautifully decorated and completely uncluttered as your house. And you know I'll help you in any way I can."

"That's kind of you, Nicole. I'm sure I'll call on you." Jilly took a deep breath. She really wasn't manic or an overwrought anal-compulsive. Or maybe she was, but just occasionally. "Are your stepdaughter and her family coming to your house this Christmas?" Jilly asked.

"No. They're going to spend part of the holiday with her mother and Alonzo and the rest of it with James's parents. I have to say I'm relieved. Sebastian and I are looking forward to having a peaceful holiday. We deserve it after last year. Plus, everyone's here for Thanksgiving." Nicole switched the focus back to Jilly. "What does George think about all this?" George Gordon was a retired accountant: kind, thoughtful, leisurely, and logical.

"Oh, George! He stays in his study at his computer working on his family tree." Jilly's laugh was tinged with hysteria. "That's kind of ironic, isn't it? He's so busy tracing his ancestors that he doesn't deal with what's going on with his real living family."

"Well, after all, Jilly, what could George do? Do you expect him to fly out to Utah, tie your daughter up, and drive her back here in the trunk of a car?" Nicole was glad to attempt to jolly her friend along. Last Christmas, Jilly had saved Nicole from losing her mind. This was what friends did for each other.

Jilly laughed. "Now that you mention it, it doesn't seem like such a bad idea. I think this Archie fellow has Felicia under his spell."

"I should certainly hope he has her under his spell if

she's going to marry him. That's the only reason to get married, isn't it? Being crazy in love with a man?"

"Nicole, you are such a romantic." Jilly rose from the sofa, picked up a poker, and poked the logs.

Actually, she realized, it was rather romantic right here in her own living room. The fire filled the house with the friendly crackles and pops and the alluring aroma of apple wood. Her furniture—handsomely restored antiques or reproductions—gleamed from frequent polishings, and needlepoint pillows she'd created herself brightened the sofas and chairs. The Christmas tree, resplendent with carefully collected antique ornaments, glittered in front of the bay window. All along the fireplace mantel paraded china Christmas figurines she'd collected since she was a child: Santa, his sleigh, reindeer, angels, Frosty the Snowman, Snoopy on a plane with his muffler, swans with holly collars. Beneath the mantel hung the elaborate felt stockings she'd made for herself, George, and their two daughters, now with Porter's, Lauren's husband, and their two children's stockings added.

"I know you're right," Jilly conceded. "I was certainly crazy about George when we got married. But I'm not so sure that's the only reason or the main reason to get married. Lauren went into her marriage with a clear head and look how well it's worked out for her. I don't think she would have married Porter if he weren't well-mannered, working for a bank, and living in Boston. Lauren knew she would never be far from Nantucket."

Nicole paused thoughtfully. "I have only one stepdaughter, Jilly, so maybe I shouldn't have an opinion, and Lauren certainly seems happy enough. But it does seem to me that your daughters are very different people. I think you need to respect that. Felicia isn't going to marry a banker and live in Boston like her older sister did."

Jilly nodded, even though Nicole couldn't see her. "You're right, Nicole. I should be grateful I have one daughter who lives nearby and calls me almost every day for a chat."

"Plus, you lucky duck, she's given you two adorable grandchildren."

Jilly paused. After a moment, she confessed, "You're right again. But you know what, Nicole? Secretly, I'm the worst grandmother in the world."

"What are you talking about?" Nicole asked, surprised.

Jilly was practically whispering, as if Lauren were standing outside the door. "I adore Lawrence and Portia. When I visit them in Boston, we have a great time. But even though they're six and four, they're like wild beasts."

Nicole chuckled. "Calves in the china cupboard?"

"In this house, yes. Well, some of our furniture belonged to my grandmother. Imagine how old those pieces are! Some of the other pieces George and I paid a pretty penny for at auctions. When we were younger it was our dream to have an elegant home. George's grandparents left him so many precious objects—porcelain bowls, Tiffany lamps, Limoges vases, figurines. We had to keep them all in storage. We couldn't put them out when our children lived with us, and it's been utterly rejuvenating to restore and decorate this house together. It's made us closer than we were when we were raising the children."

"You're not a bad grandmother because you want to have nice things," Nicole assured Jilly. "At our age, we deserve to have our home look the way we want it to look. You raised two children and had your house filled with everything from high chairs to hockey sticks. You have every right to make your house look as perfect as it does. It gives you great pleasure."

"Aha!" Jilly laughed. "I know what you're doing. You're trying to use psychology on me. You're trying to make me accept that I have to let Felicia live her own life the way she wants to."

"That's not what I said, but it's true, don't you think?"

"I guess you're right," Jilly conceded. "It's difficult, Nicole, to feel so much closer to one daughter than the other. It makes me feel guilty. But Lauren has always been just like me. She used to follow me around everywhere, pretending to help me cook and changing her baby dolls the way she saw me change Felicia. Felicia preferred riding her bike or climbing trees. I fought more with Felicia, too, especially when she was in high school. Those ripped jeans? I had to clench my jaw to keep from screaming. I'm lucky I have any teeth left."

"Well, you do have all your teeth, and love is wide and deep, and Felicia is not only coming for Christmas, she wants to be married on the island. I'd say you did a pretty good job with both your girls." In the background clinking noises sounded. "I've got to go. Cookies to bake, packages to wrap."

"Me, too. I think my project for today will be to go around the house and remove all the breakable objects, and even some of the more fragile antique furniture."

"Don't forget the bedrooms," Nicole advised.

"As if I could!" Last Christmas, five-year-old Lawrence had somehow managed to crack the spindles on an 1850 Windsor fruitwood armchair in his bedroom. "Maybe I'll buy some of those plastic outdoor chairs and put them around," she suggested with a chortle. "Nicole, thanks for the talk. You're the best."

Jilly hung up the phone and rubbed her hands together. She had some serious plotting to do.

# 2

At the same time that Jilly was talking to her friend Nicole in Nantucket, Jilly's daughters, almost an entire continent apart, were talking to each other on their cells.

Lauren was in the family room of her large faux Colonial house on two acres in suburban Boston. "You've got to be kidding me," she said. "Archie is giving you a *bike* for a wedding present?"

In their tiny apartment above a bookshop in Moab, Utah, Felicia snorted with exasperation and ran her hand through her cropped easy-care hair. "You don't even have a clue. It's a Cannondale trail bike, lightweight and—"

"I'm happy for you both," Lauren interrupted, "so can you be nice to Mom for once?"

"How much nicer can I be?" Felicia asked plaintively. "Archie and I are going to fly all the way to Nantucket for our wedding. His mother will have to fly up from Florida, but none of our friends will be able to come, because they'll be in their own homes or their parents' homes for Christmas."

"It was your idea to have the wedding on Christmas Day, after all," Lauren reminded her sister. "I don't understand why you're in such a rush. Are you pregnant?"

"No, I am definitely not pregnant. Archie doesn't want us to have kids. The planet is already overpopulated. We have to think of the planet."

"Of course you do. So why the quickie marriage?"

"Archie and I joined a special hiking tour of the Himalayas and if we're married, we'll be entitled to our own private tent. It's part of the tour policy."

"Well, that's certainly a romantic reason for getting married."

Felicia could imagine her sister rolling her eyes. "You *know* Archie and I have been planning marriage for a couple of years now. This just seems like the right time. Come on, Lauren, you have to remember how much I did to keep Mom happy when I was in high school."

Lauren snorted. "You mean when you campaigned to join the boys' ice hockey team?"

"Hey, I was better on the ice than any of those klutzy boys. No," Felicia argued, "I mean when I took ballet for four years when I wanted to play soccer. I mean all those years when I went to the prom wearing silly frilly dresses and makeup that made my face feel like it was coated with rubber. I mean wearing that froufrou maid of honor dress at your wedding when I nearly broke my ankle tottering along in those ridiculous high heels."

"You could hardly walk down the aisle in the church

wearing those clodhopper hiking boots you clomp around in," Lauren said, but without much emotion. This was a discussion they'd had many times before.

"Look, Lauren, you can't turn a cheetah into a house cat and you can't turn me into a model."

"I never said you could. What I'm saying is that if you could lower your standards a smidgen and allow Mom to have the Norman Rockwell Christmas wedding she longs for, it might go a long way toward helping her accept your marriage to Archie."

Felicia, always restless when cooped up inside, jumped up off their thrift shop sofa and began to pace. "That might never happen. Archie's like Rob Roy and Mom's like Martha Stewart. Last year when Mom and Dad came out to visit us, Mom was all Queen Elizabeth, turning up her nose at our apartment, as if we were living out of cardboard boxes."

"Didn't you eat out of cardboard boxes?" Lauren couldn't help teasing.

"You are totally loving all this, aren't you?" Felicia accused. "Yes, we did eat out of cardboard boxes because the nights Dad didn't take us out to dinner, we had pizza or take-out Chinese like we always do. Archie doesn't expect me to serve him a four course meal every night, complete with the proper wine."

"It's not the superficial stuff that worries Mom," Lauren said gently. "It's more the values stuff. Like the importance of family."

"Come on, there are all kinds of families. His parents

got divorced when he was young, and a few years ago his father died. But Archie and his mom are still a family," Felicia said defiantly. "I think his mom's totally awesome. She worked as a soccer coach and gym teacher at a girls' school in South Carolina and raised Archie all by herself."

"Okay. I respect that. Still, you have to admit that Archie doesn't really fit into our family. We stay in one place for generations. Archie is a vagabond. And he's turning you into one."

"In the first place," argued Felicia, "I've always wanted to travel. In the second place, Archie isn't turning me into anything except a very happy woman. In the third place, we have both worked our tails off as white-water rafting guides for the last five years to save money for this trip. If that isn't behaving responsibly and reliably, what is?"

"Fine," Lauren said. "Let's talk about the wedding. I have an idea I think you'll like. Let *me* be in charge."

"This is the sound of me trying not to scream," Felicia said.

"Come on, think about it. Who used to give her dolls weddings? Who thinks the way Mom does? I've already made some notes. The ceremony will be at St. Paul's Church. The reception will be at home. You should wear a plain white satin dress, and a red velvet cloak."

"I'll look like Little Red Riding Hood," Felicia objected.

Lauren continued unfazed. "Archie's last name is Galloway. I've already checked the tartan book. His pattern is mostly green. Does he have a kilt?"

"You bet Archie has his own kilt. He's so proud of his Scottish heritage I'm just grateful he doesn't play bagpipes."

"Fabulous. He can wear his kilt with all the trappings and you can wear a red velvet sash around your waist—"

"And a poinsettia in my hair." Felicia snorted.

"I'm considering having your dress trimmed with white faux fur on the cuffs and hem. I'll definitely loan you my diamond earrings."

"I don't have pierced ears."

"Of course you don't. Fine. I'll think of something else. The point is, I can make all the arrangements. Mother will enjoy working with me on the color scheme—"

"Our wedding will have a color scheme? This is a nightmare."

"Not if you let me take care of it. I can plan it all from soup to nuts. I already know what size you wear. Mom and I can plan the decorations for the house and the menus. I'm sure she'll want to invite a few of her own friends and some of the friends you went to school with."

"No, it wouldn't be fair to Archie if I had my friends there and he didn't have any. It's sad enough that his father's dead and he's an only child. Let's keep it simple. Please. I want a calm, quiet, brief ceremony."

"Fine, then. But will you let me be in charge of the details?"

Felicia felt totally itchy. She idolized her older sister while at the same time she couldn't stand being around

Lauren for more than a few days. Lauren, like their mother, was a perfectionist. Felicia had thought that when Lauren had her two children she would loosen up and that had sort of happened. But Lauren still didn't comprehend the way Felicia thought. If Lauren was an A, Felicia was a Z. If Felicia and Archie had their way, they'd be married outdoors in the sunshine, standing beneath Delicate Arch. They would be wearing hiking clothes and if Felicia carried flowers, they would be Indian paintbrush and Arizona daisies.

But Felicia loved her mother and knew how important this occasion was for her.

"I surrender. This is very nice of you, Lauren, and I know you'll make Mom happy. Are you sure you'll have time to make the arrangements and take care of your own Christmas, too?"

"Absolutely! This is the sort of project that invigorates me. Oh, Felicia, it's going to be so much fun."

"I certainly hope so," Felicia said doubtfully.

The moment she clicked off her cell, Felicia stuck it in her khaki shorts pocket, opened the apartment door, and thundered down the stairs to the street. She had to go out in the sunshine and walk. She had known this wedding business would drive her mad.

The crazy thing was that Felicia cherished Christmas on Nantucket. She always had. She loved the small town atmosphere, the security of nearby neighbors as the dark winter drew nearer. When she was younger, her parents first bought their home on the island. She'd enjoyed being an angel in the Christmas pageant the year their next-door neighbors played Mary, Joseph, and baby Jesus. That was probably the only time in her life Felicia was considered an angel. The Christmas parties back then were noisy, giddy fun, and her mother's Christmas Eve and Christmas Day meals were gastronomical delights, not to mention the adorable Christmas cookies Felicia and Lauren always baked, giggling and eating the icing as they worked.

Archie had never been to the island, and that was another reason Felicia wanted to have their wedding there, so she could show him the landscape she knew so well. But the main reason was to make her mother happy. She adored her mother and realized her tomboyishness disappointed Jilly. This was the best present she could think of. Her dad would like it, too, although he was much more mellow about everything.

Maybe her dad could convince her mother that once Felicia was married, she would have her own life with Archie, and she should be free to live it as she wanted.

# 3

A week later, George trudged up the stairs with a wicker basket of fresh laundry in his arms. He found Jilly in the guest bedroom. "Here you go, Lady Gordon, one clean set of snowman-covered sheets and a reindeer-patterned duvet."

"Help me make the bed, will you please, George?" Jilly asked. "My back is starting to ache."

"I'm not surprised," George said as he flapped out the bottom sheet and helped Jilly spread it on the mattress. "You've been working like a crazy woman on the house."

"We'll never have another Christmas like this one. I want it to be perfect," said Jilly. "Anyway, I have most of it done. Lauren and Porter will be in Lauren's old bedroom with air mattresses on the floor for Portia and Lawrence. Felicia and Archie will have her old bedroom. Pat Galloway could have the guest room but she prefers staying in a hotel. I've put on Christmas sheets and quilts anyway."

"I noticed," George told his wife. "Looks great. And I'm sure that now that the kids are older, nothing will get broken."

Jilly was quiet as she helped George finish making the bed. She plumped up the pillows in their Christmas shams and smoothed out a few tiny wrinkles on the duvet.

"We don't have any little-boy toys in the house, but I bought a few "Meg Mackintosh" mystery books I think Lawrence will like and I've put them on the bedside table. As for Portia, I left Lauren's old doll carriage and baby doll in the room for her to play with."

Suddenly Jilly collapsed on the bed, dropped her face into her hands, and began to cry.

Alarmed, George sat down, put his arm around his wife, and asked, "Hey, honey, what's wrong?"

"Oh, George," cried Jilly, "when I got out the baby carriage, it made me remember when Lauren's children were babies and slept in our daughters' crib. There it was, up in the attic, all folded up, with a mattress wrapped in plastic, and the soft baby sheets and blankets and bumpers tucked away in a plastic box. And we'll never use any of it again."

"How can you say that?" George asked. "Felicia's getting married. I'm sure she'll have kids someday."

"Yes, and she'll probably give birth in a yurt in the Gobi Desert, attended by two Mongolians and a goat."

George threw back his head and laughed, hugging Jilly to him. "You have quite an imagination."

"I don't need an imagination when I have a daughter like Felicia," Jilly said glumly.

"You really have been working too hard," George said soothingly. "You're upset over nothing. Listen, it's Stroll weekend. What are we doing sitting inside? Let's go for a walk and then I'll take you out to lunch."

"George, what a great idea." Jilly wiped tears from her eyes and stood up. "I'll change clothes and put on some lipstick."

In a flash, Jilly's mood brightened. The Nantucket Christmas Stroll took place the first weekend after Thanksgiving weekend. This annual occasion became more exciting every year, as islanders and tourists alike entered into a shimmering bubble of holiday magic with the sweet salt air glittering like fairy dust over their heads. The town blocked the use of cars on Main Street so that the hundreds of strollers could amble along, pausing to listen to the Victorian carolers in cloaks and bonnets singing to the crowds, or to watch Santa and Mrs. Claus arrive on the Coast Guard boat down at Straight Wharf.

The stores were filled with luxurious and delectable gifts, their windows decorated with artistic flair. Mermaids and snowmen, reindeer and ice skaters, gingerbread sailboats and candy canes twinkled behind the glass. The town crier strode through the town, welcoming people and announcing the beginnings of pageants, fairs, and readings.

The crowds themselves decorated the streets; it had become a custom to dress with dash for the Stroll. Women wore red velvet cloaks and wide picture hats with feathers or faux fur coats and earmuffs. Some men and women wore hats with reindeer antlers, or red and white Santa hats, or green elf caps with golden bells jingling from the pointed tip.

Jilly put on warm wool slacks and her green cashmere sweater, topped with her green wool coat. She added her special Christmas earrings, one red, one green, which flashed on and off, because she'd remembered to put the new batteries in. She added a bright crimson slash of lipstick and smiled at herself in the mirror. She felt better already.

Hurrying down the stairs, she caught up her purse and her leather gloves.

George was waiting in the front hall, looking quite handsome in his black wool dress coat, even though the buttons strained over his belly; he'd worn this coat for years. Jilly picked up the new headgear she'd purchased for him this year, a red felt stocking cap with miniature green felt Christmas trees bobbling above each ear.

"Not a chance," George said, stepping backward.

"It's specially for the Stroll," cajoled Jilly. She took the red and white candy-cane-striped muffler she had knit for him and wrapped it around his neck, kissing his cheek as she did. "Try it on. Show some Christmas spirit."

"Fine, but I refuse to wear it in the restaurant," George grumbled.

Jilly put her Santa hat on, adjusting it so that the fat white pom-pom at the end fell over her shoulder. Taking George's arm, she twinkled up at him. "Let's go!"

As they walked into town, the Gordons began to turn up their coat collars and pull their mufflers tighter around their necks. No snow had fallen yet, but the day was unseasonably cold, and when they reached Main Street, they saw that the other strollers already had rosy cheeks. They encountered some acquaintances who had their matching corgis on red and green leashes. The dogs and owners alike wore blinking Christmas lights around their necks. The Gordons patted the dogs, greeted the humans, and continued their walk.

"I'd forgotten that this has really become a dog holiday," said George.

"Well, this is a dog island, after all. And the dogs seem happy to be decked out."

Jilly pointed at a large yellow Lab wearing reindeer ears. Farther down the street, an elegant white poodle sported a glamorous headband with several sequined white snowflakes attached by springs. And trotting along happily like a well-fed pig, a very fat pug paraded down the street wearing a red satin bow around her neck.

"What a sweet little puppy," Jilly cried. "May I pet her?" she asked the owner, who rather resembled a pug herself.

"Of course," the owner said. "Her name is Poppy."

Jilly knelt and reached out a hand to the pug. Poppy stuck out a peppermint pink tongue and licked Jilly's hand.

"Hello, sweetie," Jilly greeted the puppy. She looked up at her husband. "I wish we had a little dog like this."

"Have you ever had a dog?" the pug owner inquired.

"No," Jilly answered briefly, not wanting to admit what a neat freak she was. "But maybe . . ."

The pug owner continued, "Not to be a Grinch, I only ask because I'd forgotten how much work dogs are. They have to be walked several times a day, and it's holy murder crawling out of bed early on a dark winter morning to take Poppy out. But she yips and yaps and scratches at the bed until I do. Then there's the matter of chewing. I can't tell you how many leather shoes Poppy's ruined. And she's not even a big dog, certainly not one of those eternally hungry dogs like yellow Labs who will eat anything, even the contents of wastebaskets, no matter how much you feed them."

"Goodness!" Jilly stood up. "I appreciate you warning us about all this."

The pug owner replied, "Of course I'm crazy about Poppy, and I won't give her up. Anyway, Merry Christmas!" With that, the fat little pug and her owner waddled away.

The Gordons strolled on, crisscrossing the cobblestone streets, stopping to watch Joe Zito and his puppet, Grunge, entertain a flock of children, pausing farther up the street to listen to the Victorian carolers.

"My stomach's growling," George mumbled as "Come All Ye Faithful" ended. "Let's go eat lunch before the restaurants are too crowded."

He steered Jilly toward the Brotherhood, a historic pub with fireplaces, juicy hamburgers, and a full list of wine and beers. He knew what he wanted, but Jilly stared at the menu for so long he thought she'd slipped into a coma.

"Jilly?"

"Oh . . . I guess I'll have a salad." Listlessly, she let the menu fall from her hand.

"You're kidding. No one eats a salad when it's so cold. Don't tell me you're trying to lose weight over Christmas!" Now he was worried.

"I'm not hungry, George." Jilly gazed out the window, idly watching the crowds pass by.

George stared at his wife. How could he help her? They were too old to have another baby, which was no doubt what she secretly wanted. Lauren and Porter wouldn't have another child; they'd confessed that Porter had had a vasectomy, considering two children enough. Felicia might have a child someday, but until then would Jilly remain so downhearted? His wife was an odd mixture of perfectionism and softheartedness.

He could buy her a puppy, but that meant newspapers on the floor, toilet training, long nights interrupted by pitiful howling, and eventually, as the pug owner had said, chewed shoes.

Suddenly, he had an inspiration.

"Jilly!" Reaching over, he took her hand, indicating his desire for her full attention.

"Yes, dear?"

"I'm going to buy you a kitten!"

"A kitten?" Jilly was puzzled, looking for a moment as if she had no idea what the word meant. Then she smiled, her big, happy, generous smile. "A kitten! Oh, George, what a wonderful idea! This is going to be the best Christmas ever!" Jilly declared. "Oh, George, let's order clam chowder and cheeseburgers! No, I can't wait to drive out to the animal hospital. Oh, should we choose an all black kitten? I've always fancied those, wanted to name one Salem or Midnight. Or an all white one? We could call her Snow!" Jilly nearly clapped her hands with joy at the thought. She was out the door before George had even pulled on his coat.

# 4

By ten A.M., Felicia and Archie had finished a lazy breakfast of pancakes and bacon, following an energetic session
under the bedcovers. Now they were showering, dressing,
and preparing for the arrival of friends for the Sunday NFL
game between the New England Patriots and the Buffalo
Bills.

"Archie," said Felicia in her sweetest voice, "I have a
few early Christmas presents for you."

"Oh, yeah?" Archie came out of the bathroom wearing
only a towel wrapped around his waist.

Felicia gestured toward the bed. "I bought you some
things. Would you try one of the shirts on to be sure they're
big enough?"

Archie stomped over toward the bed—he wasn't angry,
he always sounded like he was stomping—and stared down
at the pile of new clothes as if they were rattlesnakes.
"What the heck?"

"For our trip to Nantucket," Felicia explained.

Archie looked wary. "I have clothes."

"I know you do, but we're going to be on Nantucket for two weeks. It's winter and it's cold. I know we'll spend most of the time hiking around the island, but some evenings Mom and Dad will want us to eat out. They'll want us to join them at Christmas cocktail parties, and I'm sure they have a Christmas party planned, as well. They want to show you off, and you can't be wearing a torn T-shirt that says *Take a Hike*."

Archie made a face. "Come on, honey, give me a break. I've already packed my kilt, isn't that enough?"

"Do you want to wear your kilt to every cocktail party?" Felicia asked mildly. "Look, Archie, these are from Lands' End. They're not dressy, they won't scratch your neck—"

"Anything with a collar scratches my neck," Archie argued.

"—and you'll look like the handsome gentleman I know you can be."

"I don't want to be a gentleman. I never have wanted to. Where did you ever get that idea?" Archie dropped his towel and pulled on clean briefs.

"I don't want you to be a gentleman, either, but I want you to look like one for my parents. I don't think it's too much to ask. You and I have talked about this, Archie. You said your mother has never cared about appearances, but my mom's a nut job about them. Remember when she and Dad came out here, you looked a bit—um, caveman?"

Archie swooped Felicia up in his arms, threw her on the bed, and fell next to her, tugging on her hair. "As I recall, that's a look you like."

Felicia grinned. "True."

"And as much as I like your mother, she's not the one I'm marrying." Archie nuzzled Felicia's neck, kissing her ear, her cheek, her lips . . .

"Stop that!" Felicia demanded, rolling away from her gorgeous fiancé. "I'm trying to talk about our wedding. Who knows when we'll see my parents again? It will be years, probably, before you have to put on a button-down shirt." She sat up. "We are going to settle this matter before the football game starts."

"You really ask a lot of a guy," Archie muttered. "All right, which shirt do you want me to try on?"

Felicia handed him a navy-blue-and-white-checked flannel shirt that she knew would bring out the solar flare blue of his eyes. She had already unbuttoned it for him; Archie hated fumbling with tiny things like buttons.

Archie put on the shirt. He surveyed himself in the mirror. "It fits," he admitted grudgingly.

"Now try this," Felicia suggested as she handed him a navy blue blazer.

"I already have a blazer."

"I know you do. It's at least eight years old and has been in the storage unit the entire time. I doubt if it even fits you anymore, never mind the problem of trying to find it among all those boxes. We are almost done here, Archie."

Archie pulled the blazer on over the flannel shirt. It was barely big enough for him but there was no time now for her to return it for a larger size and Felicia wasn't sure there was a larger size. As long as Archie didn't do anything more strenuous than lift a glass to his lips, the seams should hold.

"Whoa, you look gorgeous," said Felicia.

"I feel like a rhino in a straitjacket." Archie took off the blazer and began to unbutton his shirt so quickly he nearly ripped the fabric. "Are you through with me now?"

"Yes. But I want to warn you: when we're on Nantucket there will be times when I will choose your clothes for you."

Archie pulled on his chinos and a clean hunter green T-shirt. "Fine. What about you? Did you order yourself a couple of dresses for this all-important impression-making occasion?"

"Actually, I did. I also bought a pair of shoes." Digging through the piles of clothing bags on the bed, Felicia took out a pair of black high heels.

Archie smiled. "You can model those for me later," he said, raising his eyebrows.

"You see," she smirked. "Clothes do make a difference."

Archie left the room and went into the kitchen to start putting together the snacks. People would be arriving soon. Felicia's best friend, Brianne, was coming with her husband and bringing the navy blue dress coat she was loaning Felicia for this trip. Felicia had plenty of cold weather gear, but nothing her mother would want her to wear out to dinner.

Picking up a dark blue corduroy dress, Felicia held it against her and looked in the mirror. She would wear the pearls her parents gave her when she graduated from high school; that should please them. She could trust Lauren to add any necessary feminine touches like lipstick, blush, or one of their grandmothers' Christmas brooches.

Suddenly Felicia sank down onto the bed, burying her face in the corduroy dress. More than any other holiday, Christmas was a time for remembering. Like a set of Russian dolls, a large one opening to show a smaller one inside, the ornaments on a Christmas tree reflected images of past Christmases. A memory of her grandmother holding Lauren's firstborn baby at their mother's house one Christmas filled Felicia with joy and sorrow. That grandmother, like her other grandmother, had since passed away. Lauren had their brooches and other jewelry, assuring Felicia that when she was ready for them, she could have her pick.

Five years ago Felicia hadn't wanted frivolous jewelry, and she hadn't wanted children. She had wanted to hike the world with Archie, climbing difficult trails, swimming across blue lagoons, and seeing sights few other mortals would see.

Now, out of the blue, like a lightning bolt, a secret desire had taken hold of Felicia. She could talk to no one about this new obsession. She couldn't understand what had happened to her, except that last week when she and

Archie were hiking the Dark Angel trail, they passed a family of three. The man and woman were about Felicia's and Archie's ages, and the man carried a one-year-old child in a backpack. The child had on the cutest cap with a long brim to shade his chubby face. When he saw Archie and Felicia, he waved his arms and giggled and babbled to them. Had she ever seen a cuter baby in all her life? Six years ago, when Lauren's first child was born, Felicia had dutifully traveled to see this miracle of procreation, and had been horrified at the amount of dirty laundry and end-less diaper changes. Lauren's house had seemed so hot, and the infant's cries shrilled through the air like a fire alarm. Over the years, Felicia came to feel great affection for Law-rence and Portia, although she also took notice of the time and hard work it cost their parents simply to keep them fed, dressed, healthy, and safe. Not for her, Felicia had thought. Never for her.

But then, last week, the sight of the chubby, bright-eyed, wriggling, giggling baby—it was like a spell from the most ancient of fairy tales. Felicia was enchanted and possessed.

"Archie, look," Felicia had whispered. "Isn't that baby sweet?"

"All babies are sweet," Archie responded. "Then they turn into adults and ruin the planet."

Felicia didn't argue. Archie was all about the planet. He was for zero population growth. He was okay with getting married, but it wasn't of great emotional importance to him. This entire wedding business at her parents' home on the island was a concession from Archie to Felicia because he understood how much it would mean to her parents. His own parents had divorced when he was young. His father never saw him. Recently they'd had news that he had died. No, Archie didn't comprehend the duties and pleasures of family bonds.

Felicia didn't dare tell him about her odd new longing. It might be a deal-breaker. Anyway, her sudden obsession would pass, she was certain. Once she was home in the bosom of her anal-compulsive, super-tidy family, the terror of ending up like her mother would remove these strange wishes for a baby from her system. Until then, Felicia would keep quiet and pretend she was the same freewheeling, carefree creature she'd always been.

# 5

Because the MSPCA didn't open on weekends unless there was an emergency, Jilly and George had to content themselves in their search for a kitten with scanning the want ads in the local weekly paper, *The Inquirer and Mirror*. No kittens, puppies, turtles, or birds were listed for sale or adoption, so George went online and checked as many relevant sites as he could think of.

No luck.

So it was Monday morning when the Gordons climbed into their pristine Mercury Mariner SUV and drove to the MSPCA. The handsome facility was new, with a desk in the foyer resembling the bridge of the starship *Enterprise*. The doors and windows were hung with fresh green garlands and red wreaths. A Christmas tree in the corner was decorated with catnip mice, dog bones, sparkling collars, and net bags of treats tied up with red silk ribbons.

"Hello," Jilly said cheerfully. "We'd like to adopt a kitten."

The young girl at the front desk had curly black hair and

a vivacious personality. "Safe Harbor for Animals does the adoptions. They're right next door."

"Great! We'll go over there."

The young receptionist looked dismayed. "I don't think they have any kittens."

Jilly sagged. She'd awakened early, dreaming of snuggling a warm, plump, little body in her arms. "Thank you anyway," she said politely, and turned to walk to the car.

But her husband said, "Wait a moment. Do you know if there are *any* animals up for adoption at Safe Harbor?"

The curly-haired girl looked baffled. "Maybe. I'm not sure—" Suddenly a smile broke out over her face. "Hey! Here comes Tim Thompson. *He'll* know. He volunteers for Safe Harbor, taking care of the animals when the director's on vacation." She ran out from behind her desk to catch Tim as he was stepping out of his pickup truck.

Tim stood very still, listening, expressionless. Good news? Bad? Jilly and George looked at each other and shrugged.

Tim followed the girl back into the building. A lean Irishman in jeans and a wool vest, he had the soulful look of a man who played sad songs on the guitar.

Without saying hello or even smiling, Tim announced morosely, "We have only one animal for adoption."

"What kind of animal?" Jilly quickly asked, imagining a potbellied pig or, worse, a snake.

"Cat."

"We'd like to see him or her," George said.

"You won't want him," Tim muttered direly. But he walked away from the front desk, down a corridor, around the corner, and began to unlock a door into a small annex.

Jilly and George dutifully followed, entering a small rectangular space filled with metal cages. Two large windows let in the dim winter light. Tim clicked on the overhead electric light and the room brightened.

"There." Tim pointed.

Jilly and George scurried up to the cage positioned at eye height. Inside, curled up in a round bed, lay an orange-and-white striped cat.

"Hello, kitty," Jilly whispered.

The cat opened its gold eyes and stared at Jilly with skepticism, then elegantly rose and stretched, as if to show off its remarkable stripes and spots.

"He looks like a jungle animal," George said.

"He's feral," Tim explained. "Captured out on the moors."

"Is he tame?" Jilly asked.

"Don't know," Tim said. "He's young, not a year old yet, so he could be domesticated. Maybe. Could be a challenge."

"Is he mean?" asked George.

"Not mean so much as he's got an attitude problem." Tim opened the cage, reached in, picked up the cat, and set him on the cushioned bench where various cat toys were scattered.

For a few moments, the orange cat hunkered down, as if

expecting to be attacked. He stared at the humans with suspicious eyes. After a moment, he stood up, stretched full-length, and paced the length of the bench, ignoring the cat toys as if they were far too foolish for him.

"He's got striking markings," Jilly noticed.

"We were hoping for a kitten," George remarked.

"No kittens. Cats don't time their litters to fit with human holidays." Tim leaned against the wall and folded his arms, as if ready to wait for hours. "He's an unusual cat," he told them. "He's not striped as much as spotted. And he's smart."

Jilly drew near the animal, and reached out a hand. "Can I pet him?"

Tim shrugged. "I don't think he'll bite you."

George warned, "Be careful, Jilly."

Jilly slowly brought her hand closer to the cat. It sat down, staring up at her. Such alert gold eyes. Would it scratch? "Hello, sweetheart," she cooed in a soft voice. Cautiously, she touched him between the ears. He didn't move. She drew her hand from the top of his head down to his neck.

The cat closed his eyes. Jilly scratched between his ears. She stroked the animal the entire length of his body. An odd stuttering noise, like a rusty old engine coming to life, emanated from the cat.

"I think he's purring!" Thrilled, Jilly dared to reach out her other hand and gather the animal up against her chest. The cat nestled against her as if he belonged there.

"He likes me," Jilly whispered. "Oh, George, let's adopt him."

"What's the fee?" George looked at Tim. "Can we take him home now?"

"Nope," answered Tim. "He's got to be neutered first."

"What does that mean?" Jilly asked.

"Castrated, testicles removed," Tim said bluntly.

George winced.

"Will it hurt him?" Jilly asked.

"No," Tim told her. "He'll be anesthetized. It's a normal procedure for male cats, to keep them from chasing female cats and spraying the furniture to mark their territory. We can probably arrange for it to be done today. It's a quiet time for the hospital. You can go off and buy the stuff you need for a cat—litter box, food—and come back tomorrow morning to pick him up. Then all you have to do is check his incision occasionally to be sure he's not messing with it."

While they were talking, the cat was nuzzling Jilly and purring so loudly the humans could scarcely hear themselves talk. Clearly he was happy in the warmth of her arms.

"Oh, George, let's do it!"

Tim told them: "There are some forms you have to fill out and fees you have to pay. The vet will also be giving him a general checkup. You can ask at the front desk how much all this will cost."

"Can you tell us what kind of food he should eat?" Jilly

asked. "Is there anything we can buy that would make him happy? For example, that round bed in his cage, would he like one of those at home?"

"We've got a pamphlet for you to study," Tim said. "You can find it at the front desk."

"Let's get the process started," George said.

Tim turned off the overhead light and opened the door to leave the room. He turned back. "You can't take the cat into the reception room unless he's in a carrying case. That's another thing you'll have to buy."

"I'll stay with him here," Jilly said, "while George does the paperwork."

"You can't," Tim told her. "You have to put him back in the cage." When he saw Jilly's expression, for the first time his own expression softened. "Sorry. Rules." And he snorted a bit to express his opinion of rules.

Jilly was aware that George thought she often got overexcited and considered it his duty to rein her in, and she appreciated his concern. Still, even though it had been his idea to get a cat, she wished he wasn't with her now in Geronimo's, the pet supply store.

They had chosen a soft round stuffed cat bed in an adorable patchwork fabric that would coordinate perfectly with the cushions on the kitchen chairs. Food and water bowls had also been found that met Jilly's standards, white china with cute blue paw prints on them. Choosing the kitty litter box and scoop was not much fun, but the box would live out in the back hall; it wasn't something people would see.

"Don't you think the cat would look gorgeous with this green velvet collar?" Jilly asked George as they stood in the cat toys aisle.

"We've agreed we're not going to let him go outside," George reminded her. "Too many cars, too many dogs, too many temptations. The cat won't need a collar if he's never going out."

"Still, the green velvet against his cinnamon hair would look so pretty, and it *is* Christmas."

"Jilly, the cat doesn't know about Christmas." George was jingling the coins in his pocket, a habit he had whenever he was restless in a store and wanted Jilly to hurry up.

Jilly had to satisfy herself with purchasing a high-end cat carrying case plus a quilted cushion that fit inside it for the cat's comfort.

"Hope he doesn't throw up—or something worse—inside there," muttered George. He was beginning to have doubts about the whole enterprise.

"Don't be silly, George," Jilly said. "I'll hold the carrying case on my lap when we bring him home and I'll talk to him the whole time so he won't be afraid."

After lunch the next day, the Gordons drove out to the Offshore Animal Hospital to pick up their new pet.

To their surprise, the doctor came out of an examination room to talk to them. He seemed rather stern, almost as if he were sizing them up as cat owners.

"I performed the neutering operation yesterday," Dr. Logan told them. "He recovered from it nicely. He's a strong, healthy, young animal with no lice or fleas."

"Lice!" Jilly was horrified.

"Gina, our receptionist at the front desk, will show you the various options we have for preventing parasites. I recommend you use something even though your cat won't be going outside. Sometimes people bring things in inadvertently on their shoes or clothing."

Jilly went pale.

"As you've been told," Dr. Logan continued, "this cat was found on the moors. He might be nervous about living in a house. I hope you will be flexible and forgiving as he learns to settle in to your environment."

"I thought cats liked lounging on cushions or on windowsills," Jilly said.

"House cats do, of course. I'm sure this one will, given time. But he is a young male born to a feral litter, used to running, hunting, and fending for himself. He will have to adapt to you and you will have to adapt to him."

"Of course. We understand," Jilly promised.

The receptionist came to lead them into the Safe Harbor annex and into the room where their new pet waited for them in his cage. George was holding the carrying case, and Gina unlatched the cage door.

"Hello, kitty," cooed Jilly.

The cat rose and came toward her slowly. When she picked him up and held him against her, he once again nestled right into the crook of her arm and began to purr.

"Oh, George, I know it's going to be all right," Jilly said. "Look how happy he is."

"He should be happy," Gina told them. "You've saved him from being put down."

"Put down?" Even George looked upset.

"We can't keep them here forever," Gina explained. "And as you know, people want kittens, not older cats."

Jilly stroked the cat's head. "You're going home with us," she whispered. "We'll give you cream, fish, and a soft place to sleep. I even made you your own Christmas stocking."

George rolled his eyes, but he willingly helped Jilly gently load the cat into the cat carrier. The cat yowled once in protest, then lay down in watchful silence.

"Isn't he amazing?" asked Jilly. "He seems to know he belongs with us."

In the car on the way home, with the cat in his carrier on Jilly's lap, she decided to bring up the very important matter of the cat's name. Privately, Jilly had several names picked out: Ginger, Honey, Cinnamon. But she sensed that George was not as enamored of this adoption project as she was and she wanted to draw him in closer.

"George, what do you think would be a good name for the cat?"

George straightened slightly and cleared his throat as he

always did before making an important pronouncement. "Well, he's got that dark orange circle between his ears, like a crown. I think we should call him Rex."

"Rex." Jilly let the name roll around in her thoughts. It certainly wasn't a name she would have chosen. But she could see how it would apply to this strong, confident animal and she was thrilled that George had actually thought about a name. "Rex it is."

When they returned to the house, George came around to carry the heavy cat carrier. They went in through the back door so they could walk through the laundry room where they'd established the kitty litter box. George put the carrier on the kitchen floor.

"Here's your new home," Jilly told the cat. "Can you smell the cat food we got for you? It's the best brand, made of real fish. This is your water bowl. We'll show you where the litter box is." She nodded at George.

George opened the carrier door. Slowly, Rex slunk out. Warily, he took a few steps into the room, the set of his ears making it clear that all his senses were on high alert. He walked over to the cat food bowl and sniffed it. He sniffed the water in the water bowl. He walked beneath the kitchen table and slowly stepped beneath the rungs of the kitchen chairs.

Then, in a flash, he took off running. He flew through

the kitchen door into the dining room, made a path around the periphery, ran into the hall, and swerved into the living room, with George and Jilly bumping into each other as they tried to follow him. He streaked up the stairs so fast he was a blur before their eyes, and a few minutes later they heard a crash.

"Oh, dear," cried Jilly. "I'm guessing that's the porcelain soap holder in the guest bathroom."

The Gordons started to climb the stairs after the animal but when they were halfway up he raced back down, nearly tripping them as he zigzagged around their feet, hurtling into the living room. A sound like dozens of bells rang out. By the time the Gordons got to the living room, they saw that the cat had jumped up on the table and knocked off the silver bowl full of red and green Christmas ornaments, which now lay scattered on the rug while the silver bowl continued to vibrate against the brick hearth.

"Where did the damn animal go?" George yelled.

Noise clattered from the kitchen. The Gordons raced in. The cat had jumped onto the counter, accidentally knocking Jilly's metal container of cooking utensils onto the floor.

"Quick," George ordered, "shut the door."

Jilly slammed the door shut, trapping the cat in the kitchen. George went for the cat, his arms outstretched, and tripped on a metal whisk, two wooden spoons, and a spatula that sent him sprawling onto the floor.

Rex raced the only way he could go, into the laundry room. Jilly managed to make it across the room and slam the door, shutting the cat in.

"Are you okay, George?" She began to pick up the kitchen utensils and drop them into the sink to wash off as her husband pushed himself up to a standing position. She was afraid to look at him. What if he insisted on taking this wild creature back? She didn't want to have an argument before Christmas. How could she explain to George that the cat was probably only trying to sense out his surroundings? Again, tentatively, Jilly asked, "George, did you hurt yourself?"

"I'm fine," George said.

Relieved, Jilly turned to face him. To her surprise, George was smiling.

"I guess I gave him an appropriate name," George said. "Wrecks the house."

# 6

The plane landed on the runway with a bump. All the other passengers breathed sighs of relief. Felicia's own heart quickened. She wanted so much for her parents to like Archie!

Her parents stood inside the terminal, scanning the arriving passengers. When her mother saw her, she burst into tears, hugged Felicia, hugged Archie, and embarrassed them all by crying, "Archie, you look so *nice!*" Felicia's father hugged her and shook Archie's hand.

Archie was wearing a blue sweater that set off his blue eyes and a handsome black wool topcoat with a Galloway tartan muffler. Felicia had taken advantage of the three-hour layover between planes; she'd insisted on dragging her fiancé into Boston to purchase the coat and muffler which, she had to admit, made him look very nearly civilized. The money spent was better for her mother than a dozen roses and a bottle of antidepressants.

The foursome hurried through the cold to the car, all talking at once. Felicia was tired—it had been a long day of traveling—and dreaded her parents' announcement of social engagements.

To Felicia's surprise, as George steered the car home, Jilly peered over the front seat to say, "I thought that after all your traveling, you two would want to stretch your legs, so when we get home why don't you show Archie the town while I prepare dinner?"

Before Felicia could answer, her mother continued, "Of course if you're tired, please feel free to take a nap or rest in front of the fire. We don't have any plans for tonight. I've made a beef stew and an apple pie. I thought we could have a quiet evening together."

"That sounds perfect, Mom," said Felicia, silently wondering what good witch had cast a spell to make her mother so relaxed.

When they arrived at the house, carried in the luggage, and joined one another for a moment in the living room, Felicia thought she understood. In her mother's arms was a handsome orange striped cat, his tail draped possessively around Jilly's wrist, and—Felicia knew she was probably imagining this—a smug, arrogant gleam of ownership in his eyes.

"Meet Rex," her mother announced proudly. "We've had him for only a week, but he's so intelligent, he settled right into our household. We'd appreciate it if you didn't let him out of the house. He was born in the wild and we don't want him to go outside and get lost—or worse. The vet told us Rex will quickly become accustomed to living in the house and we want him to be a total house cat."

"He's gorgeous, Mom," said Felicia.

"I know," Jilly said, stroking Rex. "He's extremely bright, too. Several times he's attempted to claw the sofas—I've Googled this, and it seems to be normal cat behavior—and I've learned to stop him from doing it by putting water in a spray bottle and spraying his face when he starts. He runs away at once." Jilly's face drooped. "I hate hurting his feelings."

"We're buying him a scratching post for Christmas," George said.

"In fact," Jilly added, leaning forward and actually whispering, as if the cat could understand her, "it's an entire cat *tree*!"

Felicia nodded seriously. "A cat tree. For *inside* the house?"

Jilly laughed a tinkling laugh. "Yes, silly. It's not an actual tree with bark. It's covered with some sort of shag carpet material that cats can fasten their claws in. It has three different levels, and a tiny little house at the bottom with a hole for him to hide in."

Felicia's normally mellow father leaned over the back of the sofa to pet the cat. "If you'd like, you could give him some toys for Christmas. Down at Cold Noses they have a sort of feathery thing on a long flexible stick that you can wave for him to jump at."

Felicia bit her lip to keep from laughing. Her parents were channeling all their parental energies onto the cat. Hallelujah! "If it's all right, then, before it's completely dark," said Felicia, "we'll go out and buy Rex a toy right now. I want to show Archie a bit of the town, too."

"Have fun," Jilly said, petting the cat.

Felicia and Archie went carefully out the door.

As they walked, her arm linked through Archie's, Felicia thought she was floating in a dream. The lights on the Christmas trees lining Main Street glowed, illuminating the shop windows with their holiday displays. Felicia longed to take the time to stand staring at each scene like a child, but she knew that Archie would be bored with man-made scenery. Somehow she would persuade her father to take him off for a walk on the moors so she could have some alone time with her mother.

As the sky turned from gray to deep violet, Felicia and Archie walked to Cold Noses to buy the cat wand. They strolled on down Straight Wharf, where a few scalloping boats still bobbed against the wooden dock.

"It's a picture-book town, isn't it?" asked Felicia.

"I wonder if we can get out on the water," Archie responded.

"Archie! It's December! Who wants to go out on the water in this cold?" Felicia buried her hands in the pockets of her down jacket.

"I do," said Archie. "It was fascinating to see the island

from the airplane, all the shoals and harbors. It would be great to see the island from a boat."

Felicia knew that if Archie had his mind set, there was no point in arguing. She simply took his arm and steered him along the brick sidewalk back up toward the main part of town and the Gordons' house on Chestnut Street.

"Look at our house!" cried Felicia as they reached the Gordons' yard. In all the windows of the old house, a single candle burned, casting light onto the dark street. They were electric candles for safety's sake, yet the illusion brought a feeling of history and security. The Christmas tree, blazing with small lights, covered with decorations, candy canes, and strings of cranberries and popcorn, filled the window at the front of the house.

"Nice." Archie was a man of few words.

Felicia stood on her tiptoes to kiss his cold cheek and they went inside.

A delicious smell of beef stew filled all the rooms of the house. Calling hello, Felicia hung her coat and Archie's in the closet and hurried into the kitchen to see if she could help her mother.

Jilly's cheeks were rosy from the warmth of cooking. She lifted the lid on the big stewpot, stirred with her wooden spoon, murmured to herself, and put the lid back on. In a round, down-filled cat bed, Rex was curled asleep.

"That smells yummy," said Felicia. "Is there anything I can do to help?"

Maybe it was only her imagination, but at her voice, the cat stirred slightly and peered disapprovingly at her through narrowed eyes.

"No, darling, we're all set. Let's go in the living room and have a drink before dinner." Jilly untied her apron. Leaning toward her daughter, she whispered, "I hope I made enough food. Archie is such a big man."

"Mom, he is six feet four inches and weighs two hundred twenty pounds. Stop making him sound like Goliath."

"Sorry, darling, I'm not criticizing, I'm remarking."

Felicia followed her mother into the living room where her father and her fiancé were seated in the armchairs by the fire, chatting.

The ladies settled side by side on the sofa.

"Did you enjoy your walk?" asked Felicia's mother.

"It was great," exclaimed Archie. "George, do you own a motorboat?"

George blinked. "No, although I often wish I did. Why do you ask?"

"I thought it would be fun if you and I could take a tour of the harbor in a boat and perhaps putter out to Great Point."

"In this weather!" Jilly looked horrified.

"I'm sure if we bundled up—" began Archie.

Even though she'd objected earlier, now Felicia was quick to defend her fiancé. "Mom, fishermen go out in this weather all the time. It's not the Arctic."

Felicia's father surprised them all. "I'd like to see the

land from the water, too, Archie. I do know a few fellows who have motorboats. I'll give them a call and see if we can borrow one. The harbor's beginning to ice over, but if we get out there in the next day or two we should be all right."

*Gosh,* thought Felicia, *Go, Dad!*

Jilly looked stunned. Felicia turned the topic to safer subjects. "So, Mom, when do Lauren and her family arrive?"

"The twenty-third, I think," Jilly said. "Before then, we have a number of parties to attend, and I do hope you will join us. You'll see some of your old friends. I've been meaning to tell you—Steven has bought the house next door. He's going to live here permanently!"

Felicia lit up. "Really? That's great. I can't wait to see him."

"Why don't we invite him over for dinner tonight?" Jilly suggested perkily.

"No, Mom, we just got here, and dinner's all ready." Felicia tapped her lip. "You and I will have to sync schedules, because I want to take Archie on some walks around the island and perhaps on a bike ride to 'Sconset."

"Bike ride," she echoed weakly, disappointed that Felicia didn't want to invite Steven over right now. As if she needed food for fortification (she did!), Jilly stood up. "Perhaps we should eat now."

"I'll help you carry the stew in, dear." George rose and followed.

Jilly had set the dining room table with one of her best damask tablecloths and centered it with a Christmas wreath around a mirror with a clever holiday scene of miniature ice skaters. She'd brought out the best silver and china.

"Exquisite, Mom," Felicia exclaimed, and kissed her mother's cheek.

"This smells delicious," Archie said. When Jilly took her place at the head of the table, Archie stood behind her to help seat her and push in her chair. Jilly flushed with pleasure.

Felicia beamed at Archie, who moved to his chair at the side of the table and sat down. She noticed the cat creeping into the room, stationing himself next to Jilly's chair.

"If you'll hand me your plate, Felicia," said her father, "I'll dish out—"

A loud cracking noise interrupted George. More snaps and pops, like kindling on fire, erupted into the room, and then Archie's antique wooden chair exploded into bits. Archie was dropped to the floor, the back of his head smacking the raised metal fireguard. Blood spurted over the hearth.

Rex yowled as a section of the wooden chair slammed into him. He streaked from the room.

"Archie! Are you all right?" Felicia knelt next to her fiancé who lay sprawled on the carpet looking startled.

"Let me help you up," offered George, but he tripped on some of the round, rolling rungs of the chair and had to grasp the dining room table for support, pulling the table-cloth and dishes sideways so they trembled at the edge.

"I'm fine," insisted Archie. With a groan, he sat up, leaving a pool of blood on the hearth. More blood poured down the back of his head and his neck. "It's only a small cut."

"*Nothing* about you is small!" Jilly cried.

"Mother!" Felicia snapped. She snatched her clean white napkin and pressed it against the back of Archie's head.

"Should I call 911?" Jilly asked.

"No," protested Archie. "I'm fine."

"But all that blood!" Jilly said.

"Head wounds bleed a lot," said Archie, "because there are so many blood vessels beneath the scalp. Keep the pressure on, Felicia, and the blood will stop."

"I hate to tell you this, Archie," said Felicia, "but I think you're going to need some stitches."

"I'll call an ambulance," Jilly said.

"Nonsense." George took charge. "Felicia, keep the pressure on his head. Here's your coat, and Archie's. We'll take Archie to the emergency room at the hospital. Felicia, you sit in the backseat with Archie. I'll drive."

Archie awkwardly stood up as Felicia continued to press her napkin to his scalp. Like a couple in a three-legged race, they struggled toward the front hall. Jilly ran up with a pile of towels in her hands.

"Put this around your neck, Archie, and this one over

your coat, so you don't ruin your clothes. Felicia, use this towel if there's any more blood."

"Thanks, Mom. Do you feel dizzy, Archie?" asked Felicia. "Can you see right? Are you sick to your stomach?"

"I'm fine," Archie insisted, but he stumbled as they all went out the door, possibly because in their anxiety they were trying to squeeze through at the same time.

"Call me," Jilly begged. "I'm sure you'll be okay, Archie."

"Of course he will, Mom," Felicia called as they hurried toward the car. "Believe me, Archie has a hard head."

"I'll keep dinner warm!" Jilly called. More quietly she added, "And wash up the blood."

# 7

After the other three raced off to the hospital, Jilly returned to the dining room, where she stared at the gleaming red patch of blood on the floor.

"Okay," she said to herself aloud. Picking up her cell phone, she punched in a number. She could almost hear the phone next door ringing.

"Hi, Steven," she said cheerfully. "How are you settling in?"

Steven's low voice was smooth, almost melodious. "Great, thanks. I've enjoyed the casseroles you brought over."

"I wonder if I could ask you a favor in return," Jilly said. "I have to go to the Cape tomorrow to buy some new dining room chairs. My antiques are falling apart. I need someone to help me carry them to the taxi and load them on the ferry luggage rack." As a boy, Steven had been practically a fixture at the Gordon house, enjoying innumerable meals and snacks, so Jilly felt completely at ease asking for his help.

"Um, isn't Felicia there with her fiancé?"

"Yes, but unfortunately, Archie hit his head when he broke one of the chairs. He's on his way to the hospital for stitches. I think he'll be out of commission tomorrow."

"Sorry to hear that. Is he okay?"

"He's fine. Just needs a day of rest. I think Felicia will be going over with me," Jilly added enticingly.

"Let me check something." After a moment, Steven said, "The weather should be good tomorrow. The wind will be just fifteen miles per hour. So, great. Of course I'll go."

"You're an angel!" *And I'm a bit of a devil*, Jilly thought as they made plans for which ferry to take. "See you tomorrow."

But as she carried the antique hand-painted porcelain tureen back into the kitchen, a kind of guilt itched at Jilly's heart. She dialed Nicole's number.

"Can you talk for a moment?" she asked her friend.

"Of course. Are you okay?" Nicole asked, sounding worried.

"I feel so *terrible*, Nicole! Poor Archie actually cut his head and is on his way to the hospital to have stitches! Thank heavens we haven't had a dinner party since I bought those antique chairs. I had no idea they were so fragile."

"I'm sure Archie will survive. He's a rough tough outdoors guy. Could he stand up?"

"Yes, he walked and everything. But I'm going to go to the Cape tomorrow to buy some sturdy dining room chairs."

"Excellent idea, Jilly. I'll go with you. I have some last-minute things to buy."

"Fabulous!" Now she only had to convince Felicia to come with her, and Jilly could chat with Nicole while Felicia chatted with her dear old high school buddy Steven.

"How's the stew?" Nicole asked.

"Keeping warm on the stove. We'll eat in the kitchen when everyone returns. I know *those* chairs are safe. I'd better finish scrubbing up the blood." Jilly laughed, rather wildly. "That's not a sentence I ever thought I'd say."

She put on an apron and rubber gloves. She carried in a big pail of hot water, a new roll of paper towels, a plastic garbage bag, and a scrub brush. As she cleaned, she sang Christmas carols at the top of her voice. Soon all signs of blood had disappeared. She emptied the pail, double-checked the stew, then made herself a cup of tea and sank into a kitchen chair.

A noise made her turn her head. Rex slunk out of the laundry room, a pair of George's boxer shorts hanging from his tail.

"Rex, you silly boy!"

Rex jumped on her lap and butted her chin, the way he did when he wanted her to pet him.

"Sweetie," Jilly said, laughing and stroking the cat's head, "you do look fetching in these boxers, but cats don't ordinarily wear clothes."

Rex didn't even notice when she gently pulled the boxers off his tail. He allowed her to pet him, then turned around a few times and curled up in her lap. He purred, and the purr was like a kind of calming om, a universal soothing mantra that vibrated through her body and smoothed out her racing thoughts. Jilly closed her eyes and relaxed.

# 8

Felicia decided to join her mother and Nicole on their day trip to Hyannis. Archie would be fine in her father's company, and she had so many good memories of shopping orgies like this one. On the way over, she and her mother and friends would enthusiastically list all the treasures they were going to discover at the Cape Cod Mall, because Nantucket didn't have a mall or a CVS or a Marshalls, Macy's, Talbots, Gap, or any chain store—they were not allowed on Nantucket. During the three or four hours before the fast ferry home, they would each scurry off their separate ways like desperate cavewomen foraging for hides and furs to keep them warm in the winter. On the return trip, they'd show each other their prizes, eat food they'd bought from the forbidden McDonald's, and arrive home exhausted and totally happy.

The morning was frosty and bright. A line of passengers waited on the cobblestone wharf to board the boat, and Felicia, Jilly, and Nicole were there, too. It was like old home week as neighbor greeted neighbor, but Felicia was surprised to see Steven Hardy stroll up, very GQ in his black wool coat and fedora.

"Steven!" Felicia exclaimed, delighted. "Are you going to the Cape, too?"

"Didn't your mother tell you I'm coming over with you?" Steven flashed his gorgeous smile. He looked incredible, with his dark hair neatly cut and combed, his intense dark eyes and hawkish nose.

"I'm so glad! Tell me everything. Mom says you've moved back to the island." Felicia flung her arms around her old friend's neck. Even in her excitement, she didn't miss the way her mother nudged Nicole.

"I have. With my computer, I can do my stock brokerage business from my house or anywhere."

"Fantastic! Did Mom tell you I'm engaged? I'm going to marry Archie Galloway on Christmas Day."

Jilly poked Felicia, perhaps more brusquely than she intended. "We're boarding. Get your ticket ready."

"Mom. I have my ticket ready. I've only done this a million times." She linked her arm through Steven's. "Let's find our own booth and catch up on everything."

The waiting crowd filed up the ramp and into the large cabin where they spread out in booths and on blue benches and chairs. As the Hy-Line catamaran sped over the waves to Hyannis, its passengers read, snoozed, and gabbed during the hour-long trip.

Felicia and Steven sat in a booth behind Jilly and Nicole, so they could hear Jilly describe in rapid-fire excitement the events of the previous evening.

"Rex has been with us for only a week and you know how quietly we live. It must have seemed to him like a bomb went off. I talked it over with George and we decided that during the Christmas season, Rex will be allowed to sleep in our room. And do you know, last night, he crept up on the bed and curled up next to me."

Felicia leaned forward over the table and said softly to Steven, "My mother's turning a moment's crash into a Hallmark miniseries."

Steven grinned. "Mothers have a way of doing that."

Felicia reached out and took her friend's hand. "How *are* you, Steven? You were in New York for what, five years? And you've made a ton of money? Are you married or anything? Did Mom tell you about Archie?"

Steven laughed. "Which question should I answer first?"

"All of them!"

"I'm great," Steven told her. "New York, five years. Yes, tons of money. No, not married—yet. Yes, your mother mentioned Archie. I'm happy for you, Felicia."

As she talked with Steven, Felicia flashed back to the night of their senior prom, when she had been his date. He had held her close as they swayed dreamily to a slow dance. She had nestled her cheek against his chest, inhaling his clean male scent. Their legs had touched all up and down as they moved, making her aware that Steven was not merely her friend, he was a boy. Almost a man. She hugged him closer, affectionately melancholy about the end of high school, the beginning of their new lives. She was pretty sure she felt him kiss the top of her head.

"Steven—"

Jilly interrupted them. "Nicole's brought a homemade coffee cake to eat on the way over. Want some?"

Nicole piped up, "Having something in your stomach prevents motion sickness, and it's good to fuel up before a day of high-pressure shopping."

"Sure, I'll have some," Steven said.

Jilly patted the empty space on the bench next to her. "Come sit with us for a minute."

Steven settled next to Jilly. Felicia settled next to Nicole, who broke off a piece of cake rich with walnuts and honey and handed it to Felicia.

"How's Archie?" Nicole asked.

Delighted to have a chance to talk about her fiancé, Felicia said, "He's fine, with five stitches in the back of his head. They had to cut some of his hair to reach his scalp but it doesn't really show."

"I've never seen a man with so much hair!" exclaimed Jilly. "He has so much energy, too."

"I'm looking forward to meeting him," Nicole said. "Steven, tell me what shops you need to hit today."

Felicia relaxed back in her seat. She closed her eyes. She was grateful to Nicole for changing the subject away from Archie's catastrophic tumble, which was, after all, her mother's fault for having such fragile chairs. As the ferry continued to speed over the waves, she replayed last night's scene in her mind.

It hadn't taken long for the emergency room doctor to stitch up Archie's scalp. By the time she, Archie, and her father returned home, Jilly had had a chance to calm down. The four of them sat around the kitchen table enjoying the delicious stew.

Jilly had taken the calendar down from the wall in order to point out precisely what parties they were invited to. She wanted Felicia and Archie to know they were invited to all of them but not expected to attend all of them. Whatever they felt like. They also discussed the arrival of Archie's mother, who would be coming for the wedding, but who insisted on staying at a hotel.

"My mother often likes to sleep late," Archie explained.

"She's probably exhausted from cooking for you while you were growing up," Jilly joked, looking Archie up and down.

"Mother!"

"It's all right, Fill," said Archie. "She's said exactly that many times herself."

After dinner, Felicia's father and Archie insisted on doing the dishes and tidying the kitchen, allowing Jilly and Felicia the opportunity to make grocery shopping lists. They were all in good spirits when they retired for the night.

So perhaps it was going to be okay, Felicia thought.

They had survived the breakage of a valuable chair. Anything else would be minor. And she had to give her mother credit for apologizing about the chair instead of fussing over the loss of her cherished antique.

Rubbing the condensation off the wide window, Jilly watched as they glided past waterfront houses, boatyards, and wharves and arrived at the Hyannis dock. "We're here!"

The group gathered up their purses and empty duffel bags—the bags would be filled by this evening. They carefully walked down the ramp from the boat to dry land, shivering as the frigid air hit them.

"Let's hurry," Jilly urged. "We want to get one of the taxis."

"No need," Steven told her. "I've hired a car and driver for the day."

The three women stopped dead in their tracks and stared up at him.

"You what?" Felicia demanded.

"Over there." Steven pointed to an enormous black SUV, white smoke steaming from the exhaust pipe as it waited by the curb. "Jilly said she needed help moving some chairs to the boat, so I thought I'd better hire something big. The driver will take us to all the furniture stores and anywhere else we want to go. Oh, and I've made lunch reservations at Bleu in Mashpee. It will be a twenty-minute drive, but worth it."

Felicia hugged Steven and kissed his cheek. "You're an angel!"

Jilly smiled complacently. "Yes, Steven, you certainly are."

It was dark when the group finished their shopping. Steven and the driver helped load their Christmas loot and six new dining room chairs, carefully packed, onto the baggage carriers.

"I'm flying back," he told them. "I've got some plans for this evening."

The flight to the island took only fifteen minutes, but was expensive, while the fast ferry took an hour, a perfect time to relax.

Jilly was disappointed Steven wouldn't be with them for another hour, but she hid it well. "Thank you for this marvelous day!" Jilly told him. She was so restrained she didn't even ask him if he had a date, and who it was, and if they were serious, and where they were going tonight and . . .

Felicia hugged him and kissed his cheek again. "Steven, it's been so great spending time with you. Thank you for everything."

They went their separate ways. The women boarded the ferry, collapsed in a window-view booth with a long table between two padded benches, set their bursting duffel bags on the floor, and plopped their shopping bags on the table.

Jilly used her cell to phone a friend with a pickup truck who promised to transfer the chairs from the luggage rack to her house.

"There," Jilly said, "that takes care of the chairs. His cab's too small for all of us, though. George is coming, anyway."

Nicole suggested, "Let's have some hot chocolate."

Jilly and Felicia thought that was a brilliant idea. The warm drink gave them the energy to rave about the marvelous presents they'd discovered, the amazing sales, the adorable new wrapping paper, and the Christmas trinkets they'd bought for themselves. And how handsome Steven was. How sophisticated. The car and driver! The French restaurant with wine! His adorable sense of humor.

"Don't you just love him?" Jilly prompted Felicia.

Felicia answered truthfully. "I've always loved Steven." She saw her mother shoot Nicole a meaningful glance.

As the ferry entered Nantucket Harbor, Jilly said, "I wonder what George and Archie did today."

"I'll bet Dad took Archie to one of the beaches," Felicia said. "It's a sunny day, perfect for a long walk."

Jilly frowned. "I'm not sure your father is up to a walk, especially in this cold weather."

"Mom," Felicia said, "Dad is still a young, healthy man. You two act like you're ready for your rocking chairs."

"I'm certainly ready for one now," panted Nicole as they made their way down the steep ramp with duffel bags and packages in their hands.

Jilly peered at the crowd waiting on the wharf. "I don't see George."

"Let's walk to the intersection," Felicia suggested. "Maybe they wouldn't allow him to drive the car down here."

They struggled along until they came to the corner of Main and New Whale Street. No sign of George. Jilly flipped out her cell phone and hit George's number. "It goes to voice mail," she told the others.

"He's probably on his way," Felicia said. "Let's wait a while."

But the wind that had been so lazy during the day was waking up, blowing harder on the island than it did on the mainland, chilling the backs of their necks, flipping their hair into their eyes, and making the December darkness seem even colder than it really was.

"Enough," said Nicole. "I'll call Sebastian to come pick us up."

Her husband arrived within five minutes. The women scrambled into his car, grateful for the warm air from the heater. Chestnut Street was only a few blocks away. They all talked at once, telling Sebastian about their day, but they went silent as they pulled up in front of the Gordon house. No lights were on. George's SUV was not in the drive.

"That's odd," Jilly said.

"They're probably down at the wharf waiting for us." Felicia laughed. This sort of thing had happened before.

The women kissed and said goodbye. Sebastian helped carry the duffel bags and other packages up to the house and waited while Felicia turned on some lights.

"Thanks, Sebastian."

"Let us know if you have any problems." Sebastian didn't need to finish his thought. Jilly was clearly worried about where her husband had gone.

Like her mother, Felicia dropped her packages in the front hall. She trailed Jilly to the kitchen.

"George always leaves me a note on the Peg-Board," Jilly murmured, as much to herself as to Felicia. "I'm sure he wouldn't have—oh, look, he did leave a note!"

In George's blunt block printing, the note read: *Archie and I have borrowed Ed's boat and gone off for a little exploring. See you at dinner.*

Felicia breathed a sigh of relief. "Well, that explains it. They should be back any moment. More than anything, I want a hot bath."

"Are you kidding?" Jilly's voice was strained. "It's eight o'clock at night. It's been dark for hours. I don't have any messages on my voice mail. Do you?"

Felicia scrolled through her phone. "I don't have any messages from Dad or Archie."

"I'm going to call Ed Ramos and see if George brought the boat back." Jilly picked up the phone book and found Ed's number. She punched it in. "Ed, I'm so glad I reached you. Has George brought the boat in yet?"

Felicia didn't have to hear Ed's words to know what his

answer was. Her mother went completely white and sat down hard on a kitchen chair.

"All right, Ed, call me if you hear anything." Jilly stared at her daughter with frightened eyes. "Archie and George took Ed's boat out from Madaket Harbor around ten this morning. He hasn't heard from them since."

Felicia nodded calmly, thinking fast. "Okay, Mom, let's not panic. Let's think this through. I'm going to run upstairs to see if Archie left his cell phone here. He hates carrying it. You look for Dad's cell."

Felicia found Archie's phone just as she thought she would, lying on the dresser. She hurried back downstairs to the kitchen.

"I found George's phone on his desk in his study." Jilly tossed the device onto the kitchen table. "What did he think he was doing, going out on the water without his cell phone?"

At that moment, Rex strolled into the kitchen, obviously awakening from his nap in the laundry basket. He rubbed around Jilly's ankles, purring.

Jilly picked him up and held him against her for comfort. "Oh, Rex, if only you could talk and tell us what you overheard. Where did they think they were going?" Helplessly, Jilly looked at her daughter. "What should we do?"

The landline phone rang. Jilly set the cat on the floor and snatched up the receiver. "No, Sebastian, we haven't heard from them. They left a note saying they were going out on Ed Ramos's boat but they haven't returned it. How long do you think we should wait before contacting the Coast Guard?"

Felicia sat very still as her mother hung up the phone.

Jilly was trembling. She clutched her hands together, in an attempt to calm down. "Sebastian thinks that, given the dark and the cold, we should contact the Coast Guard now and not wait. Also, he suggested calling the police and the hospital."

"You call the Coast Guard, Mom. I'll use my cell to call the hospital."

The hospital had no record of any men brought in that day. As Felicia hung up, there was a knock at the door. She ran to answer it.

Nicole and Sebastian stood there. "We came to see if there is anything we can do to help."

The three hurried to the kitchen. Jilly was leaning against the refrigerator wringing her hands. When she saw them, she gasped, "I spoke with John West, the commanding officer of the Coast Guard. They said a small motorboat has been anchored at Great Point for about four hours. No sign of"—Jilly couldn't bring herself to say the word *life*—"people."

Everyone was silent, riveted by their own thoughts to various possibilities, most of them frightening. It was one thing to be out on the water in an open boat in this cold weather if you wore warm clothing. And if it was daytime. If it was night, when the temperature plummeted, it was dangerous to be out in an open boat. Ice floes were already forming on the harbor water. Hypothermia was always a danger.

Felicia's thoughts swirled through her mind: her father. Her darling Archie. Her poor mother. Her sister. Christmas. The wedding. The cold night. Memories of people who had fallen overboard and drowned near the island. Stories of people who had jumped overboard to rescue someone else and both had sunk deep into the unforgiving water. Her legs felt like jelly under her.

"Sit down," said Sebastian. "You, too, Jilly. Let's not go to the worst-case scenario. Let's take a moment to think."

"I'll make tea," Nicole said.

Jilly sat down. Immediately Rex jumped up into her lap, pressed himself against her, and began to lick her chin. Automatically her hands went to his soft thick fur. She stroked him absentmindedly. "John West said they haven't been able to make contact with the boat anchored at Great Point. They're sending one of their own boats over to check it out. It's possible it's not Ed's boat. It's possible George and Archie are on their way back to the Madaket Harbor now—although nothing shows up on the Coast Guard radar."

"Is Archie a good sailor?" Sebastian asked.

"He's not very familiar with boats," answered Felicia. "But he's a good strong swimmer," she added, trying to reassure herself.

Nicole set steaming mugs of tea in front of Jilly and Felicia. "Should we call the police?"

Jilly's laugh was more of a shriek. "Yes, because George and Archie probably got drunk in a local bar, got into fights, and got tossed into jail."

The front door opened and male voices boomed into the house. For a moment, everyone froze. Then, all at once, they crowded into the hall and raced down to see who was there.

"Hello, everyone! Is that coffee you're drinking? I could use a hot drink."

George and Archie stood there, warm, happy, and rosy-cheeked in their parkas and gloves, nothing wet, nothing dripping, nothing torn, nothing bleeding.

With a sob, Jilly cried, "Where the hell have you been?"

Behind George, Archie winked at Felicia.

"Having an adventure, my dear, having an adventure!" George roared heartily. He strode into the house with the air of a conquering hero.

Archie followed more quietly, a smile twitching at the corners of his mouth.

"Really, George, we've been worried sick. We've called the Coast Guard and the hospital and Ed Ramos doesn't know where his boat is—"

"It's safe and sound over on Great Point." George peeled off his waterproof jacket and wool cap. The dryness of the air made his gray hair stand up as if electrified.

"But what happened?" Jilly demanded.

George shook his head. "Believe it or not, we ran out of

gas." He glanced at his future son-in-law. "It's not Archie's fault. I should have known to check the fuel gauge. Fortunately, we were close to the beach, so we paddled in, anchored the boat, and walked home." He practically crowed the last words.

Jilly's hand flew to her chest. "*Walked* home? In this weather? That's over fifteen miles!"

"And much of it was a trudge through heavy sand," George said proudly. Less boastfully, he added, "We did catch a ride with a guy coming into town from Wauwinet Road."

"But, Dad," Felicia spoke up, "why didn't you call to tell us you'd be late, or to ask for a ride?"

George looked sheepish. "We left our cells here. Didn't think we'd need them, and you two were over on the Cape. Once we hit paved road and were off the damned sand, we hit our strides, and frankly, I didn't want to stop walking."

Felicia glanced at her mother, who managed to express anger, relief, and affection at the same time.

"Did you ladies have a good time shopping?" George asked.

"Don't you ever, ever go off like that again without taking your cell phone!" Jilly said, her voice shaking. She shot an accusatory glance at Archie. "I would have thought you, a seasoned hiker, would have more sense!"

Before Archie could respond, George put his arms around Jilly and pulled her to him in a tight embrace. He kissed the top of her head. "It's totally my fault, Jilly. I'm so sorry if I worried you. I promise I'll never go off without my cell phone again."

Sebastian suggested, "Let's have a drink to celebrate the safe return of the explorers."

They gathered in the living room. Jilly phoned the Coast Guard to report the safe return of the two men. Felicia hurried into the kitchen to prepare a board of cheese, crackers, sausages, and chips for the hungry hikers. As she worked at the counter, she felt two arms circle her waist.

Leaning her head back, she purred, "I'm awfully glad you're back."

Archie said, "Your dad was great. He's a real trouper."

"Oh, dear," Felicia moaned. "You're turning my father into a manly man."

"I don't think your mother will mind," Archie said.

When they returned to the living room, Felicia saw that Archie was right. Her mother was sitting as close to George as she could without sitting on top of him. And she was holding his hand, something Felicia hadn't seen for years.

"Here's a little snack for you." Felicia set the board on the table.

Her father hardly noticed the food, he was so revved up. "Archie got to see a part of the island few people see!"

"Archie, how's your head wound?" Felicia asked, although she knew from experience how hard-headed he was.

"No problem," Archie told her. "Feels fine."

"But weren't you cold?" Jilly asked.

"Not at all!" thundered George. "The walk warmed us up."

Felicia curled up next to Archie, watching her parents fondly. She hadn't seen her father so animated in years. Archie and George both now practically inhaled the food. George talked as he chewed, and Jilly didn't even seem to mind.

At Jilly's feet, Rex sat with watchful eyes, waiting for bits of cheese and sausage to fall to the floor. Felicia saw Rex pounce on a morsel of cheese and eat it. She saw her mother watch and held her breath. Food on the carpet?

Jilly simply smiled beatifically. Looking at her daughter, she murmured, "Isn't it helpful, having a cat? I won't have to vacuum."

# 9

Lying next to her happily exhausted husband who was snoring like a hippo, Jilly tossed and turned all night long. She was pleased and slightly amused that George had returned from his watery outing not only alive but convinced of his superman status, but in truth, she was also alarmed. That escapade could have ended so very differently! Truly, they were lucky to be alive, or at least not in the hospital with hypothermia. Or was it hyperthermia? Around Archie, everything was hyper.

Archie seemed like what George would call a perfectly decent fellow, and heaven knew he was handsome, but he was so energetic! So young, fit, muscular, and healthy. He wouldn't understand how George, at fifty-eight, had slightly elevated blood pressure and a troublesome hip. Tomorrow he would ache all over, but because company was in the house, he would try to hide it and would appear merely ill at ease. George wouldn't want to expose his age-caused weakness to his future son-in-law.

Jilly had to admit Archie was awfully attractive in a Liam Neeson way. (But wasn't Liam Neeson Irish, not Scottish? It was questions like this in the middle of the night that made Jilly afraid she was becoming senile.) But what kind of husband would he be—and would he ever want to be a father? First, he breaks an antique chair, then he lures an old man into dangerous waters in December— Archie was reckless, and that did not bode well.

It had been marvelous watching Felicia and Steven reunite—how happy they had been to see each other. Felicia had hugged him, she'd been all over him. So maybe something else could take place to throw the two together . . .

Jilly fell asleep, plotting.

The next morning after breakfast, Felicia told her parents she was taking Archie out to walk around the island for the day. And yes, for sure, they were going to join the Gordons for tonight's cocktail party at the Somersets'.

The moment her daughter and Archie were out the door, Jilly called Nicole. "Did you invite Steven to your party tonight?"

"Good morning to you, too," Nicole responded.

"Sorry, Nicole, good morning. It's just that—"

"Jilly. Deep breath. Take one," Nicole ordered affectionately. "Yes, I did invite Steven. Yesterday on the boat, and again this morning I phoned and left a message on his machine."

Jilly sighed with relief. "You're the best friend in the world. Isn't Steven handsome?"

"Yes, but Archie is, too. And, Jilly—"

"I've got to go. See you tonight."

That night the Somersets' house was crowded from wall to wall with guests. Jilly chatted with friends, but always kept a careful eye on Felicia and Archie. At last her surveillance paid off: she saw Steven approach the couple. Felicia spoke and the two men shook hands.

With the sneaky swiftness of an FBI agent, Jilly crossed the room and became very busy refilling her cup with Christmas punch from the big silver bowl on the dining room table. It took her a long time to do it because she spilled some (on purpose), found a paper napkin to wipe it up, and fussed around ladling more, all in the interest of overhearing the conversation a few feet away from her.

"Yes," Archie was saying, "Felicia has told me all about you."

Steven laughed. "I hope not. You know you're lucky, getting this gorgeous woman for your wife." Steven wrapped a companionable arm around Felicia and hugged her against him.

"I'm well aware of that," Archie replied, bristling.

"We've always been each other's biggest fans," Felicia

added, snuggling into Steven. "We were each other's date for senior prom. I have to show you the picture, Archie. We were so gorgeous!" Looking up at Steven, she smiled.

"I'm sure you were," Archie answered, and to Jilly's eavesdropping ears, his tone was growing antagonistic.

Felicia pulled away from Steven. "Archie and I are going to travel to the Himalayas after our wedding! Isn't that exciting?"

Archie still glowered at Steven. "Oh, look, Lisa just arrived. Excuse us, Steven, I want Archie to meet her." Felicia took Archie's arm and tugged him away from Steven toward the living room.

Jilly wandered in the other direction, ending up in the living room talking with old Sherman Waterson, who had bad hearing and worse breath.

All the next day, Jilly schemed and plotted, realizing how hopeless she was at strategy. She'd never read Machiavelli; she'd never even played chess. But in desperation, she did her best.

It was four o'clock. Darkness was falling. At six they would all go to the Ernsts' Christmas party. Jilly was in the kitchen, carefully covering a plate of gingerbread with ClingWrap when Felicia came in, carrying cups and glasses she'd gathered from around the house to put in the dishwasher.

"Thanks, darling," Jilly said, adding casually, "oh, and

would you mind taking this next door to Steven?" She held out the plate of gingerbread.

Felicia was bent over the dishwasher, rearranging glasses—everyone thought she knew the best way to pack the dishwasher—so Jilly couldn't see her face.

"Why does Steven need gingerbread?" Felicia asked.

Jilly trilled a laugh that sounded fake even to herself. "He doesn't *need* gingerbread, silly. I just like sending him over seasonal treats now and then. He's all alone, you know, in that big house. Have you been inside his house? It's delightful. Lots of bedrooms for children."

Felicia stood up. She stared at Jilly. "Mom. What do you think you're doing?"

Jilly widened her eyes in innocence. "Well, I'm trying to give our good old friend a little Christmas cheer."

"Why not take the gingerbread over yourself?"

"Oh, I have so many things to do . . ."

"*And?*"

*The hell with it*, Jilly thought. No more game playing. She wasn't any good at it anyway. "And I thought you might like to talk with Steven about marriage before it's too late."

"You want me to drop Archie and marry Steven?" Felicia asked. Both her hands flew to her mouth in shock and her expression was so odd Jilly couldn't tell whether her daughter was laughing or crying or both.

"I just want you to *think*—" began Jilly.

With a strange croaking noise, Felicia shook her head and ran from the room.

Jilly didn't mention the gingerbread again.

As they left for the Ernsts' party, Jilly and Felicia pretended that all was normal in a stilted, fragile way, remaining so subtly out of sync that George and Archie didn't notice. The party was such a crush, Jilly quickly recovered her good mood.

Paul Miller approached them, addressing Archie. "Hey, aren't you the young man who went out with George in Ed Ramos's boat and walked all the way home from Great Point?"

This question was asked over and over again. To her surprise, Jilly realized George's and Archie's foolish actions had raised them in the town's estimation. George was no longer a retired accountant, he was a crazy eccentric like the rest of the year-rounders. George glowed with pride as he recounted his adventure, which became more embellished with each telling. Before she knew it, Jilly was telling her own friends about it, almost as if it were some adorable prank instead of something that scared her half to death.

Over the next few days, Archie was the model son-in-law-to-be. During the day, he went out with Felicia to hike for hours on the moors or beaches. In the evenings, he showered and dressed in his blazer, organized his wild red hair into a semblance of normality, and joined the Gordon family at several cocktail parties. Felicia remained polite but distant to her mother, as if she were avoiding an argument—or as if she were contemplating her mother's wise words? Jilly could only hope.

At home during the day, Jilly kept busy baking for Christmas day and all the guests. George often went off for a hike with his daughter and Archie, but Jilly never felt alone. When no one else was around, Rex came out from the laundry basket and lay in his pretty round bed in the kitchen, keeping her company. If she settled in the family room to wrap presents, Rex joined her there, folding himself up on a pillow and watching her carefully, hoping she would dangle a ribbon for him to try to catch.

"You're a clever little fellow, aren't you? I'm amazed at how well you've adapted to life in a house. And I must say all the treats I've been feeding you have made you fill out quite nicely. Your coat is glossy and silky now. We shouldn't have named you Rex. We should have named you Noel or Christmas but of course George wouldn't like that. You're probably too proud to accept a name like that, anyway."

Rex would listen as if he understood her every word, his golden eyes glowing with intelligence. He was also the only living being in the house who didn't argue with her. She had discovered it calmed her remarkably to spend time alone talking to him, and secretly she was pleased that the cat always sat next to her. He was definitely *her* cat. She could say anything to him and he wouldn't take offense. What a treasure!

One night the four attended the Festival of Trees at the Nantucket Historical Association on Broad Street. In the grand historic rooms that once had been a candleworks factory, dozens of live evergreens had been decorated by artists, scholars, and merchants in dazzlingly creative and innovative ways. A few trees were actually artistic creations fashioned out of lobster traps and buoys, or books read by a book club over a series of years, or the wooden parts of an ancient sailboat. Caterers passed champagne and canapés as wild cries of delight filled the room to the highest point of the ceiling where the skeleton of a forty-six-foot sperm whale hung, reminding them of the island's history.

The glittering array of Christmas trees was equaled by the sparkling jewelry and dresses on the women and the colorful holiday vests, velvet jackets, or cummerbunds on the men. *Everyone* was here, and Jilly watched her daughter introduce Archie to them all.

Steven Hardy was also there, handsome, elegant, and alone. He kissed Jilly's cheek and shook George's hand. "Merry Christmas."

Jilly kissed Steven's cheek. "Merry Christmas, Steven," she cooed as she thought frantically of a way to draw him into their little group, but he only nodded a polite hello to

Archie and Felicia, then walked away. Jilly saw Felicia staring after him—was that a look of regret on her face? Or did Jilly only hope it was?

The third Sunday in December, the Gordons and Archie attended the annual Christmas pageant at the Congregational Church where well-known members of the town acted out the ancient nativity story. Dolly and Mike Mills, who had a baby three months old, played the parts of Mary, Joseph, and Jesus. Elementary schoolchildren in halos and wings were backup singers for Tricia Carr, a senior in high school and on her way to Juilliard. The Kastner family played the part of shepherds, complete with three woolly sheep from their farm, and three of the town's selectmen appeared as the Three Wise Men, which added a great deal of levity to the occasion.

When the congregation sang "Away in a Manger," Jilly's thoughts drifted. She knew this was the calm before the storm. Tomorrow Lauren, Porter, Lawrence, and Portia would arrive. In three short days Christmas would be here. Not only that, Felicia and Archie would be married and twenty people would gather in the house on Chestnut Street for the wedding reception.

Jilly was a great one for making lists. At night she lay in bed mentally reviewing what she had checked off and what still needed to be done. She couldn't wait to see the gown Lauren had made for Felicia. Lauren had such exquisite taste. If the children could keep from wrecking the house . . . if the weather cooperated so they could play outside . . . if Archie didn't lure George or Felicia out for some other extreme escapade . . . if the planes made it to the island in time for Archie's mother to arrive . . . if Archie's mother was not too difficult to deal with . . . if she'd ordered a large enough turkey . . . if Rex didn't slip out the door with all these people coming and going . . . if Felicia would stop acting so politely cold toward Jilly . . . if only Felicia were going to marry Steven . . .

If only Jilly could get one good night's sleep!

# 10

In her childhood bedroom, Felicia also tossed and turned through the night.

Her first few nights there, she'd found it amusing to sleep in her girlhood twin bed while her gigantic fiancé lay snoring in the twin bed next to her, beneath a lavender, violet-dotted duvet. They'd had fun messing around and making love in the twin beds, enjoying the challenge of not making noise. She'd relished the sight of her fiancé's huge shoes beneath her tall white bureau with the mermaid-shaped pulls.

But now, as the first white light of day dawned, Felicia found herself realizing how much work her mother had done to make this bedroom such a private girlish sanctuary. Jilly had made the lined, white muslin curtains trimmed with lavender grosgrain ribbon and the tiebacks adorned with felt flowers. Jilly herself had painted the walls a pale violet with marshmallow white woodwork. And it had been Jilly who discovered the old desk at the Hospital Thrift Shop, brought it home, sanded it smooth, and painted it white, with iris twining up the sides and bunnies and birds in the grass. Okay, it wasn't a professional job, but it was darling, and Felicia was fond of this little room.

Lauren's room had been rose-themed until she turned fifteen, at which point she went into an earthy-crunchy hippie save-the-earth phase and hung posters with peace signs and pictures of U2 all over her walls. Lauren's desk had become a repository for her eye shadow and lipstick, CD player and piles of CDs, and tie-dye scarves. Funny how Lauren had ended up as much a happy homemaker and mom as their mother.

Felicia had never changed her room because she'd seldom spent time here. When she entered junior high, she went mad for sports—swimming, girls' hockey, gymnastics, and baseball. She didn't have time even to consider the decor of her room although she did alter its looks with the piles of different uniforms she tossed on the chairs, over her desk, and on the floor. Her mother had attended all her games and never fussed about the piles of dirty uniforms to be washed.

Lying here on her soft bed, as daylight dawned, as her new life was about to begin, Felicia struggled to deal with her deepest fears, that she would never have a baby. At the same time, she was insulted that her mother didn't appreciate how wonderful Archie was, and how much Felicia loved him. She and Archie would be here only three more days. After the wedding and reception, they were moving to a hotel for the night before having a delayed Christmas dinner with the family. Then they were flying to California to begin the first leg of their honeymoon.

Lauren and her family were arriving this morning and Archie's mother was flying in this afternoon. With all the coming and going and cooking and eating, Felicia and Archie would be only part of a massive shifting family celebration, like two arms of an octopus.

And Felicia's mind was like a goldfish, swimming in circles, going nowhere. Felicia threw back her violet duvet, slipped into her robe, left her fiancé with his big feet sticking out of the end of a twin bed, and dashed across the hall for a quick shower before the day began.

# 11

"Bring two cars," Lauren had advised over the phone from Boston, while in the background her husband, Porter, yelled, "Bring a U-Haul!"

Felicia remembered her sister's words as she and Archie helped Lauren, Porter, Lawrence, and Portia carry their backpacks, suitcases, duffel bags, and mysterious brown boxes from the baggage claim at the Nantucket airport. She was trying not to feel overwhelmed at the astonishing amount of luggage her sister's family required, but she reminded herself that first of all, they had brought Christmas presents and more important, Lauren had brought not only Felicia's wedding gown, but undoubtedly a dress for Lauren to wear to the wedding which would be much more eye-catching than Felicia's.

Oh, drat, there she went again. Why was it that the moment she set eyes on her older sister, Felicia morphed from a happy normal woman into a sniveling green-eyed monster? But damn, Lauren looked amazing. Lauren was tiny and curvy in all the right places. Even her long highlighted blond hair was curvy. While Felicia wore a North Face down parka—she was only going to the airport after all— Lauren was clad in a form-fitting black suede coat with black faux fur around the cuffs and hem and high-heeled black boots. Her matching black faux fur hat gave her a sophisticated air. Her only normal accessory was her husband, Porter, a nice enough looking man wearing a camel's hair coat and a genuinely happy smile.

"Portia! Stop! I told you, watch for cars! Lawrence, are you sure you don't have to use the bathroom before we get in the car? Portia, don't drag your backpack!" Lauren fired out orders to her children as they progressed in a ragged cluster through the parking lot to the cars. "What did you say, Felicia?"

"I asked how your trip was."

Before Lauren could answer, Lawrence yelled, "I want to ride in the big car!" while Portia jumped up and down, begging, "I want to ride with Daddy."

"I want to ride with Daddy, too!" yelled Lawrence.

Archie, who had experience with groups on rafting tours, silently opened the trunks of both vehicles and began loading in the luggage.

"Porter, don't forget we have to put the booster seats in for the children." Glancing at Felicia, Lauren told her, "It's the law in Massachusetts."

Felicia had a slightly wicked idea. "Archie, honey, why don't you take Porter and the children in Dad's SUV, and I'll drive my sister in Mom's car?" She felt guilty sticking the exuberant children with Archie, but he was a good sport and this would give her an opportunity for a few private moments with her sister before they hit their family home.

Once everyone was buckled in and Archie had driven away with his babbling cargo, Felicia turned and gave Lauren a good long look. "You're as gorgeous as always," she said. "You're like a model from a catalog."

"I'm glad you think so." Lauren sighed. "I feel like a shrieking old hag on a broomstick. I'd like to hire an army sergeant on mornings like this when I need to be sure we're all dressed, packed, and out the door in time for a plane." Glancing at the cup holder, she smiled. "You remembered! Iced tea?"

"Three tea bags strong, no milk, no sugar."

Lauren grabbed up the go-cup and took a big swig. "You have no idea how much I needed that! How are the 'rents?"

"Good. Mom is in her usual pre-holiday frenzy. Dad mostly stays out of her way. But oh, guess what, they have a cat. He's new, and spends a lot of time in the laundry room, but I think it's excellent that Mom has a pet."

"Yeah, it's her substitute baby." Lauren slurped more tea.

Felicia wanted to confide her new baby yearnings to her sister, but the ride from the airport was only about ten minutes and she didn't want to start talking about something so intimate when she knew they'd be interrupted. "So you brought my gown?"

"I did. Here's my strategy: I brought videos for the kids.

You know I never allow them to watch television or videos or YouTube or play games on the cell phone. This is my secret weapon." Lauren laughed naughtily, the kind of laugh Felicia had never heard from her sister before. "Do I surprise you? When you become a mother, you'll discover depths of cunning within you that you never knew existed."

"Um, okay . . ."

"After lunch, Porter has been assigned the responsibility of taking the kids out for a walk through town to use up some of their crazy energy. When they return, they'll be allowed to watch *101 Dalmatians*. This will superglue them to the television and then finally give us plenty of time to play dress-up with your wedding gown!"

"I'm impressed," Felicia admitted. Secretly she thought, how could she expect anything else? Lauren always knew exactly what to do.

When they arrived at the house, Archie had just parked the big SUV in the driveway. Jilly and George had come outside to welcome everyone. The family was hugging, kissing, and cooing with delight. When Felicia parked her mother's car behind the SUV, and Lauren stepped out, Jilly greeted her as if she hadn't seen her oldest daughter for years.

"Stand back," George whispered to Felicia, hugging her to him. "I think your mother's going to explode with happiness—having her two girls home."

It took a while for the men to carry in the luggage as Lauren directed what went where. Jilly and Felicia knelt in the living room, supervising Lawrence and Portia as they brought Christmas presents in hand-decorated parcels out of a duffel bag and placed them beneath the Christmas tree.

"I wrapped that one, Grandma Jelly," six-year-old Lawrence proudly announced to Jilly.

"We made the wrapping paper!" his little sister announced, pointing to a package in white paper covered with rainbow swirls.

"They're beautiful!" Jilly said, clapping her hands.

Felicia had never seen her mother's face glowing with such tender joy as now when she interacted with her grandchildren. Lawrence's brown curls bobbed as he spoke, and his eyes were bright and clear. Portia resembled her mother, Lauren—and now Felicia saw traces of Jilly in the lines of Portia's sweet round cheeks and pointed chin. Here's where the image of angels came from, Felicia realized. Such shining innocence, such pure trust, such unquestioning happiness. When Lawrence climbed on his grandmother's lap, the curve of his shoulders carried the same lines as Felicia's father. Life on earth may be limited, but grandchildren were the promise of the eternal.

Felicia had tears in her eyes. She had envy in her heart. She knew she had to discuss the possibility of having children with Archie soon.

Portia, noticing Felicia's tears, rushed to her and held her hands. "We brought you a special present, Auntie Felicia. We made it ourselves!"

Not to be overshadowed, Lawrence leapt off Jilly's lap and ran to Felicia. "Yeah, Auntie Felicia, and Mom said I get to be ring bearer in your wedging!"

"Wedding." Portia corrected her older brother wearily, as if this were a burden she had to bear.

"Wedging sounds rather appropriate," Felicia said to her mother, who returned a smile.

Felicia hugged the children to her. "Archie and I have special presents for both of you, too." Inhaling the sweet scent of their flawless skin, their lush hair, their sweet breath, she closed her eyes simply to be in the moment.

And it was only a moment before her nephew and niece wriggled away, eager to be on to the next thing.

# 12

Because the children had spent so much time sitting on a plane, George, Archie, and Porter took the children out to play in the snow before lunch. When they returned with rosy cheeks and big appetites, the children were yawning.

When the meal—with no broken chairs—was finished, George asked, with an odd adolescent grin, "What are you girls doing this afternoon?"

Lauren jumped up. "We're going to try on wedding clothes."

"Great! Archie and Porter and I are going back out for a, um, little jaunt," George announced. He was almost snickering.

The women were delighted to see the men bonding, even if they kept exchanging guilty looks. Probably off to buy some idiotic present, Jilly thought. "Have fun!" she told them, waving them away. The men went out into the cold winter day.

"Just give me a moment to settle the kids with a video,"

Lauren said, herding her son and daughter into the family room.

Jilly went to Felicia and took her hand. "Sweetheart, before we go upstairs, I want to apologize for anything I said that hurt your feelings."

A huge sigh passed through Felicia. Her shoulders relaxed. "Thanks, Mom. But you know—"

"I'm ready!" Lauren announced. "Let's go up to Mom's bedroom—it has the most space and the full-length mirror."

The three women hurried up the stairs. Felicia removed her jeans and sweater. Jilly moved a pile of clean laundry from the armchair so she could sit and watch this once-in-a-lifetime moment.

"Of course that won't be the lingerie you'll wear beneath your dress," said Lauren, eyeing Felicia's sports bra and white cotton underpants.

Felicia rolled her eyes. "This is what I have. This is what I wear. Do you have a problem with that?" she challenged her sister.

"I absolutely do have a problem with that! This is for your wedding day. I've made you an exquisite gown. You need something new, sensual, extraordinary, and feminine."

"You said it, Lauren. This is for *my* wedding day. I'm not you. Plus, come on, no one will see."

Jilly listened to her daughters argue with a smile. Taking a deep breath, she relaxed. This was like Throwback Thursday up close. All their lives, her two very different daughters had held different opinions and neither one had been shy about expressing how she felt. Sometimes this had led to terrible fights, slammed doors, and even floods of tears. But now they were grown up, and Felicia was finally getting married, and the matter of her second daughter's underwear was only a feather blowing in the breeze.

"Could I please see my dress?" Felicia said.

Lauren lifted a suitcase onto the king-size bed, unsnapped and unfolded it. Carefully she unzipped it, obviously enjoying this dramatic moment. The suitcase revealed layers and layers of white tissue paper. Then white satin gleamed, and Lauren lifted out the gown.

Jilly and Felicia gasped. Long-sleeved, full-length, the dress had an empire waist and a gently rounded neckline. Lauren helped Felicia step into the dress, and zipped up the back.

"Now wait," ordered Lauren.

Unfolding more white tissue paper, Lauren lifted out a red velvet sash which she wrapped around the high waist of the dress. She tied a simple bow in the back and let the long ends of the sash trail to the floor.

"And I thought you'd like this," Lauren said to her sister, carefully sliding a white circlet covered with miniature roses into her hair.

Felicia's eyes sparkled. "Lauren, this dress is perfect."

"I thought you'd like it. No ruffles, no frills, no chiffon, not a speck of lace. What do you think, Mom?"

Jilly opened her mouth to speak and broke into tears.

She had never imagined such a perfect moment when one daughter made the wedding dress for the other daughter and they were all here together in a room in peace and happiness. "The dress is astonishing, Lauren. Felicia, you look *beautiful.*"

Lauren absolutely glittered with satisfaction. "And I've got something more." More rustling of tissue paper, and Lauren lifted out a red velvet cape with a red velvet hood. And then, a muff of white faux fur.

When Felicia looked skeptical, Lauren laughed. "You won't want to be cold on the ride in the horse-drawn carriage from the church to our house."

"I thought we were going in cars, or walking if it's a nice day," Felicia said.

Lauren shook her head. "You are SO not walking in your wedding dress! Anyway, it's all arranged. I've spoken with Travis Cosgrove and reserved an open carriage and two horses. And guess what! The horses are white, and their harnesses will be red leather with golden jingle bells!"

Felicia glanced at her mother. Jilly looked as if she were floating on a cloud on her way to heaven. *It's only one day,* Felicia thought, and said, "Thank you, Lauren. That's very thoughtful of you."

"The children will be so excited to see the horses!" Jilly exclaimed. "I wonder if there's a way they could ride in the carriage with you."

"Mom, don't be daft. Why would a couple who just got

married have two children with them?" demanded Lauren, rolling her eyes at her mother.

"I think it's a darling idea," Felicia said. "I'd like to have the kids ride with us."

"All right, then," Lauren relented. "That's really nice of you, Felicia."

"Let's see your dress, and the children's clothes," suggested Jilly.

For the next hour, Lauren slipped into her green velvet matron of honor dress, and Jilly put on her red silk suit, and the three women took turns admiring themselves and one another in the mirror.

They didn't notice that day had turned into evening until Jilly cried, "Gosh, look at the windows. It's dark out there already."

"I'd better go see what the kids are doing," said Lauren.

"I'd better go start dinner," said Jilly.

"I wonder where the men are," said Felicia.

The women scurried around, carefully hanging their dresses on padded hangers and sliding them gently into the closet. Lauren returned the thousands of sheets of tissue paper to the suitcase, closed it, and shoved it beneath her parents' bed.

"I'm getting an ominous feeling," said Jilly anxiously as they went down the stairs. "We stayed up there too long."

"Oh, dear, I hope the children haven't been peeking at the presents," said Lauren.

But they found the children happily stuck to the sofa, watching cartoons on television.

"Is the movie over?" Lauren asked.

"It was over a long time ago, Mommy," Portia replied, not taking her eyes off the TV screen. "We're watching the Cartoon Network."

"How did you know how to work the remote controls?" Lauren asked.

"Duh," her son muttered, shaking his head.

"The main thing," pointed out Jilly, "is that everything is all right."

And then the door opened and the men came in.

# 13

The three men stood shrugging in the hall like schoolboys outside the principal's office. George's right ankle was splinted and wrapped in a protective blue boot. He leaned on crutches.

Jilly rushed to her husband. "George! Darling, what happened?"

"Wiped out on a moped," George told her, unable to wipe the pride off his face.

Jilly slammed to a stop. "A moped? What were you doing on a moped?"

"I wanted to show Archie a lot of the island and while the weather is so nice I thought it would be fun if we rode mopeds. You can see a lot more that way."

"But, George, you've never ridden a moped before."

"So what?" George spoke as if he were wearing a Tarzan leopard skin and beating his manly chest. "It's easy."

"Then how did you end up on crutches?" Jilly inquired, a hint of annoyance in her voice.

"I went around that curve on the parking lot at Jetties

Beach, hit some shells, and wiped out." George seemed to take pleasure in saying the words "wiped out."

"How badly are you hurt?"

Shyly, George lifted his left hand. "Sprained wrist, sprained ankle, nothing serious."

"Nothing serious? How are you going to walk your daughter down the aisle on crutches with your hand in a bandage?"

Lauren interceded smoothly before her mother's voice rose any higher. "Dad, let's help you into the living room where you can sit down."

In an awkward cluster, the men removed their hats, coats, and gloves. The women stayed close to George, ready to support him as he hobbled into the living room. He fell into a chair. Felicia took his crutches and leaned them on the arm of the chair next to him in easy reach.

"Are you in any pain, Daddy?" Felicia asked.

"A little, perhaps," George admitted with a brave smile.

"Can I fetch you a drink, Dad?" Lauren offered.

"If he's on medication, he shouldn't drink," Jilly pointed out.

"They only gave me ibuprofen," George told them. "A nice big scotch would help a lot right now."

"A scotch?" Jilly's voice went soprano again. "Since when do you drink scotch?"

"Archie bought a bottle of single malt."

Archie held up the bottle. "For medicinal purposes," he said with a smile.

"I'll have some, too," Porter announced, dropping into a chair. "We've had a dramatic afternoon. A scotch will go down well."

Jilly took a deep breath as her nurturing instincts overruled her desire to lecture her husband. "You're probably hungry, too. I'll bring you some munchies."

"We'll help," Lauren said, pulling Felicia along.

In the kitchen, Lauren gently pushed her mother into a chair. "Sit down, Mom. We'll fix the snacks. You have a glass of red wine. You're shaking."

Felicia poured the wine and set it before her mother. "Dad's going to be fine, you know, Mom. He's okay. He's not badly injured. You shouldn't worry."

"I'm not worried," Jilly admitted, "I'm furious. What the hell did he think he was doing, riding a moped two days before your wedding? I'm sorry, Felicia, but I can't help thinking it was Archie's influence."

Felicia snapped, "Mom, that is so unfair."

"Really?" Jilly shot back. "Do you think *Porter* came up with that idea? Porter's hardly the type to take a ride on the wild side."

"Hey!" Lauren hurried to Porter's defense. "I'll have you know Porter can be WAY wild when he wants to."

"Do tell," Felicia teased.

Jilly interrupted. "Never mind who started it, your idiot father went along with it and now look at him. You children have to remember he's not a young man anymore. He can't keep up with your husbands. He knows better than to ride a moped, especially before your wedding, Felicia. I truly want to *shake* him, I'm so angry."

"Calm down, Mom." Felicia emptied a bag of chips into a bowl and spooned salsa into a smaller bowl. "Here. Cut some veggies into strips for the hummus dip." She put a chopping board, knife, and fresh vegetables in front of her mother.

"I'm going to have to phone the Howards to give our apologies." Jilly forcefully beheaded some celery. "They have the best parties, too. But I can't have George weaving around on crutches, getting in everyone's way."

"You go, Mom," Felicia said. "We'll stay home with Dad."

"I just might do that," Jilly said, vigorously beheading a carrot.

Lauren took a plate of veggies in to her children, who were still captivated by the television. She returned to the kitchen, dumped a can of mixed nuts into a bowl, and joined her mother and sister as they carried the snacks into the living room.

". . . fishermen dump scallop shells down by the jetties," George was saying, obviously unable to urge his mind off the awesome moment when he wiped out on a moped. "It's a gritty, uneven surface."

Settling into chairs and sofas with their glasses of wine, the three women listened patiently to George recount his drama. Finally Jilly couldn't take it anymore.

"You know, George, we're going to miss the Howards' party tonight."

George frowned. "What a shame. They always have great food. Perhaps you can go with Felicia and Archie, Jilly."

"I think I will," Jilly said. "Would you mind being in charge of Lawrence and Portia? Do you think you could manage them? We'd only be gone for an hour."

"I'll read to them," George said. "We've got lots of good books."

"But, Dad, will you be okay without someone to help you?" Felicia asked.

"Of course I will," George huffed.

A knock sounded at the front door.

"Who can that be?" Jilly wondered aloud.

"The police, to arrest Daddy for reckless moped driving," Lauren joked.

Felicia went to the door. A short, lean, tanned woman stood there, shivering in a zip-up golf jacket.

"Is this the Gordon house?"

Oh my God! This was Felicia's future mother-in-law! "Yes," Felicia managed to say. "Yes, it is."

"I'm Pat Galloway. Archie's mother."

"Oh!" Felicia held the door open. "Please! Come in! Oh, man, we forgot to meet you at the airport! You see, we've had a bit of a drama this afternoon—" She stopped, took a deep breath, and composed herself. "Mrs. Galloway, I'm Felicia. Archie's fiancée. I'm so pleased to meet you."

"I'm thrilled to meet you at last." Pat Galloway leaned forward to kiss Felicia on the cheek. "You're as pretty as your pictures."

"Thank you. Let me take your coat."

"Not yet, if you don't mind. I'd forgotten how cold it is up here in the north."

Felicia ushered Pat Galloway into the living room.

Archie jumped up from his chair like a jack-in-the-box. "Mom!"

All heads turned as Archie strode across the floor to hug his mother. With his arm wrapped around her shoulders, Archie announced proudly, "Everyone, meet my mother, Pat Galloway."

# 14

Jilly greeted the tiny, shivering woman and brought her to a chair close to the fire. Of course she was cold, the woman was all skin and bones and muscles. Not an ounce of fat on her. Her salt-and-pepper hair was cut sensibly, rather like Derek Jacobi as Brother Cadfael. Her skin was as tanned as one of Jilly's favorite Coach bags; no doubt Pat came from Florida. That also explained her choice of clothing, Jilly assumed. While everyone else wore turtlenecks and wool sweaters, Pat wore tartan golf slacks, a long-sleeved rugby shirt, and the ridiculously inadequate windbreaker. Instead of winter boots, she wore high-topped sneakers. Those at least would be practical on Nantucket's uneven brick sidewalks.

Jilly was so busy gawking at her daughter's future mother-in-law that she failed to notice how her husband was struggling to stand up to meet Pat. George gripped one of his crutches, leaned on it, and rose shakily. He bent to grasp the other crutch with his bandaged hand, teetered, tottered, and fell back onto the sofa, his crutch hitting the brass bowl of chestnuts, walnuts, and pecans still in their shells on the coffee table. Everything flew. The nuts barreled across the floor like large marbles.

"George!" Jilly ran to help him wobble back into his chair.

"Sorry."

"Did you hurt yourself?" Jilly asked.

"No," said George, looking slightly embarrassed. "I'm all right."

All the others were gathered around Pat, everyone talking at once.

"Stay there, please, George, and don't move. I've got to pick up all these nuts before everyone else trips over them and we're *all* on crutches."

Jilly quickly sank to her knees—not as easy a movement as it used to be—and began to gather up the nuts and return them to the bowl. She had collected most of them when she heard Felicia say, "Mom, what are you doing on the floor?"

"Gathering the nuts," Jilly answered factually, realizing as she spoke that this made her sound slightly demented. A childish part of her wanted to make sure everyone knew the scattered nuts were George's fault, especially because as she looked up she met the sensible green eyes of Archie's mother.

"Hello up there," said Jilly, trying to make a joke out of it. "The bowl of nuts got knocked over and I wanted to pick them up before anyone tripped on them." There, she thought, she hadn't mentioned George's clumsiness.

"I'm pleased to meet you," said Pat. "I apologize for showing up at your house like this, but no one met my plane and I couldn't wait to see everyone."

"We're so glad you came," Jilly told Pat. She set the bowl of nuts on the table and rose. "We've had a rather disorganized day because the men went off on mopeds and George had an accident."

Pat turned her vibrant green eyes toward George. "An accident!" Pat said the word as Jilly would say *"chocolate."* "How exciting. How did it happen? Were you on a dirt road? Was it hilly?"

George shrugged carelessly. "I hit some grit and wiped out." He sounded as if this happened every day.

"Did you have to go to the hospital?" Pat asked hopefully.

"I did," George announced triumphantly. "Porter and Archie were on mopeds too. They helped me onto the back of Archie's moped and took me to the hospital. Of course we had to take a taxi home."

Jilly was torn between guilt at not having asked George how he got to the hospital, and concern that three mopeds were dispersed around the island, driving up the charges on George's credit card.

"Did it hurt terribly to ride on the back of Archie's moped after your fall?" Pat inquired.

Proudly, George nodded. "I knew I'd done something pretty bad to my ankle because I couldn't move it without pain, and the same thing with my wrist."

"I've heard that a sprained wrist can hurt more than a broken one," Pat said with sympathy.

*Oh, brother,* Jilly thought. All the others had settled back into their seats to sip their drinks and listen to George's dramatic account of how he had "wiped out."

"Pat," Jilly asked, "may I get you a drink?"

"That would be nice," Pat said. "Could I have a Manhattan?"

Jilly froze. She didn't know how to make a Manhattan and she was wondering where she had put her cocktail recipe book and whether she had the ingredients for the drink in the house.

Fortunately, Archie came to her rescue. "Mom, no bourbon. We've got wine and scotch."

"No bourbon?" Pat asked, surprised, as if her son had told her they all drank out of jam jars. Then, without waiting for an answer, she said, "Scotch on the rocks would be perfect."

"Coming right up," Jilly said cheerfully.

As she prepared Pat's drink in the kitchen, Rex swaggered out of the laundry room, rubbed against her ankles, and meowed. He'd had his dinner, but Jilly opened a can of Fancy Feast and gave him a tiny bit more.

"Obviously we're not going to the Howards' party now," she whispered to Rex. "I'd counted on everyone enjoying the Howards' gourmet canapés and returning to the house stuffed to the gills. Instead, I've got to prepare some kind of dinner."

Rex meowed again. Jilly thought he sounded concerned.

"I do have the makings for sandwiches, of course, but I don't want to serve them to Pat, especially since we forgot to pick her up at the airport. Pat seems remarkably good-natured about this. If she's going to be Felicia's mother-in-law, I want her to feel welcome and comfortable here."

Rex left the food bowl to wind around Jilly's ankles, purring. It was as if he were saying: *I feel comfortable here. I'm sure she will, too.* Cats were remarkably sensitive creatures.

In the freezer, Jilly had a lasagna she'd made for one of the evenings after Christmas when Lauren, Porter, and their children were still here. She took it out, microwaved it for a couple of minutes, then put it in the oven.

Rex watched thoughtfully. "It will be ready in thirty minutes," Jilly told him. "I'll serve a green salad with it and dessert can be—"

"Mom, what are you doing in here?" Felicia stood in the doorway. "You've been forever fixing Pat's drink."

"Oh, my goodness," Jilly said, hitting herself on the forehead. "I thought I would start dinner—"

"Give me Pat's drink and I'll take it in to her."

"No, no, I'll take it in." Jilly didn't want to be rude, hiding away in the kitchen. Carrying the drink to the living room, Jilly thought: *Broccoli? Green beans?* Lauren's children hated salad but Lauren insisted they eat one green vegetable at every meal. *Broccoli*, Jilly thought, she would sauté some broccoli.

Pat almost snatched the drink out of Jilly's hands. "Thank you so much! I really need this after the day I've had. First my plane out of Miami was delayed, then we had to circle for forty-five minutes before we could land in Boston, and the flight from Boston to Nantucket felt like a roller-coaster ride."

"Well, we're so glad you're here. Enjoy your drink. There's more where that came from." Jilly offered Pat the platter of sliced vegetables and dip.

"Thanks." Pat picked up a carrot.

"Have you checked into the hotel yet, Mom?" Archie asked.

"I did. It's great," Pat told her son. "This seems to be a first class little village." To Felicia, she said, "You grew up here, right?"

Jilly sank into a chair, took a sip of her own drink, and relaxed as the conversation flowed. Really, it was a splendid thing to have so many people she treasured gathered here together—even though she still thought George had been an idiot to ride that moped.

"What a divine house you have," Pat told Jilly. "Your Christmas tree is like something out of a storybook. And look at all those presents!"

Pat's praise and Jilly's drink spread a warm sensation of satisfaction through Jilly. She felt rather earth-motherish, capable of dealing with spontaneous events with aplomb. "I've put a lasagna in the oven. It will be ready in thirty minutes."

"But, Mom," Lauren objected, "I thought we were going to the Howards' cocktail party."

"I think it will be much cozier to stay here," Jilly said, "and besides, I don't want to put any stress on your father's ankle. We'll have to wait on him hand and foot for the next day so he can walk Felicia down the aisle." She flashed George a loving look. He beamed with pleasure at her words. Jilly rested in her chair and studied the Christmas tree. It was glorious, as it should be, for she had spent hours positioning the lights and ornaments in the right spots. The appetizing aroma of cheese and tomato sauce drifted out from the kitchen. Her family was all here, safe and content.

This was turning into a perfect family evening.

# 15

In the living room of the house on Chestnut Street, Felicia surreptitiously studied her future mother-in-law. Quiet, Archie had described his mother. *Quiet.* Who could understand the male mind? Perhaps he meant that his mother was athletic, preferring golf, tennis, and swimming to conversation.

What did Pat think of Felicia? Did it matter terribly? Archie's family wasn't as close as the Gordons. Archie seldom visited his mother, although he often phoned her and sent her gifts from exotic lands.

Perhaps everything was all right. The wedding was in two days and then she and Archie would go on their honeymoon.

"If you'll excuse me," said Jilly, rising, "I need to prepare a few things for dinner."

"I'll help you, Mom," Felicia offered.

"I'll wrestle the children away from the television set," Lauren said. To the room in general, she warned, "Prepare yourselves for screaming. Porter and I don't let our children watch television very often and they've been stuck to the TV practically all day. But they're good children, I promise."

In the kitchen, Felicia tossed a green salad while her mother got out a sauté pan. From the family room came the predicted sounds of anguished protestations, before Lauren, Portia, and Lawrence appeared in the kitchen.

"I want you to go out in the backyard and run around the yard six times without stopping," Lauren told her children.

"Mom!" Portia and Lawrence protested simultaneously.

Lauren folded her arms over her chest and glared like a drill sergeant. "Do it, now, or no dessert."

Heads hanging, feet dragging, the children went out the back door, down the stairs, and began to plod wearily around the yard.

"Lauren," Felicia said, "shouldn't your kids have on coats or hats in this cold weather?"

"My children are like little furnaces," Lauren told Felicia. "And they'll heat up even more—watch."

Portia and Lawrence hadn't made it around the yard once before they turned the run into a race accompanied by arm waving, war cries, and general screaming. This year, snow had come early and the snowy ground was already coated with a thick layer of ice. The kids slid on it, fell down, rolled around, giggling and whooping.

"You see," Lauren said. "They won't want to come in. They have no idea it's cold out."

Felicia and Lauren set the dining room table with their mother's poinsettia place mats and matching napkins. Jilly also had an entire set of Christmas plates that they put around the table.

"Gee, Mom," Felicia teased, "do you expect us to use regular silverware?"

"I've looked in all the catalogs," Jilly answered, taking Felicia's question seriously, "but I haven't found any Christmas silverware or utensils."

Felicia and Lauren grinned at each other, as they had so many times in the past, silently mocking their mother's passion for themed dinnerware.

"Has anyone seen Rex?" Jilly wondered. "He likes to hide in the laundry room. I hope he didn't sneak out the back door."

"I'll get the kids in the house and have them wash their hands," said Lauren.

"I'll organize everyone in the living room to come into the dining room for dinner," said Felicia.

"I'll sauté the broccoli," Jilly said. "Everything else is ready." She poured olive oil in the pan, switched on the heat, and after a moment, added the broccoli.

Felicia had just stepped into the living room when she heard a commotion. She rushed back to the kitchen. Through the open doorway, she saw her mother kneeling next to an overflowing laundry basket. Jilly was petting Rex. At the same time, Lauren was holding the back door open to the mudroom which was at the far end of the laundry room. Through the open door, her son and daughter burst into the house.

"Look! A cat!" yelled Lawrence.

"A kitty! Mommy, look, a kitty!" shouted Portia.

"Quiet voices, please. Use your quiet voices," said Lauren quietly, as if to remind them what a quiet voice was.

As Felicia watched, the cat, half covered with laundry, froze into a physical red alert, ears back, eyes wide, aware of the sounds of a predator.

"Can I hold the kitty? Can I? Can I? Can I?" asked Lawrence.

"No, I want to! I want to hold the kitty first!" yelled Portia.

Jilly was attempting to gather the cat into her arms protectively, while at the same time she tried to rise from her knees and turn her back to the children.

Lauren awkwardly bumped into Jilly as she tried to squeeze past her mother to reach her children. She managed to grab Portia's shoulder and Lawrence's arm. "Settle down!" Her voice was less quiet now.

"Here, kitty, kitty!" shrieked Portia in her high, eardrum-shattering small girl's voice.

"Children, please be quiet," begged Jilly. "Rex has never met children before. He's afraid of you. You have to be as quiet as little mice so he'll like you."

"I'll be quiet!" bellowed Lawrence.

"Lauren, perhaps you could take the kiddies back outside for a moment," suggested a slightly flustered Jilly.

Misunderstanding, Portia stretched her arms out. "I'll take the kitty outside!"

"Kiddie!" Jilly snapped. "Not kitty, kiddie!" She'd never used an angry voice with her grandchildren before. It startled everyone in the room, including the cat.

"Fine, Mom, I will, as soon as I can move around you." Lauren was also getting her dander up. She was mad at her children and not that thrilled with her mother, either.

Jilly backed against the wall, clutching the orange cat to her chest. Before Lauren could step past her, Lawrence wriggled out of his mother's hand and squirmed to Jilly's side.

"Hi, kitty kitty," Lawrence yammered, reaching up a hand to pet the cat.

Rex shot out of Jilly's arms like a squeezed banana out of its skin. In a flurry of orange and white fur, he streaked down the hall and into the living room.

"Oh, no!" exclaimed Jilly. "Rex will be afraid of all those people. He's not used to groups."

Bumping into one another as they ran, Lauren, Jilly, Felicia, Lawrence, and Portia sprinted down the hall and into the living room.

Pat jumped to her feet, horrified. "Oh, dear, a cat!"

The cat had taken refuge behind an armchair next to the Christmas tree.

"He won't hurt you," promised Felicia. "He's more afraid of you than you are of him."

"I'm allergic to cats!" Pat proved her claim by exploding in a giant sneeze.

"We'll get him, Grandma Jelly," Lawrence said. The little boy dropped to his knees and crawled behind the armchair where his father was sitting.

Porter stood up, the better to observe his son. "Be careful, Lawrence, the cat might scratch you."

Jilly said defensively, "Rex has never scratched anyone!"

Lauren hastened to back up her husband's warning. "There's always a first time."

"He went behind the Christmas tree," Lawrence reported.

"He'll tear up all the pretty wrapping paper on the presents!" cried Portia.

"Don't crawl on the presents, Lawrence," Lauren ordered. "You might break them."

At the mention of the presents, Lawrence subsided.

"I'm sure poor Rex is traumatized by so much noise," Jilly said, wringing her hands.

Felicia put her arm around her mother. "Why don't we all go in the dining room and have dinner? That will give the cat some peace and quiet."

Her mother nodded. "That's a good idea, and dinner is ready."

"But what if the cat pees on the presents?" asked Pat, anxiously digging in her purse for a tissue.

"Why would the cat pee on the presents?" demanded Jilly, rather insulted.

"That's what cats do," said Pat. "They'll pee on anything and you can never eradicate the stink."

"Rex has never peed on anything in the house except his litter box," Jilly retorted indignantly.

"Yes, but you only got him a few days ago," Lauren argued.

Four-year-old Portia burst into tears. "I don't want pee on my presents!" she wailed.

George, the hero of the hour, rose shakily on his crutches. "I'll poke my crutch behind the tree. That will force him out."

"Please don't hurt him," begged Jilly.

"I wouldn't dream of it," George said. He sat on the arm of the chair next to the Christmas tree, steadied himself with one hand, and with the other, slowly maneuvered his crutch over the piles of presents and behind the Christmas tree.

All around him, everyone, even the children, watched in breathless silence.

George yelled, "I think I poked him!"

The cat yowled, the wrapping paper rustled, the Christmas tree shuddered, and dozens of ornaments fell from the tree as Rex fled up the trunk to the very top where he attached himself with all four claws to the handmade, spun cotton angel.

"Oh, George!" cried Jilly.

"Step back, Lawrence and Portia," their mother demanded. "You might get cut on some of the broken ornaments."

"Here, kitty kitty!" called the children, as if he were at the top of a building instead of a tree.

Rex's fur stood up all over and he had a wild look in his eyes. His back feet scrambled furiously to find more secure footing on the quivering slender branches.

"Quiet voices," Lauren encouraged.

"A-cheese!" Pat sneezed.

Perhaps Pat sounded like a predatory animal. It certainly seemed so to Rex, who reacted to the noise with a frightened hiss and an arched back. More ornaments fell to the floor.

Felicia took a practical approach. "How are we going to coax him down?"

"We've got a stepladder," George told them. "It's in the garage."

"No, it's not, George," Jilly reminded her husband. "Remember we brought it in to decorate the tree. I think we put it in the hall closet."

Porter said, "I'll get it," and left the room. A moment later he called, "It's not in here."

"A-cheese!" sneezed Pat loudly and juicily.

"Hiss!" hissed Rex. The Christmas tree wobbled back and forth, threatening to topple.

"Oh, boy," Lawrence yelled with glee. "It's gonna crash!"

"I think the stepladder is in the back hall by the washing machine," Jilly called.

"I don't want the tree to fall down!" Portia burst into tears again.

"We don't need a stepladder to reach the cat," Archie announced. He stepped up onto the cushion of the armchair, reached up, and hoisted the cat by the scruff of his neck. Rex protested loudly, flailing at the Christmas tree with his front paws and growling deep in his throat. Twisting like water in Archie's hands, he went upside down and faced Archie, claws extended, hissing and snarling like a mountain lion. His contortions threw Archie off balance. Archie fell off the chair, dropping the cat. He landed on his back with a loud crunch as he hit the presents. Rex rushed out of the room, thundered up the stairs, and disappeared.

"The presents!" cried the children and Lauren.

Felicia hurried to help Archie up from his inelegant position. "Are you okay?"

"I'm fine." Archie awkwardly tried to find a place for his feet. "Maybe a bit embarrassed."

An ear-piercing shriek bleated through the house, so shrill and overpowering everyone in the room automatically covered their ears with their hands.

"Now what?" George asked, eyes wide.

"Maybe it's the police!" suggested Lawrence hopefully.

"It's the smoke alarms," said Jilly. "Oh, no, I think the broccoli is burning." She ran from the room.

"I've got to help Mom," Felicia told Archie. She raced away into the smoky kitchen to find her mother dumping blackened broccoli into the sink.

"Open the back door!" Jilly ordered. Felicia hurried to do that as Jilly said, "I'll open the windows, too. Stay by the door. I don't want Rex to get out."

Felicia went into the laundry room, opened the back door—there were no screen doors here on Nantucket. She stood guarding the door, waving her arms in the air to help the flow of fresh air enter the house and deactivate the fire alarms. Finally they shut off. The cool air felt good and so did the momentary peace. She was worried about her mother, who had gone to such great effort to make everything perfect for this Christmas holiday.

Returning to the kitchen, she asked, "How's the lasagna, Mom?"

"The top is more brown than I'd like, but I think it's fine for eating. I'm sorry to say the sauté pan is ruined and so is the broccoli but I'm sure the children will remain healthy without broccoli for one night." Jilly was leaning against the counter, looking dazed. "I don't know if I can return to the living room. All those broken ornaments . . ."

Felicia gently took her mother by the arm and led her to a kitchen chair. "Sit down a minute and rest. There are plenty of adults in the living room who are capable of picking up. Besides, not all of the decorations are broken. Relax a moment."

In the living room, Felicia found everyone involved in gathering up the fallen decorations, putting the broken ones into a paper bag and the good ones into a book bag that Lauren had taken from the front hall.

"This way," Lauren said, "Mom can look through them. If one of them means a lot to her, perhaps she can glue it back together."

"Good idea." Felicia returned to her mother in the kitchen. "You'll be surprised, Mom, when you see the tree. You won't know that anything happened."

Jilly opened her mouth then closed it. "I'm sure you're right," she said, too overwhelmed to disagree.

# 16

While her mother relaxed in the kitchen, Felicia leaned against the living room door, scrutinizing the mess and wondering where to start.

Pretty little Portia was sitting on her mother's lap, sobbing at the top of her lungs. "The presents are ruined! The presents are ruined!" Lauren hugged her little girl close, stroking her hair as she reassured her that the presents were fine.

Beneath the Christmas tree, Lawrence crawled around like a CIA agent, sneakily peeling back the torn paper, tearing it more to peek at what was inside.

Porter was on his stomach on the floor, tightening the screws in the green plastic device that held the Christmas tree while Archie supported the trunk and directed him. "The left screw. It's leaning to the right. No, the other way!"

Felicia's father had taken sanctuary in the armchair farthest from the Christmas tree. His head had fallen to his chest and he seemed to be mumbling to himself.

And standing by the fireplace, Archie's mother, Pat, continued to sneeze her eccentric, high-pitched sneeze.

Wading through the fallen ornaments, Felicia made her way to Pat. "Why don't you step outside for a few moments for a breath of fresh air? Maybe that will help your allergies."

Pat glanced up gratefully, her face centered by a puffy red nose. "That's a good idea, dear, but it's so cold outside. Perhaps I'll call a cab and go back to the hotel."

"Oh, no, please don't leave yet. Dinner's almost ready. Why don't you let me loan you one of our down coats," Felicia offered. "It will keep you nice and warm."

"All right," Pat agreed unhappily. Handkerchief to face, she allowed herself to be led to the front hall where she donned one of Jilly's down jackets. Regarding herself in the mirror, ensconced in so much puffy bulk, Pat croaked, "I look like a sofa."

Felicia laughed. "We all look that way here in the winter. Let's go out."

The two women stood side by side on the front steps of the house on Chestnut Street. The Gordons' house was right in the middle of town, one of the few houses that hadn't been turned into a commercial establishment. It was a magical location, especially at Christmas. On the shops all around them, small lights twinkled like colorful stars. The harbor was only three blocks away and they could hear the deep booming horns of the ferries as they arrived and departed. The evening air was cold and salty, flowing into their lungs like an elixir.

Heels clicked and laughter rang out as people hurried from nearby restaurants and the movie theater.

"Would you like to take a walk?" Felicia asked.

"Not in this snow." Pat looked down at her sensible sneakers. She breathed for a while, then said in a confessional tone, "You have much more family than Archie and I."

Felicia couldn't tell if this was a good or bad thing.

Before Felicia could ask her future mother-in-law to clarify her remark, Pat shivered. "I'm ready to go in now."

It was noisier in the living room than it had been ten minutes ago. Lauren was standing over Lawrence with her hands on her hips, smoke practically steaming from her nostrils.

Her son stood glaring at her with a fierce face and clenched hands. "I didn't tear the wrapping paper! I didn't!"

*Yes, he did! I saw him do it! He's lying!* Felicia thought, but wasn't certain what the appropriate action was. After all, Lawrence was her nephew and in general a darling boy.

"Lawrence, because this is Christmas season, and because we're at Grandma Jelly's house, I'm not going to punish you for lying." Lauren knelt down next to her son and put her hands on his little shoulders. "This is a crazy time, isn't it?"

The rigidity of anger slowly melted from the little boy's body. He nodded.

"It would be so nice if you could help me stack the Christmas presents up in a nice pile again," said Lauren.

"Okay, Mommy."

"I want to help, too." Portia jumped off the chair and knelt next to her mother.

*How does she do it?* Felicia wondered silently. How did her sister manage to transform a furious little monster back into a sweet little boy? How did Lauren even manage to love her children when they were shrieking, nasty-faced maniacs? How did perfect Lauren live with such imperfection?

"I don't know if I can do it," Felicia whispered. "I don't know if I will ever be capable of being a mother."

Next to her, Pat chuckled. "It's sort of a learn-as-you-go job. Believe me, when I was raising Archie, I didn't play golf. Some days my hair never got combed."

"Excuse me, ladies, I want to take this out to the mudroom." Porter held up the brown paper bag filled with broken ornaments. He slid past them into the hall.

"The tree is stable again," Archie told them. "We can start rehanging the decorations."

"Dad," Felicia joked, "you stay over there in your chair with your crutches out of the way."

George joked, "Oh, you mean I can't do my tap dance now?"

The ornaments had been gathered into a pile on the coffee table next to the brass bowl of nuts. For a while the family worked in relative harmony. Lauren and her children restored order to the pile of Christmas presents while Archie, his mother, and Felicia hung decorations on the tree. Felicia looked down to see her nephew, so engrossed the tip of his tongue was caught between his teeth, carefully sliding a red ribbon over a torn part of wrapping paper so that the tear didn't show. At this moment Lawrence looked absolutely angelic. She saw Lauren glance at Porter. The two looked down at Lawrence and then at each other with smiles of pride and pleasure.

Jilly came to the doorway. She looked calmer now.

"Is anyone hungry?"

The family made their way into the dining room where the two children immediately got into an argument about who got to sit next to Grandma Jelly. Finally the table was rearranged so that Jilly sat between. She seemed happy with this arrangement.

As they ate rich, cheesy lasagna, tossed green salad, and warm garlic bread, they discussed tomorrow: Christmas Eve day.

"I've made a list," Jilly told them. "Maybe after dinner and after the children have gone to sleep, we can all sit down and go over the list. Christmas morning will be busy opening presents. Then lunch. The wedding is at three in the afternoon. About twenty people will be coming back

to the house for a little party. I'd like to have everything—"
She paused.

"Perfect," George said with a knowing little snort.

"No," said Jilly. "I'm not going to aim for perfection. I'd
simply like to have everything in some kind of order. After
all, it's not every day your daughter gets married!"

# 17

The long evening was over. Dinner had been served and eaten. With Lauren's and Felicia's help, the dishes had been stacked in the dishwasher and the kitchen cleaned, ready for breakfast tomorrow morning.

The children, protesting loudly, had been put to bed on air mattresses in Lauren's old bedroom. The adults had gathered in the living room to go over the to-do list for the next day. Jilly had restrained herself from rehanging every object on the Christmas tree. This was not a tree in a boutique or a museum, she reminded herself, it was the tree for a family, and she was pleased that her grandchildren had helped put it back together. She tried not to mind that the lower ornaments were hung in clumps, leaving some branches completely bare, while the upper branches seem to have been decorated by the color-blind.

At any rate, she was too exhausted to lift her arm to move one single star. What a day this had been! Felicia was cuddled up next to Archie on the sofa. Pat listened to George recount his wipeout with great detail; he looked content in spite of his wrist in a splint and his crutches. Porter and Lauren had UPSed "Santa" presents to Nantucket last week and they snuck off to the garage where they'd been hidden to take them out of the cardboard and start assembling them. Jilly thought back with affection to those days with young children when the anticipation of Christmas morning brought her and George as much pleasure as seeing the presents they bought their daughters being unwrapped.

Finally everyone went his or her separate way. Archie borrowed George's car and drove his mother to the hotel, asking Pat to call him when she wanted to be picked up the next morning. Porter and Lauren went up to bed. Felicia and Archie helped George make his clumsy, bumbling progress up the stairs and into the bedroom with Jilly following behind carrying one of his crutches. Then the almost-newlyweds went to bed in Felicia's childhood bedroom and Jilly began the arduous process of helping George out of his clothes and into his pajamas. This involved supporting him as he hobbled into the bathroom, brushed his teeth, and surveyed his body in the mirror. He greeted every bruise from his wipeout as a badge of honor and continued to point out the bruises until Jilly expressed the proper dismay at their size and color.

Once George had fallen onto the bed, Jilly propped up his ankle on several pillows. She gave him two Tylenol PM tablets with a glass of water. He was asleep almost at once.

At last she was able to organize herself for bed. She was

exhausted, and also a little maudlin. With George out of commission, no one was around to rub her tired shoulders or compliment her on her dinner, or tell her that in spite of everything, this was a wonderful family holiday. Someday she knew she and George would sit around talking about this crazy day and laughing. Now she lay in bed feeling irritated and unable to sleep. With his foot elevated, the blankets on the bed had all drifted over to George's side. His snore was like a chain saw. Jilly got up, put her robe back on, and dug an old blanket out of the back of the closet to wrap around herself. She lay back down on her side, feeling oddly lonely even though the house was full. She used to enjoy having a full house. The terrible truth was, she was getting old. She couldn't do it all the way she used to, or if she could do it all, she couldn't do it with the same enthusiasm. She had heard that as people grew older they became cranky and she wondered if this was what was happening to her. It made her so sad to think of becoming a cranky old woman.

A slight shift in the air alerted her to movement. She opened her eyes. Rex had been hiding under the bed, and now in one fluid leap, he jumped up next to her. He sat on the edge of the bed and regarded her for a long time with his gold eyes.

"Hello, pretty boy," whispered Jilly. "You have a full bowl of cat food in the kitchen but I'm too tired to carry you down to show it to you. Anyway, I have a pretty good idea you'll find it in the night. I'm sorry you were so frightened today. Human beings must seem a bit uncivilized to you."

Rex began to purr. The gentle, resonant purring soothed Jilly's edgy nerves. She closed her eyes. After a moment, she felt the cat turn around once or twice. Then he settled right next to her in the curve of her hips. His warmth was as soothing as a hot-water bottle. He continued to purr.

Jilly slept.

# 18

The morning of Christmas Eve dawned cloudy and cold. Felicia woke early, as always, and tiptoed to the window to look out at the new day. She was surprised to see that while she slept, Mother Nature had blanketed the island with several more inches of pristine white snow. The temperature had fallen even lower—she could tell by the frost lacing the window and by the iciness of the floorboards beneath her feet. Her parents, frugal Yankees that they were, always turned the heat down during the night.

Hurrying back to bed, she slipped beneath the delicious warmth of the covers. It was only a little before seven, and it sounded as if everyone else in the house was still asleep.

"Come over here," Archie mumbled sleepily.

She didn't have to be asked twice. The twin bed was scarcely large enough to hold both of them, but that was fine with her. She was very happy to nestle up against her soon-to-be-husband. She lay with her back to him, snuggled close against him, and with a mischievous smile she pressed her frozen feet up against his warm legs.

"Hey!"

"Sorry, but my parents haven't turned the furnace up yet."

"A big blizzard swept through last night."

"How do you know?"

"Got up to pee. Heard the wind howling, and took a look out the window. I'm surprised it didn't wake everyone up. I watched for a long time. It's been a while since I've seen a good old New England blizzard."

"I like your mother," Felicia said, "but I don't think she's prepared for this weather. We'll have to buy her a decent coat and some gloves and a hat."

Archie groaned. "That means I should get out of bed."

Felicia stroked his hand. "Not quite yet. I'd like to talk about something."

"I hate when you say that."

"Portia and Lawrence are so adorable. They're funny, and clever, and sweet."

Archie didn't reply.

Calmly, she continued, "Seeing them makes me rethink this entire zero population growth idea, Archie."

Archie said nothing. So it was going to be this kind of discussion, Felicia thought, feeling her blood pressure rise, the kind where she babbled and Archie stonewalled her with silence. She didn't want to start this day with bad feelings.

"Oh, never mind." She pulled away from him and put her feet on the floor.

"Why don't you just marry Steven and have kids with him?" Archie muttered.

Felicia burst out laughing. "I think I'll stick with you." She was still laughing as she showered and dressed. It cheered her immeasurably that Archie could be jealous.

She went downstairs, leaving Archie in bed, talking to his mother on his cell.

Felicia discovered Jilly wandering around the house in her robe, carrying two large poinsettia plants in her arms.

"Mom?"

"Nicole just texted me that poinsettias are poisonous to cats!" Jilly looked down at the flowers in her arms with consternation, as if they might bite her. "I have to remove these from the house, but if I put them outside they'll immediately freeze and die. I don't know what to do. Plus, how am I going to decorate the house for Christmas? And the church for your wedding?" Jilly quivered with so much anxiety it seemed she was about to achieve liftoff.

"Mom, does the cat ever go in the basement?"

"I don't know," Jilly replied helplessly.

"We can make sure that he doesn't go down there by shutting and locking the door from the kitchen," Felicia told her sensibly. "We'll take the plants down to the basement. We'll lock the door. Tomorrow we can take the plants to the church. After all, Rex isn't coming to the wedding."

Jilly laughed a rather demented laugh. "Oh, of course he isn't. Silly me! I think I've had too much coffee to drink.

There are so many things to do. I haven't even scrambled the eggs yet."

Felicia gently relieved her mother of the two poinsettia plants, led her to the kitchen, and set the plants on the top basement step, shutting and locking the door to the basement.

Turning to her mother, she asked, "Have you had anything to eat yet?"

"I don't think so. I was just drinking my coffee when I got Nicole's text."

"Why don't you go upstairs and dress?" Felicia suggested. "I'll scramble the eggs and make toast."

"Darling, you're so kind, thank you so much. I hope you don't think I'm going senile."

"Not at all. You've always been this way," joked Felicia, relieved and delighted to see her mother smile.

Lauren came into the room, wearing a red cashmere sweater, jeans, and pearls. On her it worked.

"Don't bother about scrambling eggs," Lauren said. "I made my cheesy egg deluxe casserole. We only have to nuke it in the microwave when everyone comes down."

Felicia stared at her sister. "What? You got up and cooked in the night?"

"Of course not, you nut job. I made it at home, brought it here in my insulated food carrier, and stashed it in the refrigerator for today. I knew Mom would have a lot to do and I wanted to stave off the crazies." Lauren tugged Felicia toward the kitchen. "You can set the table while I put the cinnamon rolls in to warm."

"Where are the children?"

"Porter's helping them dress for the day. They noticed it snowed more overnight and they can't wait to run outside."

Jilly kissed both daughters' cheeks. "Such good girls! I'm going to shower and dress, and then I'll help your father get up." She sounded calmer.

"If you need any help lifting Dad, call Porter," Lauren told her mother. "Dad's really too heavy for you to try to lift."

"Good idea, Lauren. Thanks." Jilly headed up the stairs.

Impressed and slightly daunted by her sister's super-helpfulness, Felicia bit her lip. All the old emotions of being second-best came rolling over her in a wave. Then she heard a metallic scraping sound. Running to the front door, she looked out to see that Archie had dressed and gone outside. He'd found the shovel in the garage. He was shoveling a path to the door.

"Archie's shoveling the sidewalk!" Felicia called up to her mother. *Take that,* she thought smugly, *my man is doing some heavy lifting without even being asked.*

# 19

Jilly stood beneath the soothing hot shower and repeated to herself quietly: *Slow down. Slow down.*

She could force her body to move with less haste. She took her time washing with her favorite perfumed soap and stood for a while enjoying the pounding of hot water between her shoulder blades.

But her mind raced.

George and Jilly had spent fifty thousand dollars on Lauren's wedding. Lauren had had six bridesmaids, a Vera Wang wedding dress that Lauren and Jilly had traveled to New York to find, one hundred guests at a sit-down surf and turf dinner at the yacht club, and a band from Boston. But that wasn't all. The day after the wedding, which had been in June, half of the guests had remained for a champagne brunch on a boat hired to take them around the harbor.

Jilly was aware that Felicia thought her parents preferred Lauren. And it was true that Lauren was more like Jilly's idea of a perfect daughter living a perfect life. Lauren had always been tidy, punctual, sweet, and dainty. Felicia had always had scraped knees, bruised elbows, torn clothes, and hair that in spite of constant brushings stood out all over like a bouquet of cowlicks. Actually, the short hairdo Felicia wore now was very becoming and the best look Jilly had seen on her second daughter.

Of course Jilly and George loved both daughters equally, if love could be measured in a container on a scale. But the truth was, Jilly didn't understand her younger daughter. Jilly and Felicia had such different ways of living that Jilly would have thought Felicia was adopted if she hadn't given birth to the girl herself.

Still, it was of the utmost importance to Jilly that Felicia didn't feel she was being slighted on her wedding day. On the other hand, Felicia hadn't spent a year consulting with Jilly about the wedding. She hadn't spent even an hour. She'd pretty much dumped the announcement on Jilly as if it were a barely significant matter. She hadn't given Jilly the opportunity to share the experience of planning the wedding in the same intimate and memorable mother-daughter way Lauren had.

And imagine having your sister make your wedding dress without even giving your opinion on how it should look! Imagine not caring who attended your wedding and reception afterward! Felicia hadn't arranged for flowers in the church or at home, or for music at the church, or for a photographer. Jilly could foresee Felicia saying at the last minute, "Hey, Mom, grab my cell phone and snap a shot of me and Archie on our wedding day."

Knowing that her second daughter was too busy barreling over life-threatening rapids, Jilly had taken certain matters into her own hands.

She had ordered masses of red and white roses and red and white carnations interspersed with evergreens in gigantic glass bowls to be set around the house. The church was already decorated for Christmas so she had planned no flowers for the church, but now she would take the two poinsettia plants to set in front of the altar. They would look jolly and the cat wouldn't be able to reach them. For Felicia, she'd ordered an arrangement of white baby roses attached to Jilly's mother's white leather Bible to carry down the aisle. She had boutonnieres ordered for the men, including Lawrence, and a circlet of flowers for Portia who would be carrying a small Nantucket basket of rose petals and scattering them along the aisle. She ordered a white gardenia corsage to wear on her dress because she enjoyed the scent, and if the bride was going to be loosey-goosey, she could at least treat herself to a gardenia. She had ordered a small white silk pillow for Lawrence to carry as the ring bearer. It occurred to her she needed to speak with Archie about this; she could only hope they were going to exchange rings instead of tattoos.

She'd arranged for music. When she heard that Archie was going to wear his Galloway tartan kilt, she had spent hours searching for someone who could play the bagpipes to pipe the newlyweds out into the world after the ceremony. She hadn't found anyone, which turned out to be a good thing, because when she told Felicia on the phone she was trying to find a bagpiper, Felicia had cried, "Oh dear Lord in heaven, Mother, get a grip!" So Jilly had asked three talented young women, one who had a portable piano (an electronic portable piano! How fast the world was changing!) to sing at the ceremony. Laura, Susan, and Diane had consulted with Jilly, who suggested Pachelbel's "Canon" and Beethoven's "Ode to Joy." The three women had called Archie and Felicia in Utah because they knew Lauren and Felicia and insisted it was only correct to consult with the bride. So of course everything changed. Jilly had to compromise. The three women were instructed to play Pachelbel's "Canon" before the ceremony and Aerosmith's "I Don't Want to Miss a Thing" after.

Aerosmith! And the song was from a movie named, of all things, *Armageddon*. Jilly still couldn't believe it. Her daughter was going to be married to the music of *Armageddon*.

At least she'd been able to arrange the guest list for the reception at the house. There would be the immediate family, of course, and Archie's mother, Pat. Madeleine Park, who had been the girls' favorite babysitter, would attend with her husband, Lloyd. Nicole and Sebastian Somerset, who were Jilly's and George's ages and their best friends on the island, were attending and so was Father Sloan, the Episcopal priest who would perform the ceremony and who was recently widowed. He would provide a nice male counterpoint to Pat. Finally, even though they were slightly older than Lauren and Felicia, Jilly had invited the three women musicians, Laura, Susan, and Diane, and their husbands. Since Felicia didn't want any of her old high school friends invited because Archie wasn't inviting any of his, this made a nice full house with a mixture of ages.

Jilly was having Greta and Fred White prepare platters of delicacies for the late afternoon party at their home. She'd ordered a wedding cake from Wicked Island Bakery. The cake would be carrot cake covered with white frosting. In a moment of frivolity, Jilly had told Ronna to construct the icing like a slide down the four-layered cake, as if it were going over rapids with the bride and groom seated together at the top, ready for the ride of their lives. Jilly was actually quite proud of this idea.

Usually the Gordons had Christmas Day dinner in the evening, but because of the wedding, they would be eating catch-as-catch-can for lunch and reception goodies for dinner. December 26, they would sit down to their Christmas meal, and even the newlyweds would stay for that. Today Jilly had to pick up the twenty-pound fresh free-range turkey and a few other fresh items from Annye's Whole Foods. She had already bought three pounds of chestnuts to roast over the fire after the wedding celebration, but she needed to run by the liquor store for the case of champagne she'd ordered. She'd counted on George picking this up, but now of course with his crutches he was grounded. Jilly didn't want to impose on Lauren and Porter because she knew they had a few things to get ready for Christmas for their children. Plus, Lauren had already helped so much by bringing down some casseroles for their holiday stay. Because tomorrow was Christmas when all the shops were closed, Jilly had to pick up the flowers and the cake today.

She also had to hurry over to Marine Home Center and buy a new pan to replace the one she'd ruined burning the broccoli.

What else? One thing eluded her . . . it was on the edge of her mind . . . she often wished someone would invent a kind of white board that attached to the shower wall so she could make a list while she showered, when her thoughts came more easily.

Yes! Photographer. Porter had an excellent camera with an infinite number of lenses and dials. He had volunteered to take photographs. So. Everything was under control.

Reassured by her thoughts and the peaceful moments in the shower, Jilly dressed in her favorite red corduroy dress that she took out especially for the Christmas season. She added a touch of cherry lipstick and inserted her adorable blinking light earrings.

George remained sprawled on the bed like a giant sea turtle, watching her with a pitiful expression on his face.

*Proud of your glorious wipeout, are you?* Jilly wanted to ask, but sympathy won. "How do you feel today, darling?"

George rubbed his left arm. "Terrible. I ache all over. I can scarcely move. I don't think I can even crawl out of bed."

"Maybe you'll feel better once you shower and dress," she suggested cheerfully.

"Maybe. I certainly won't be able to do it without some help."

"I'll find Porter."

"Can't you do it? I hate having a stranger see me in such a pathetic state." George cocked his head to the side and gave her his best puppy-with-a-wounded-paw look.

Downstairs one of the children screamed, a normal playing scream. Somewhere in the house a door slammed. Wind battered the bedroom window with splats of snow. Voices scattered through the downstairs.

Jilly sat down on the bed. "George, it is the day before Christmas and the day before Felicia's wedding. I have many things to do and my milk of human kindness has run dry. You have one perfectly good arm and leg, and your bruises may hurt, but you are not incapacitated by them. If you want to stay in bed all day, that's your choice. If you want me to ask Porter to help you, it's your choice. But I've got things to do."

"Well, merry Christmas to you, too," George muttered.

"Hello, everyone!" said Pat, breezing into the Gordons' bedroom. Today she wore a violet-and-blue-striped turtleneck with her green tartan golf slacks. Perhaps she was color-blind. "Sorry to disturb you like this, but Lauren told me to come on up." Pat's arms were full of packages. "George, I brought you some things."

In a twinkling, George morphed from a pitiful old patient to a strong ex-soldier, maybe even a Navy Seal, as he pushed himself up against the headboard, yanked the covers up to his chest, and ran his hands over his disheveled hair.

Jilly looked on, astonished, as Pat arranged her bony athletic rear end on the bed next to George. "Now. Jilly, you might want to take notes." She lifted several bottles out of the paper bag. "First, Epsom salt. Of course you know about it. Soak your body in a warm—not hot, warm—bath with two cups of the salt for fifteen minutes. Next, Burt's Bees Muscle Mend. Rub it on wherever you're sore. Next, I'm sure you're taking aspirin regularly for the pain and as an anti-inflammatory, right?"

"Right." George nodded. His eyes were bright and to Jilly's eyes it seemed he'd grown younger right before her eyes.

"Okay, trust me on this. Google it if you want. These are Boiron Arnica montana 30c pellets. It's a homeopathic medicine, made from mountain daisies. It helps your muscles mend, and so does this—blackstrap molasses. Pour a big helping of it into your coffee. You'll heal faster."

Jilly watched Pat with her face frozen in a look of—she hoped—interested gratitude, but what she felt was guilt.

What kind of wife was she to have so completely ne-
glected thinking of how to make her husband, her darling
husband of thirty-five years, feel better?

George was questioning Pat about each medicine. He
and Pat went into such detail they sounded like they were
prepping him for an Olympic event.

To her surprise, Pat stood up, straightened her shoulders, and announced, "Now. Jilly. How can I help you?"

Jilly was speechless.

"Do you have dinner organized for tonight? Because if
you're going to the grocery store, I could go with you. I'd
like to buy some stuff and make dinner for everyone. I'm an
excellent cook if I say so myself, and I do."

"We traditionally have clam chowder for dinner on
Christmas Eve," Jilly replied weakly.

"I can make clam chowder," Pat said. "Or you can make
it and I'll be your sous-chef. For sure I can help you carry
groceries in from the car. That's always such a pain."

"Pat, that's so nice of you."

Pat grinned and flexed a muscle. "I'm small, but I'm
mighty."

Jilly's spirits lifted. "But I don't want you to catch cold.
I have tons of sweaters. Tell me your favorite color and I'll
loan you one. Wool?"

"Wool's not my favorite. Makes me sneeze. Got any
fleece?" Over Jilly's shoulder Pat spotted an orange fleece
jacket. "There's one. Perfect."

*Perfect*, Jilly thought, looking at Pat in green, violet,

and orange. "As long as you're warm." Looking at George, she said, "Are you ready for us to help you up and into the bathroom?"

George flushed bright red, obviously embarrassed to appear feeble in front of such a vigorous woman. "No, no," he said brusquely. "You two go on. I'll be there in a minute."

As they went down the stairs, Pat said, "Your customary Christmas Eve dinner is clam chowder, you said. What if I took over and made a Cajun seafood gumbo? It's like clam chowder, but with spices and stuff in it."

*But this is New England,* Jilly thought, appalled. *This is our family tradition!* "Well . . ." she began.

As they reached the bottom of the stairs, Lawrence and Portia barreled past them, knocking the mail off the hall table, screeching, "Where's that cat? Where's that cat?"

Lauren followed, looking exasperated. "Lawrence! Portia!" She disappeared into the kitchen.

On the other hand, Jilly remembered, the children didn't like clam chowder.

Through the door into the living room, Jilly saw the Christmas tree, so oddly and rather revoltingly decorated after yesterday's accident. It was a bizarre spectacle now, but it was certainly one unlike any other, and it was one she would always remember. She and George had caused it, in a way, by bringing Rex into the household. The cat had ripped the stuffing right out of her vision of a perfect Christmas, and for a moment Jilly flashed back to the days when her daughters were young, younger than Portia and

Lawrence were now. When wrapping paper and ribbons littered the floor and the children couldn't sit still for a holiday dinner but wriggled and dropped gravy on the tablecloth and George gave her a new vacuum cleaner when she longed for a romantic piece of jewelry. Jilly smiled. Those days glowed in her thoughts. Family life was messy, Jilly realized, and no matter what Jilly had fantasized for her daughter, Felicia loved Archie. That made no-nonsense muscular Pat almost family. And frankly, it was pretty nice to have some help.

"I'd be delighted if you made your Cajun seafood gumbo," Jilly told Pat. "We'll pick up the ingredients when we go to the store."

# 20

It was almost ten o'clock before the family in the house on Chestnut Street sat down to breakfast.

George had managed to bathe and dress himself, but Jilly had to change his bandage and Porter had to help George maneuver his bad ankle and his crutches down the stairs.

Portia and Lawrence, who'd eaten cereal earlier that morning when they woke, begged not to have to eat Lauren's gourmet cheesy egg casserole; Lawrence said it looked like a snot pie. Desperate to have some adult time with her family and a nice hot cup of coffee, Lauren once again settled her children in front of the television set where they watched a movie appropriately named *Frozen*.

Surprisingly, Rex had developed an appetite for the children's game of Chase the Cat, probably because they never could catch him. This morning he trailed the children from room to room, always keeping at a distance. He settled on an armchair in the family room facing Lawrence and Portia as they faced the television. For a long time he watched them, prepared for any sudden movement on their part. Soon his golden eyes closed and he fell asleep.

Lauren and Porter, Felicia and Archie, Pat and Jilly and George sat around the kitchen table eating breakfast and planning their day.

"Archie and I have a brief meeting with Father Sloan at eleven at St. Paul's," Felicia told everyone.

"Would you like me to go with you?" asked Jilly.

Felicia pretended surprise. "Oh, like there's something you've forgotten to mention to him about the ceremony?" Her mother gave her a reproachful look. Felicia continued, "It's going to be short and sweet. Basically it will satisfy the legal stipulations of marriage and I hope it will satisfy your wish that we get married in an Episcopal church."

Jilly bridled. "You're making it sound as if I'm forcing you to do something you don't want to do."

Felicia glanced at Archie and then at her sister. Now that she'd met Pat, she would bet that Archie's mother would have come to a ceremony on the top of a mountain with an interfaith minister saying a few words. But Jilly was a traditionalist. She had been a magnificent mother and Felicia wanted to please her. Besides, Felicia and Archie were sort of omni-religious, they were Buddhist and inter-faith with a touch of Episcopalian.

"I'm sorry, Mom, I don't mean to rag on you. Archie and I wanted to have our ceremony in this church on this is-land with you and Dad and Pat and our family in attendance. We're really grateful for all you've done to make it a beautiful day. I hope we haven't overwhelmed you."

Jilly beamed. "Thank you, darling. I think I would feel a bit snowed under"—she laughed at her words—"except Pat has asked if she can ride along with me today to fetch the flowers and the groceries and the cake. Also, she's going to make a Cajun seafood gumbo tonight."

"I was planning to pick up the champagne—" George suddenly remembered. For the first time he looked down at his sprained ankle with disappointment.

"Don't worry," said Porter. "I'll pick it up for you."

"I'm going to iron our dresses for the wedding tomorrow," said Lauren. "I'll clean up the kitchen, too, while the children are quiet."

Porter leaned forward across the table and whispered to his wife, "Remember, we still have to put together the S-A-N-T-A gifts." To everyone at the table, he whispered, "They're more complicated than we foresaw, especially the miniature kitchen."

"We'll do that this afternoon," Lauren told him.

"Do you need a car to go to the church?" asked Jilly.

"Of course not," Felicia told her mother. "It's a nice winter day for a walk." She pushed back her chair. "In fact, we should hurry along."

This Christmas Eve day was colder than usual. Often in December, a few brave roses still bloomed in protected spots on Nantucket, but today all trellises, flowerpots, and window boxes were filled with geometric snow sculptures, perky accompaniments to the evergreen wreaths on the doors. Felicia and Archie wore their warmest snow gear; still they were glad to step into the warmth of St. Paul's church.

Father Sloan was waiting for them by the altar. A tall, distinguished-looking man with a head of silver hair and piercing blue eyes, he hailed them in his deep baritone voice.

"Good to see you, good to see you. Don't you have perfect weather for a Christmas wedding?"

Felicia had known Father Sloan since his hair was blond. She admired him and considered him part of her life, and really, it was very cool to have him meet her big strong handsome fiancé.

"Yes, Father, we do. Father, this is Archie Galloway."

Archie stepped forward to shake hands.

"Wonderful to meet you, wonderful to see you. Felicia, you're looking marvelous. Now, I'm sorry to say this, but I've got a meeting in a few moments. Always another meeting, always another meeting. Let's quickly go over the basics of the ceremony. I have your email about which passages from the Bible and the Book of Common Prayer you want to use. I think we should have a quick walk-through. No need for a full-scale rehearsal."

Felicia returned to the entrance of the church and waited as Father Sloan and Archie took their places in front of the altar. All at once as she stood by herself, she experienced a rush of excitement and even anxiety about what was to happen tomorrow. She knew she wanted to marry Archie, but she hadn't imagined the ceremony. As she walked slowly down the aisle toward the men, she had a silly moment of feeling as if she were in a Miss America contest clad in only her bathing suit. When it came to leading a group of novices on a hike or instructing them in how to use a raft on a river, Felicia was perfectly at ease. But the thought of walking along this red carpet beneath the high wooden rafters with twenty people watching her was daunting. Thank heavens her father would walk her down the aisle. And thank heavens he would be on crutches, because if anyone laughed she could assume they were laughing at him.

"Well done, well done," said Father Sloan. "I'm not going to read through the ceremony with you. You have all the passages marked on the email. Your mother has already talked with the musicians about where to put their porta-ble piano. You wanted an informal, low-key wedding, so I think it's going to work out just right. Any questions?" He looked at his watch and was halfway out the door as he spoke.

After the minister had rushed off, Archie whispered, "That went well, that went well."

"Shh. Let's sit down a moment before we return to the Arctic. Do we have everything under control?"

"I'm pretty sure your mother does. My question is: do

you still want to go through with this? Are you ready to be a married woman who will love, honor, and obey?"

"You know we got rid of that *obey* word."

Archie reached out and took her hand. "Okay, I was being facetious. But are you sure this is what you want to do?"

A surge of anxiety slammed inside Felicia's heart. "Of course I am, Archie. Aren't you?"

"I love you, Felicia, and I want to be with you all my life. But being here in the center of our families makes me realize there's more to marriage than discounts on tour tickets."

Felicia waited, trying not to be terrified. "Go on."

"I know there are all kinds of families." Archie cleared his throat. "And most families involve children."

Felicia almost moaned. Had her rambunctious nephew and niece put Archie off the idea of marriage? "Archie—"

"Hello? Merry Christmas! Happy holidays!" An apple-cheeked woman in a Santa Claus sweater appeared in the sanctuary with two large pitchers in her hands. "Don't mind me. I only need to top up the flowers with water. Go right ahead with what you were doing."

Felicia stood up. "We were just leaving. We've got a lot of shopping to do before tomorrow."

"Oh, I know! There's always something at the last minute, isn't there?"

Felicia and Archie zipped up their parkas, pulled on their mittens, and went out into the frigid day. It was so cold and windy they had to walk with their heads down to protect their faces. This was no way to continue their serious talk. They hurried down the street, around the corner, and into Murray's Toggery.

"Merry Christmas!" The salespeople were all dressed in red or green, with Santa hats dangling bells to their shoulders.

"I brought my list," Felicia said, thinking as she pulled her paper out of her pocket that she was more like her mother than she'd realized. "We have presents for everyone already. What else did you want to do?"

"I thought I'd better buy a down jacket for my mother."

"Good idea. I'll get her some gloves, a hat, and a scarf."

"Merry Christmas!" Last-minute shoppers rushed in out of the cold, talking to themselves about what they'd forgotten to purchase for Grandmother or Uncle Ed or their unmarried daughter's dog.

*Will we be like that?* Felicia wondered as she wandered into a different part of the store from Archie. *Will we be buying our mothers sweatshirts that say: "My grandchild is a dog"?* In spite of the cheerful Christmas music playing in the air, her heart for some odd reason went leaden.

# 21

"I think we did exceptionally well this morning," said Pat as Jilly pulled into the driveway. Sitting in the passenger seat, Pat was a comical sight in one of Jilly's coats, several sizes too large for her. It made Pat's head look too small.

Jilly's mouth twitched as she held back a laugh. "I agree. As soon as we lug all our booty into the house, we deserve a nice cup of coffee and one of the pastries the bakery gave us."

"How nice they were to give you those chocolate croissants for free," Pat said.

"It's one of the perks of living in a small town." Arching an eyebrow, Jilly added, "But don't forget, I did pay a fortune for the cake."

"I should pay for something," Pat murmured thoughtfully. "Aren't the groom's parents supposed to pay for the rehearsal dinner?"

"You're cooking it tonight. That's good enough for me. Okeydokey, here we are." Jilly switched off the engine, stepped out of the car, and opened the trunk. Leaning in, she lifted out a very large cardboard box. "Thank heavens Archie shoveled the driveway so thoroughly! The last thing I want to do is fall while carrying this masterpiece."

"I'll go ahead of you and open the door," suggested Pat.

"Great idea. Let's go through the side door right into the laundry room."

Walking with extreme care, Jilly made it up the driveway and into the house. She set the cake in its box on top of the dryer. Then she returned to the car to help Pat bring in the flowers, more groceries, and the heavy turkey. They set everything on the small table where she folded the laundry and began to remove their heavy outdoor gear.

Pat checked her watch. "It's already lunchtime."

"I've got cold cuts and cheeses. Everyone can have what they want."

"You're totally organized for this holiday," Pat said, impressed. "I wish—"

What she wished was interrupted by a scream from the family room. A moment later, Lawrence thundered into the kitchen with a red face.

"Rex ate my tuna fish! Mommy, Rex pulled my sandwich off the plate and ate the tuna fish."

"Drat that cat!" Lauren said, right before she saw Jilly and Pat enter the kitchen. "He's only an animal," she added lamely, not wanting to upset her mother by insulting her cat. "It's all right, Lawrence, I'll make you a peanut butter sandwich." With a rather frantic look in her eyes, Lauren asked Jilly, "Mom, where do you keep your peanut butter?"

"Oh, dear, we don't have any." Jilly had never seen her perfect older daughter in such confusion except during the first few days after her first child's birth. "I have a lot of cold cuts in the refrigerator for lunch today. I thought we could all make what we want. Does Lawrence like ham, roast beef, cheese, or corned beef?"

Lawrence burst into tears. "I want tuna fish!"

Archie, Felicia, Porter, and limping George came into the kitchen to observe the commotion.

"Rex ran upstairs like his tail is on fire," George said.

"Lawrence, did you pull Rex's tail?" asked Jilly.

"I had to, to get him off my sandwich," wailed Lawrence.

"Mother, I can't believe you're siding with the cat over your grandson," Lauren snapped indignantly, tears in her eyes.

"Darling, of course I'm not siding with Rex over Lawrence."

Portia came into the room with a plate in her hands. "Here, Lawrence, you can have my sandwich." Looking at the adults gathered in the room, she explained, "I like cheese sandwiches best. Lawrence likes tuna fish best."

"You already took a bite out of it," Lawrence observed sulkily.

"Want me to put it back?" Adorable little Portia made vomiting noises onto her plate.

The men laughed, the women gasped, and Lawrence giggled. "Gross." He happily snatched the plate out of his sister's hand and stomped off to the family room to watch more TV.

"I'll bring you a cheese sandwich," Lauren told her daughter.

"Thanks, Mommy," said Portia, and skipped after her brother.

"The children are always crazy at Christmas," Lauren apologized, taking bread from the wrapper.

"I remember," Jilly said. "It's almost too much for them to bear, waiting for Santa to come, wanting a certain present and not knowing whether Santa will bring it. Plus all the parties, the time off from school, not to mention the weather forcing them to stay indoors."

"I'd like to spend some time with the children," said Felicia. "Why don't Archie and I take them for a walk after lunch? We can look at the store windows and go down to the harbor and see the ice freezing around the boats."

"That would be super, Felicia." Lauren sighed. "Then Porter and I could finish the presents."

"Do you mind if I go with you?" Jilly asked. "I haven't been able to spend much time with my grandchildren this visit."

"That's great, Mom," said Lauren. "And Porter and I will stay here in case Dad needs anything."

"And I have a great idea!" Jilly said. "Why don't we invite Steven to join us?"

"Why would that be a great idea?" Archie asked.

"Well, poor fellow, he's all alone next door . . . It just seems the neighborly thing to do," Jilly explained. Then she saw her two daughters, her darling, adorable girls, giving each other *that look* and sputtering with repressed laughter. She didn't know exactly what it meant, but from years of practice, she could interpret it as their "Mom is such an idiot" expression.

"Fine. We won't ask Steven. I'm going to start making sandwiches," Jilly announced, moving to the kitchen counter. "Who wants roast beef?" She took the mustard, mayonnaise, lettuce, and tomatoes out of the refrigerator, setting the containers down sharply on the counter.

"I might take a brief nap," Pat said, "before I start preparing dinner."

Athletic Pat needed a nap? Just like that, Jilly's mood improved.

The children were not at all pleased about having to leave the family room for the cold outdoors. They fussed and whined and pouted as their parents ushered them to the bathroom and then bent to the backbreaking task of suiting the children up for the cold.

The moment they all stepped outside, Portia and Lawrence flung themselves into the snow with glee, rolling around in the high drifts like dogs in summer grass.

"Don't get snow inside your boots," Jilly advised. "We're going to walk down to the harbor to see the ice."

"Stay on the sidewalks and when you come to a street, stop," ordered Felicia. "You have to hold someone's hand to cross the street."

Because their house was right in the center of town, all the streets around them had been recently plowed and sanded, which was good for the cars but made the sidewalks into hills and valleys of mounded snow. This only added to the children's fun. The air was frigid and a breeze was blowing from the east, occasionally sprinkling their faces with snow falling from the tree limbs. Lawrence and Portia thought this was hysterically funny.

Already at two in the afternoon, the cloudy sky imparted an aspect of twilight to the village. All the street and shop lights were on, casting a golden gleam on the icy cobblestones and brick sidewalks. The small Christmas trees lining the street sparkled with light and rustled with handmade decorations made of Popsicle sticks and twine, aluminum foil and rubber bands, or pictures of children and their pets carefully laminated and hung with fuzzy colorful pipe cleaners.

"Look at this gingerbread village!" Jilly called to the children.

They ran up to the window. "Awesome!" yelled Lawrence. "Can I have a gingerbread man?"

"Me, too!" cried Portia.

"We just had lunch," Jilly reminded them. "Maybe we'll stop here on the way back home. Let's go see the boats in the ice first."

The town was busy with last-minute shoppers bustling in and out of the stores with bags and lists in their gloved hands. Friends called, "Merry Christmas!" to each other as they hurried along. Dogs waiting inside cars scratched at the windows, barking at the dogs fortunate enough to be walking with their owners down the sidewalks. Random melodies such as "Frosty the Snowman" and "Rudolph the Red-Nosed Reindeer" tinkled over the streets as shop doors opened and closed.

"Now that's a big tree!" Archie stopped in front of the thirty-foot evergreen in front of the Pacific National Bank. Every branch and needle was layered with thick white snow illuminated by the small lights wrapped around the tree. Archie hefted Portia up to ride on his shoulders.

"It looks like it's covered with Marshmallow Fluff!" Lawrence ran up, took a handful of snow, and put it in his mouth. "Nope, it's snow."

Next to the giant tree, someone had built a snowman, complete with carrot nose, black coal eyes and mouth, and a holiday red bandana around what would have been a neck if he'd had one.

"Let's build a snowwoman next to him!" Portia suggested.

"Let's wait and build one in the yard at home," Jilly told her. "We've got to keep walking."

At Mitchell's Book Corner, enticing children's Christmas books were displayed in the window: Jan Brett's *Home for Christmas*, Chris Van Allsberg's *The Polar Express*, and Dr. Seuss's *How the Grinch Stole Christmas*. Jilly was pleased to see her grandchildren gazing upon the books with the same wistful expression they had when they looked at the gingerbread.

"Can we buy a book for Grand-Auntie Pat?" Portia asked.

The adults stopped, shocked at the child's thoughtfulness.

"That's a brilliant idea!" Archie told them. "Come on, kids, let's go in and I'll show you what she likes."

Felicia's heart melted as she watched Archie shepherd the children into the store.

"Oh, look!" Jilly cried. "There's Steven! Across the street by the pharmacy. Let's go say hello. Wait, who is that man he's with? He's awfully handsome." Jilly tugged her daughter's hand.

"Mom," Felicia snorted. "That's probably his boyfriend."

Jilly gaped. "His *what?*"

"Mom. Steven's gay."

"Are you sure?" Jilly squinted to get a better look at Steven, who was talking with his friend. His *boy*friend. How had she missed this?

"I've been his best friend for years. Of course I'm sure."

"Does Lauren know?"

"Everyone knows. Except, I guess, you and Dad." Felicia

put her fingers in her mouth and wolf-whistled, catching Steven's attention. He waved and headed across the street, his handsome companion with him.

As the men cut through the crowd, working their way toward them, Jilly's mind swirled. Steven was gay? Steven was *gay*. Steven was gay, Felicia loved Archie and his world, Lauren was happy with her family, and Jilly's feet hurt. Secretly, she was looking forward to a quiet evening with a book, her husband, and a cat. How things changed. Jilly nodded to herself as she realized she had no control over her grown-up children. She hadn't had for years. What a lot of emotional energy Jilly had wasted, trying to make life fit into a gilt-edged picture frame. Life was much more like her chaotically redecorated Christmas tree that even now was probably dropping needles on the carpet.

"Jilly, Felicia, hello!" Steven stepped onto the sidewalk and quickly kissed both women's cheeks. "I'd like you to meet David Hagopian, my partner."

David smiled and nodded hello.

"Your business partner or . . ." Jilly arched an eyebrow, working for a sophisticated look.

"Both, since you ask," Steven replied. "David's going to be moving in with me in a couple of weeks."

"That's swell, Steven," Felicia said. "I'm so happy for you."

"I am, too," Jilly gushed, feeling a little bit tipsy. "My, what a lot of romance in the air this Christmas. Steven," she continued spontaneously, "why don't you and David come to Felicia's wedding?"

Steven exchanged glances with David. "We'd love to."

Felicia hugged Steven. "Oh, good. I'm so glad!"

Just then Portia and Lawrence exploded out of the store, followed by Archie. Introductions were quickly made while the children jumped up and down yelling about their purchases.

"We got Grand-Auntie Pat a picture book!" Portia announced.

"About golfers!" Lawrence added.

"Women golfers," Portia clarified.

"That's brilliant, children," Felicia said, stamping her feet and rubbing her arms to keep warm. "But I'm cold. The wind's picking up. Let's walk on down to the harbor."

Jilly and the others said goodbye to Steven and David, then hurried along over the brick sidewalks. The children skipped ahead of the adults, stopping to gaze in shop windows, and obediently waiting at the crosswalks for an adult to hold their hands. Best of the Beach had a sale, and so did the Four Winds Gifts, with red or green Nantucket sweatshirts hanging on the door. The Jewel of the Isle jewelry shop sparkled with treasures, and farther down the street, shoppers rushed in and out of Cold Noses.

"Oh, children," cried Felicia, "let's go get Rex a present!"

Jilly was pleased that her daughter had thought of buying Rex a present. Silly, she knew, but in such a short time she had come to think of Rex as part of the family. She had even crafted a little stocking with Rex's name on it made from felt she had cut out and pasted on one of George's old wool socks. She'd bought a gray furry rat filled with catnip to put inside.

She'd bought a gift for Steven, too, because she'd thought he'd be alone. It was only a tie, a nice silk tie from Murray's Toggery. She'd give it to Archie instead. Or— David had such gorgeous brown eyes—if she had time, she'd buy a red tie for him.

Everyone had fun at the animal boutique. Portia chose a play toy resembling a pink parrot wearing a tutu. Lawrence discovered a wind-up gray plastic mouse that skittered across the floor and would provide exercise for Rex—if Lawrence ever stopped playing with it himself.

When they stepped outside, they discovered the wind had become even stronger, shaking the bare branches of the trees in the Nantucket Harbor Stop & Shop parking lot and whisking small tornadoes of snow all along the long wooden wharfs. Straight Wharf was crowded with people as passengers hurried to catch the Hy-Line headed for the mainland or dragged their rolling suitcases behind them up the wharf toward the taxi stand.

"Let's go this way," suggested Archie, heading along the sidewalk of New Whale Lane between Straight Wharf and Old South Wharf.

About one hundred years ago, fishermen had built small

wooden shacks on the wharves to keep warm in while they mended their nets and traps. Now with the gentrification of Nantucket, these wooden shacks had been restored and beautified and transformed into elegant shops. In the twenty yards between the two wharves, a narrow boat basin led to the harbor. Ten or fifteen feet deep, depending on the tides, the water here was shallower than out in the harbor. Here, small boats for scallopers and fishermen could tie up. In the summer, charter fishing boats waited for customers but in the winter, especially this cold winter, many of the boats had already been taken to dry dock. Mallards and gulls floated in this protected rectangular water bowl.

"Grandma Jelly!" yelled Lawrence. "Look at the ice!"

Jilly, Felicia, Archie, and the children stood on the weathered wooden boards at the edge of the dock, peering down into the boat basin where three small, well-worn Boston Whalers, fastened by ropes to the pilings, were rapidly becoming locked in ice.

"It's like a skating rink!" said Portia.

"Not down here it isn't." Lawrence, always ready to argue with his sister, ran down the dock toward the open harbor. Here the ice was not as solidified. Instead, it floated around the boats in thick, circular floes.

Portia skipped down the dock after her brother, calling, "Let me see!"

Jilly, Felicia, and Archie ran after the little girl who was only four years old and even in her pink puffy parka seemed tiny on the narrow dock. "Don't run!" they appealed as they ran.

"These things are cool!" Lawrence lay on the dock with his head hanging down for a closer look at the miniature icebergs.

"Lawrence, get up," Jilly ordered. "These boards are covered with gull poo."

"Really?" Lawrence cackled as if this was the funniest thing he'd ever heard, but he did stand up. "I thought the white stuff was snow. Grandma Jelly, why is the ice frozen solid up by the sidewalk but there is no ice past the docks?"

Jilly hesitated. She turned to Archie. "Maybe you can answer that question better than I can."

"The ice freezes in the boat basin first because there's less movement of water. The wind stirs up the harbor water more because it's not protected by the wharves."

"Oh, look, a mommy and daddy duck!" Portia scampered back down the dock, clumsy in her pink snow boots, waving and yelling, "Hello, duckies!"

All three adults ran back after her. Archie caught her as she was trying to climb on the ladder down to the ice, and swung her up onto his shoulders.

"Sweetheart," Jilly reminded her granddaughter in a serious voice, "we asked you not to run on the dock. There's ice on the wood and it's slippery. You could easily fall in."

"Okay, Grandma Jelly," Portia sweetly agreed, clutching Archie's wool hat. "Hey, where's Lawrence?"

The three adults whipped around to stare at the end of the dock.

No little boy.

They thundered down the dock, Archie holding on to Portia's ankles as he ran.

Looking down, they spotted Lawrence sitting on a round ice floe, waving at them.

"Way awesome," called Lawrence. "I've got my own little boat."

"Oh my Lord," whispered Jilly, her hand to her chest where her heart had begun to race.

"Put me down!" begged Portia, kicking her legs against Archie's shoulders. "I want to go out on the ice, too."

Felicia knelt on the dock. She spoke slowly, attempting to keep calm as her nephew bobbed in the icy water. "How did he get there? Oh. Look. A wooden ladder." Rising, she glanced around. "I would think they would keep some kind of life preserver here somewhere. We could throw it to him and haul him back."

"Haul him back?" Jilly repeated, and then gasped as she realized what was happening. The outgoing tide was slowly, gently, almost unnoticeably, but irrevocably carrying Lawrence on his ice raft out into the surging open harbor.

Archie carefully set Portia on the dock. Sternly, he said to the little girl, "Portia, I want you to hold your grandmother's hand and don't let go." As he stood up, he said to Jilly, "Keep hold of her hand and don't let go, okay?"

Jilly nodded, understanding from Archie's expression the gravity of the matter. Lawrence was light enough to sit on the ice floe without breaking it, but he didn't have a paddle or oar to navigate with. In the few seconds she had been talking to Archie, the ice raft had moved a few more feet away from the dock toward the open harbor where the wind made the waves leap and splash.

"I can't find a life preserver anywhere," Felicia told her fiancé. "Should I run over to the Ship Chandlery?"

"No time," Archie said, stripping off his down parka.

"Hey," yelled Lawrence. "I'm getting wet." He started to stand up.

"Lawrence," Archie called, "don't stand up! You'll make the ice tip back and forth if you move. Stay still. I'm coming to you."

By now, other pedestrians, their arms full of Christmas packages, had gathered on the other dock to see what was going on.

The wind howled and blew sleet against everyone. Archie took off his heavy winter boots. On the other dock, a woman shrieked, "The little boy's going to drown!"

Alarmed at her words, Lawrence moved onto his hands and knees, huddling in the very center of the ice circle. "Archie? Can you get me?"

"Call 911!" a man on the other dock yelled.

"Call the Coast Guard!" someone else yelled.

"Where's my brother going?" Portia asked her grandmother. "Is he going to be okay?"

"Of course he is," Jilly said. Kneeling down, she wrapped her arms protectively around her granddaughter. They were both shivering with cold.

"Archie?" Lawrence called again.

"I'll be right there," Archie called to the boy, and jumped feetfirst into the water.

Here at the end of the dock, with the tide halfway out, the water was only eight or nine feet deep, yet still deep enough to completely swallow Archie. For a moment Felicia couldn't see him, and then he suddenly erupted from the water and began swimming toward Lawrence. By the time he reached the child, waves were breaking over the circle of ice, soaking the edges and also soaking his hands and feet. Lawrence started to crawl toward Archie, but Archie, treading water near the ice floe, said in a quiet but firm tone, "Don't move, Lawrence. You'll only make yourself wet. I'm going to tow you in."

Jilly looked up at Felicia. "What *is* Archie doing?" Instead of catching hold of the child, Archie seemed to be involved in some complex maneuver underneath the water.

"I have no idea," answered Felicia, her cold hands clenched anxiously.

As they watched, Archie pulled his belt out of the water and used his fist to hammer the buckle with its sharp prong into the edge of the ice.

"Sit still and hang on, kid," Archie said to Lawrence with a grin. "I'm taking you for a ride."

Holding the end of his belt in one hand, Archie lay on his side and did an awkward sidestroke back toward the pier. Because the tide was going out, it took him longer than Felicia thought it would and as they came closer she could see the first white patches of frost nip on Lawrence's cheeks. The little boy was shuddering with cold, but he was smiling broadly.

Archie drew abreast of the dock and wrapped his belt around one of the rungs of the ladder. Bobbing in the water, he managed to grip Lawrence under the arms and lift the little boy toward the dock where Felicia lay with her arms outstretched to catch him.

"Lawrence, you were going way out!" said Portia with wide eyes.

Lawrence's feet, legs, and arms were soaking wet but his torso was dry. Felicia tore off her own parka and wrapped it around him, pushing the hood up over his head. Archie grabbed the rungs of the ladder and hauled himself up onto the dry dock. He was completely dripping with ice water.

From the other dock, cheers and applause broke out. Several people took pictures with their cell phones.

"That's my son-in-law!" Jilly cried to the crowd. "Isn't he brave?"

"Mom." Felicia hugged her mother. "Settle down."

"I'm just so relieved," Jilly said, and burst into tears. "Felicia, thank goodness we have Archie in the family."

"Can you pose for me, holding the boy?" requested a

man with an expensive camera in his hand. "Hang on a minute, I have to adjust the lens."

"Clueless idiot," Archie muttered, pulling on his parka and his boots. "Come on, gang, let's hail a cab and hurry home and dry off." His teeth were chattering and his lips were blue. Felicia remembered that fifteen minutes in water below the freezing point caused death.

"Are you okay?" she asked but Archie didn't wait to answer. Lifting Lawrence from her arms, he ran down the dock toward the taxi stand on the cobblestone street with Felicia, Jilly, and Portia right behind.

Archie opened the passenger door of the first cab. "Chestnut Street."

The two women and the little girl slid into the back of the cab.

It was only a few blocks to the house on Chestnut Street, something that irritated the cab driver, but Jilly dug a twenty dollar bill out of her wallet, flung it at the man, jumped out of the cab, and sprinted to her front door to unlock it.

Portia squeezed in first and ran down the hall crying, "Mommy! Daddy! Lawrence almost drowned!"

# 22

General mayhem followed Portia's jubilant announcement. Pat, Lauren, and Porter bumped into each other as
they hurried down the hall. In the living room, George
struggled to stand on his crutches and accidentally kicked
the cat, who dashed, affronted, from the room. Jilly, Felicia, and Archie talked all at the same time in increasing
volume to be heard over Portia who jumped up and down
in time to her chant: "Lawrence almost drowned!"

Lauren clutched her son, carried him into the living
room, and plopped right down on the rug by the blazing
fire. She yanked off his wet boots, socks, and snow pants,
and began rubbing heat into his feet with her hands. Jilly
hurried up the stairs, snatched several blankets from the
cupboard, and took them down for Lauren to bundle
around Lawrence. Porter hurried into the kitchen to make
a mug of instant hot chocolate in the Keurig and brought
it to his son to drink, sloshing it on the rug and burning his
hands—but not badly—as he ran.

In the front hall, Felicia helped Archie strip off his sodden heavy outer clothing. Together they ran up the stairs and into the bathroom, where Archie removed the rest of his clothing and jumped into the shower, turning the water on full and hot.

Felicia stood by the shower curtain holding a towel. "Do you want some hot chocolate?"

"I want some brandy!"

"I'll be right back." Felicia raced down the stairs.

Everyone else was still in the living room, gathered around Lawrence and Lauren, asking questions and offering suggestions. Should the little boy go to the hospital? Did the Gordons know a doctor who would come by the house to check on him? Were his toes blue?

Lawrence's toes were pink. Jilly found a thermometer and Lawrence held it in his mouth for a full five minutes while everyone waited, scarcely breathing. His temperature was normal.

"I'm too hot!" the little boy objected.

Trembling with worry, Lauren decided, partly because his sharp elbows were digging into her side, that he was fine. "Very well, you can get off my lap, but you have to put on your pajamas and two pairs of socks and sit on the sofa with Granddad underneath this blanket until I say you can move."

Grumbling, Lawrence obeyed. He snuggled up to his grandfather. George hugged Lawrence close to him and whispered, "You had your own wipeout, I guess." They grinned at each other—two daredevils.

When Archie came down the stairs, dressed in dry clothes and looking perfectly healthy, the state of red alert dropped.

"I'm starving," Archie said.

Pat, who could hardly hold her gigantic son on her lap, nearly burst with the chance to be helpful. "I have just the thing! I'll bring you some of my Cajun seafood gumbo."

"That sounds good," said George, "but I need a drink and I'll bet Archie does, too."

And so it happened that Christmas Eve was spent with everyone gathered in the living room by the Christmas tree. Pat dished her gumbo into bowls for the others to carry in to the various invalids. She put the rest in one of Jilly's soup tureens, carried it into the living room, and set it on the coffee table. Porter took on the responsibility of giving everyone glasses of wine or milk. Jilly sliced the baguettes she'd bought that morning and handed them around so people could dip the bread into their sauce.

It was only when Felicia came in carrying a handful of napkins and paper towels that Jilly realized how this Christmas was changing the decor of her perfect living room. Slushy spots from people's boots darkened the living room rug. Her adorable granddaughter accidentally spilled the gumbo sauce, rich with tomato, onto the carpet, and a few other spots here and there implied other mishaps. The Christmas tree still looked as if it had been decorated by a committee of drunks and the presents beneath the tree were lopsided, the colorful bows limp and uneven. At least the fireplace mantel, a focal point of the room with its cheerful Christmas stockings hanging down and the old-fashioned holiday figurines parading across the top, still remained intact and festive.

As she looked around the room, she noticed the cat sitting in the living room doorway staring directly at Jilly with exasperation.

"Oh, my goodness!" Jilly cried. "I forgot to feed you." Jumping up, she hurried into the kitchen. She opened a can of cat food and dumped it into Rex's bowl.

Rex sniffed it, then looked up at Jilly with disdain. Jilly stared at Rex.

"What's wrong?"

As if he understood her question, Rex meowed and walked over to the stove where the pot still held some Cajun seafood gumbo.

"You can't eat gumbo. It's too spicy for a cat."

Rex responded by rising up on his hind legs and clawing at the stove with his front paws, as if desperate to reach the pot of seafood.

"Do you actually think I'm going to give you expensive scallops and shrimp? You have perfectly decent cat food right there."

Rex responded by jumping up on the kitchen counter next to the stove.

"No! Absolutely no cats on the kitchen counter!" Jilly picked Rex up and set him on the floor.

Rex stared at Jilly with an expression a Charles Dickens

orphan could have learned from, then spun around and slunk beneath the kitchen table, his eloquent back to Jilly.

"Oh, dear, I didn't mean to hurt your feelings!" Guilt flooded Jilly. And after all, it was Christmas Eve.

With a slotted spoon, she carefully lifted out four of the scallops, three of the shrimp, and a nice big piece of cod. She rinsed them under the faucet to remove all traces of spicy tomato sauce and to cool them. She set them on the cutting board and chopped them into tiny pieces. She spooned them onto a plate and set them on the floor next to Rex's bowl.

Rex stared at her suspiciously. Slowly, he strolled across the kitchen floor to the plate, and took a nibble of the fish. He took another bite. He began to purr as he ate, his tail slowly waving in appreciation.

Jilly smiled. Now everyone in her family was happy.

# 23

Christmas morning dawned bright and clear. Felicia opened her eyes and thought: *I'm getting married today!*

"Are you awake?" whispered Archie.

"Mmmmm," Felicia responded, crawling into his bed to be next to him.

Archie wrapped an arm around her and pulled her even closer to him, fitting his knees behind hers and pressing his feet up against her feet.

"You're all nice and warm," Felicia murmured. "How do you feel? Any aftereffects from your big adventure?"

"I feel great," said Archie. "I think Nurse Felicia's special patient care services last night provided the perfect cure."

Felicia smiled smugly. "Good to know. If you're cold on any of our travels, I know exactly how to warm you up."

"We're getting married today," Archie said. "Hard to believe, isn't it?"

His words sent a chill through Felicia. "Why is it hard to believe?"

"I guess because marriage is such a settled kind of thing. It's what old people do."

*Holy moly,* Felicia thought. *Were they going to have an argument on their wedding day?*

"We're going to grow older whether we're married or not," she reminded him sensibly.

"I know that," said Archie. He stroked her hair and her shoulder in silence; she understood that he was gathering his thoughts. "Being here this week, with your family and my mother all in the same house, has been a revelation for me."

Her stomach clenched. "In what way?"

"Well, and I don't want to piss you off, but when I first met your nephew and niece, I kind of wanted to check into a nice quiet hotel or at least pitch my own tent in the backyard."

"But we deal with children all the time on our rafting tours," Felicia reminded him. She forced herself to take deep breaths. She was afraid of what was coming.

"Yeah, but it's not the same as being with children you're related to. And when we lead our tours, we have a pretty good idea of what accidents can happen and how to deal with them. Living with children means that you've got to be prepared for *anything.*"

Felicia shuffled around so that she was lying facing Archie, with a few inches between them. She wanted to see his eyes. "As I recall, you were the one with Dad when you got stranded at Great Point. You were the one with Dad when he wiped out on a moped."

"Yeah, but he's an adult. He has to take responsibility for himself." Archie met Felicia's eyes and then did something that made her even more anxious. He sat up in bed, stuffing pillows behind his back, and stared at the opposite wall as he talked. "With kids, it's different."

Felicia sat up also, pulling the sheets up around her shoulders defensively. "Go on."

"If we get married, that sort of implies that we'll have children someday, and settle down and live in a house." Archie folded his arms over his chest. "Doesn't that frighten you?"

"Of course it does," Felicia answered honestly. "But there are all sorts of ways to live a life. I've never been as anal as my sister and I never intend to be."

"So does that mean you never want to have children?"

Felicia's heart sank. They had been putting this conversation off for a long time. Today it all had to come out in the open.

"I want to have children . . . someday." She couldn't look at him as she spoke.

"I was pretty sure I never wanted to have children," said Archie. "And if one of my children ever did something as dangerous as what Lawrence did, I think I'd die of a heart attack."

Felicia nodded. "I think you have to be brave to have children."

"Do you think you're that brave?" asked Archie.

Felicia brought her knees up to her chest and wrapped

her arms around them. "I've always assumed I was wicked brave. I've gone over Class five-point-nine rapids. I've done ice climbing and scuba diving in a cave. You've seen me, Archie, you know how capable I am."

"But having children seems to demand a completely different level of courage," Archie said. "Are you up for that?"

*Am I brave enough to be honest with this man I adore and don't want to lose?* Felicia asked herself. "Yes. I want to have children even though I don't know whether I have enough courage for the experience. Your mom told me it's a learn-as-you-go kind of thing."

Archie expelled a long sigh. "Oh, man, how did I get so lucky? I never knew I wanted children until I met Lawrence and Portia. And nothing I've done has ever made me feel as good as rescuing Lawrence yesterday."

Felicia couldn't help it. She started to cry. Archie wrapped his arm around her and pulled her against him. "I'm not saying we should have children right away. We're young, we want to travel, and we don't know where we'll want to settle eventually. But at least we both now know that someday we want to have kids."

Felicia snuggled against him, burying her nose in his hairy chest and dripping tears down his skin. "Archie, I love you so much."

"Then I think we should get married today."

"What an excellent idea!" She couldn't help it again. She kissed him all over his face.

# 24

On Christmas morning, Jilly woke up sneezing. "Can you believe it?" she asked her husband snuggled beside her in bed. "I've got a cold."

George tugged the down comforter closer around his shoulders. "Of course I can believe it. It's a stress cold. You've always had a cold at Christmas, at least when the children lived here."

"True. I had a cold when the children lived here but it always started the day *after* Christmas. Not on Christmas Day! I don't want to be sneezing at Felicia's wedding."

"No more hints necessary." George threw back the comforter, got up with the help of his crutches, and pulled on his robe. "I'll go down and start the coffee, turn up the thermostat, and make a fire. Do you want me to bring you some orange juice?"

Jilly could imagine George on crutches, coming up the stairs sloshing orange juice on each step. "No, thanks, I'll come down. It's Christmas morning. I can't believe the children are still asleep."

Jilly settled in the most comfortable armchair in the living room. George had discovered he was good with only one crutch, so he brought her a tall glass of orange juice that he set on the table next to her. Rex came in, considered the situation, and jumped up to sit on Jilly's lap like a living hot-water bottle.

It had been the tradition for the Gordon family to celebrate Christmas morning in their pajamas and robes and slippers, which was a good thing because the moment their eyes opened, Lawrence and Portia skittered down the stairs and into the living room, with their sleepy-eyed parents straggling along behind them.

When the two children entered the living room, they shrieked with such joy Rex streaked from the room.

"Look, Mommy," cried Portia. "Santa brought me a *kitchen*! It's so sweet!"

"Awesome, dude, Legos! Oh, wow, it's the Star Wars set! How did Santa know?"

The children's faces radiated genuine surprise and wonder. Lawrence was probably in his last year of believing in Santa Claus but the fact of these unexpected gifts under the tree made his eyes shine like stars. Portia was opening and closing the doors of her little kitchen cupboards, squealing with glee when she discovered pots and pans, dishes and cups, and a fake Cuisinart that turned and tinkled music when she pushed a button.

*She's so much like her mother*, thought Jilly.

The rest of the household gradually came into the living room, carrying their mugs of hot coffee. It was seven in the morning. No reason to hurry. The day was bright and sunny and if the children needed to work off some energy before the wedding, they could play in the backyard. As far as Jilly was concerned, no one was going very far from the house today until they went to the church for the wedding.

The family exchanged presents, and what a lot of presents there were. So many people and so many combinations! Even Rex, who sauntered back into the room, blasé and nonchalant, as if he hadn't just run for his life, got Christmas gifts. Lawrence lay on his belly in the hall, winding up the trick mouse and watching Rex chase it, and later Portia dangled the feathery bird from the wand for Rex to jump for. He caught it easily, wrenched it from Portia's dainty hand, and carried his prize under the sofa. Archie wrestled the cat tree into the living room and set it by the window—George was going to do it but of course couldn't because of his sprained ankle. Rex saw it, clawed it, and sprinted to the highest shelf, where he proceeded to curl up and fall asleep.

By nine o'clock they all agreed to take a break and enjoy breakfast. Lauren and Felicia, taking pity on Jilly with her cold, went into the kitchen to work together, whipping up a big batch of pancakes, frying a huge platter of bacon, and scrambling eggs with cheese.

Felicia returned to the living room. "Mom, the cat's begging for some scrambled eggs. Do you ever feed him real people food?"

Jilly rose from her chair. "I'll come feed him. I want to be sure the eggs aren't too hot and I don't want to give him too many at one time. I don't know how they'll agree with him."

"Geez, you would think that cat was a child," Felicia teased her mother.

The family gathered around the table for breakfast. The children bolted their food and ran outside to the backyard to play catch with a Velcro ball and Velcro mitts. Fortunately the ball was green; it would stand out when it landed in the snow. When the children got cold, they came back inside and the present opening resumed. Jilly brought in a large paper bag and a large plastic bag, one for recycling trash and the other for keeping bows, ribbons, and wrapping paper that wasn't too wrinkled to be used again. Lauren and Felicia exchanged amused glances.

Finally all the presents were opened. It was almost time for lunch but no one was hungry because of the huge breakfast.

Always organized, Jilly took charge: "Everyone go take showers and get ready for the wedding. We'll leave for the church at one-thirty. Pat and I will clean the kitchen from breakfast and put out some sandwiches and fruit for you to munch on if you're hungry now. Felicia, don't let Archie see you in your wedding gown and don't put it on until Pat, Lauren, and I are there to help you."

"Who's going to help me dress?" asked George.

"I'll help you of course, don't worry," Jilly told him. She had enormous amounts of patience on her daughter's wedding day.

Lauren and Porter bathed and dressed their children. They settled them on the sofa in the family room watching a video while they put on their wedding finery.

At twelve-thirty, Nicole Somerset knocked on the front door. "Merry Christmas!" she greeted Jilly, kissing her on the cheek. "I've come to fetch the poinsettias to put them in the church. Is there anything else you need me to do?"

"I don't think so, Nicole." Jilly pulled her friend into the front hall for warmth while they talked. "Archie has stacked the bottles of champagne for the reception on the back porch. We certainly don't need to use the refrigerator today. I've called the caterers and they're dropping the food off in about an hour. Archie's mother, Pat, is a whirlwind of energy and she's already tidied up the living room and dining room and vacuumed them both. I can't believe it, but I think we're good to go."

Nicole followed Jilly down the hall and through the kitchen. Jilly opened the basement door and rescued the poinsettia plants from the top step. As they were shutting the basement door, the two women noticed Rex curled up in the laundry basket.

"I think the poor guy's exhausted from all the commotion this morning," Jilly told Nicole.

"If you're lucky, he'll sleep all day," Nicole said. "Cats need lots of sleep."

After that, everything moved swiftly. Jilly helped her husband shower and dress, then gave George to the tender mercies of Porter and Archie, who were responsible for getting him to the church in time to walk Felicia down the aisle. Pat, Jilly, and Lauren clustered in Felicia's bedroom to help her dress.

"I thought you might want to wear this," said Pat. Handing a blue silk garter embroidered with tiny white roses to Felicia, she explained, "It was my mother's. She and my father were married for sixty years. Now you have something borrowed *and* something blue *and* something old."

"Thank you, Pat, this means so much to me. I'll treasure it." Tears swelled in Felicia's eyes.

"Don't you dare cry!" Lauren ordered. "You'll ruin your makeup. Besides, I want to give you something, too." She handed Felicia a small turquoise box tied with a white ribbon.

Felicia opened the box and found a thin silver bracelet from Tiffany's lying on a cushion.

"Something new, you see, and after the wedding you can tuck it away here at the house so you don't lose it when you're trekking through Outer Mongolia." Lauren had tears in her eyes.

Jilly, who had promised herself she wouldn't cry, felt

tears sting her own eyes as she watched her two daughters hug. Noticing that Pat was standing by herself, she went over and wrapped her arm around the other woman's shoulders. "I'm so glad you're here."

Porter yelled up the stairs. "We should go!"

Lauren kissed her sister's cheek. "See you at the church."

Jilly watched out the window as Porter drove George, Lauren, Archie, and the two children in George's SUV.

"The coast is clear!" Jilly exclaimed. "Let's transport you to the church, Felicia."

"Mom, you're acting like some kind of CIA operative. Archie has seen me before, you know."

"True, but he's never seen you like this." Jilly, Pat, and Felicia stared at the bride in the mirror in her long white satin gown with the bright red ribbon and the circlet of flowers in her hair. She wore more makeup than usual, meaning that she wore pink lipstick and mascara. She didn't need blush because her skin was glowing with happiness and her cheeks were flushed with anticipation.

Jilly helped to slip the red cape over Felicia, hood up for warmth. Together the four women went out to Jilly's car to drive to the church.

Once they arrived in the foyer of the church, Jilly got choked up all over again when she saw her grandchildren standing—wriggling—in wait for the ceremony. Portia wore a darling red velvet dress and a circlet of red roses in her hair and she carried a Nantucket lightship basket full of red rose petals. Lawrence was wearing gray flannels and a navy blue blazer with a rose boutonniere. He held a white satin pillow in his hands and Porter knelt next to him.

"I'm going to put these rings on the pillow now, Lawrence. The ceremony is about to begin. No messing around, you understand? This is important."

Lawrence nodded, gritting his teeth together and looking rather tortured as he tried to keep still.

From the sanctuary, came the familiar strains of Pachelbel's "Canon." Everyone invited was already there, seated and looking cheerful and expectant. *Could it happen?* Jilly wondered. *Could it really happen that this funny little ceremony could go off with some kind of elegance?*

The minister came in in his white robes with a purple stole draped around his shoulders. Porter escorted Pat down the aisle to her seat in the front pew, then took his place near the altar as Archie's best man. Lauren, a movie star in her green velvet dress, escorted Jilly to her seat next to Pat, because this was the way Felicia wanted it, and it was good for Pat not to sit alone. Lauren stood at the altar, facing the door at the back.

The music paused. A hush fell over the sanctuary. The familiar notes of "Here Comes the Bride" sounded through the church. Lawrence wobbled down the aisle, holding the pillow with both hands; he had gone white with terror at being in front of all these people. Little Portia followed, pink with pride, scattering rose petals.

Felicia entered the sanctuary, with her arm through her father's. George had given up his crutches and was using a cane for the ceremony. It lent him an amazing dignity and Jilly cried in earnest now because she cared for him so enormously. Looking at her second daughter's face, she saw the same enduring emotion radiating from Felicia's eyes as she looked at Archie waiting for her by the altar.

# 25

As Felicia walked down the aisle, her brain split into two parts, the way she'd read brains do during times of trauma. One part of her consciousness made her aware of the small party of guests standing and smiling at her. The other part had turned into a chattering monkey, babbling: *Don't trip on your long skirt! Gosh, Lauren is so beautiful! She'll always be more beautiful than you! Portia and Lawrence are so adorable; I wish I had had this videotaped. No, I don't, that would make me really nervous. If Dad leans on me much harder, we're both going to tip over onto the floor. I should have checked the mirror to see if I have anything in my teeth. No, wait, Lauren looked me over, she wouldn't have let me walk down the aisle with something in my teeth. Oh, gosh, there are Lloyd and Madeleine Park. She was my favorite babysitter of all time. Goodness, she's gotten older. How nice that Mom and Dad asked Pat to sit with them. There's Steven and David. I wonder if they'll be getting married soon. That will give Mom something to do! The Somersets have been such good friends to my par-*

*ents; I'm glad they're here.* Archie. *There's Archie. He looks so happy. Oh, wow, we're going to get married, if I don't trip on this dress before I make it to the altar.*

She had performed so many daring feats in her life. She was perfectly capable of standing in front of a group of complete strangers and telling them in no uncertain terms how to fasten on their life vests or where to sit in a raft. The group in the church was small and most of them were family and Felicia was so very happy—and still she was trembling like a sail in a gale force wind.

When she reached the altar, Archie reached out and squeezed her hand. All at once everything was unquestionably all right.

The ceremony took place without interruption, except for the moment when Lawrence looked up at his mother and whispered loudly, "When is that man going to stop talking? When can I give Archie the rings?" Of course the tiny congregation heard his words and a ripple of laughter passed through the group.

Finally, Lawrence's starring moment appeared; he held up the pillow to Archie, who removed Felicia's ring, and to Felicia, who removed the other ring. And in a golden blur, rings and vows were exchanged, and Archie was kissing her with more ardor than was probably appropriate in front of other people. It brought applause from the congregation.

To the melody of "I Don't Want to Miss a Thing" Archie and Felicia, man and wife, proceeded down the aisle to the church foyer. Everyone else followed, and Porter slipped in front of the married couple to throw open the wide church doors. On the street, waiting for the newly-weds, was a stately open black carriage trimmed with gold, pulled by two white horses wearing festive harnesses of red. When they shook their manes, the golden bells on the leather jingled.

"Oh, boy! Horses!" Lawrence was down the steps in a flash. Portia followed him and Lauren followed her and Porter followed them all, crying, "Slow down. Don't scare the horses. Remember, they don't know you."

Pat took Felicia by the hands. "At last I have a daughter." Eyes shining, Pat kissed Felicia's cheek.

Jilly helped tie the red cape around Felicia, then hugged her hard. "You are completely dazzling. We'll see you back at the house."

George shook hands with Archie, kissed Felicia on her cheek, and said, "Congratulations. Enjoy your ride. Where's Porter? I need to sit down."

The newlyweds ran down the steps under the shower of rice thrown by the Somersets and the Millses. Porter had already lifted his children up into the carriage where they sat on either side of the driver who wore a black dress coat, a red-and-white-striped muffler, and a black top hat. Archie handed Felicia up into the carriage, then stepped up himself to sit next to her, as close as he could squeeze, on seats of tufted red leather. Archie wore wool socks that came to his knees, but he was grateful for the red wool blanket that had been thoughtfully provided and tucked over both their laps.

The Gordons had consulted with the driver of the carriage to plan an extensive route along the one-way streets of the core part of town so that the rest of the wedding party would have time to get to the house on Chestnut Street to greet the newlyweds when they arrived. So the party clip-clopped merrily down Fair Street, down Main Street, along Centre Street, Broad Street, Federal Street, and back up Main. Pedestrians on the sidewalks, children on new snowshoes, and dog walkers with their pets on candy-cane-striped leashes waved and cheered at the carriage as it passed. Portia waved back enthusiastically. Lawrence was fixated on the horses, firing questions at the driver about how much they weighed, how old they were, what they ate, and where they went to the bathroom.

As they progressed slowly along the narrow streets, Felicia saw their reflections in the shop windows. They really did look like some kind of dream come true. Archie held her hand in his and often leaned to kiss her. The movement of the carriage was slow and stately, like floating on a cloud. Lauren had been wise to insist they ride in a carriage after their wedding. It made the day, to use her mother's word, *perfect*.

Archie whispered to Felicia, "When we stop traveling

to have our own children, let's bring them back here every Christmas for a ride in the horse-drawn carriage."

Tears filled Felicia's eyes. "Oh, Archie, what a brilliant idea!"

"Lawrence," Portia yelled, "they're kissing!"

# 26

The church was only a five-minute walk from the Gordons' house on Chestnut Street. Knowing that it would take Porter a few moments to help George into the car, Jilly decided to walk—run, actually, in the most dignified possible manner—to the house to be sure it was ready for the arrival of the newlyweds and the guests. Porter drove George back in Jilly's car and Lauren drove her mother's car back. Pat walked with Jilly, sprinting along in an easy glide, so the two mothers were the first to walk up the sidewalk, unlock the door, and step into the front hall.

Everything here was shipshape. The antique mirror above the hall table had been polished to a gleam. Jilly hung her coat and Pat's in the hall closet. Together they went into the living room.

And came to a dead halt.

Scattered all over the living room floor were fragments of Jilly's holiday figurines that had once paraded across the mantel. Santa's apple-cheeked head lay next to Rudolph's nose and an angel's wings framed Frosty's white belly.

Other pieces had been shattered too completely to be recognizable. They glistened on the rug like jelly beans.

"Oh my gosh, what happened here?" Pat gasped.

What had happened was obvious: "Rex."

In the middle of the debris, the orange cat lay limp, his head pillowed by a gray catnip rat, its tail extending from the darling Christmas stocking Jilly had made for him.

"When we gave Rex his presents this morning," Jilly said, figuring it all out, "we forgot to give him his stocking. It was hanging from the mantel and he must have been able to smell the catnip from the floor. It looks like he jumped up onto the mantel, walked along the edge until he could reach down and snag his stocking. Somehow he got the stocking and the rat onto the floor. He pulled the catnip rat out, and there he is."

"He looks like he's drunk," Pat observed.

"I'm sure he is." Jilly looked around the room. "People will be here any moment." She felt oddly calm.

"You do something with the cat and I'll start sweeping up the mess," Pat suggested. "Do you want me to save the pieces of figurines?"

Jilly shook her head. "At the moment, I'm too overwhelmed by everything to make one more decision." She lifted the cat, who opened one eye and snuggled against her. She carried him upstairs to her bedroom and laid him on the floor, so he wouldn't roll over, fall off the bed, and hurt himself—who knew what could happen to a drunken cat? Then she left the room, shutting the door tightly behind her.

In the living room, Pat was efficiently dealing with the mess. Jilly hurried back to the kitchen to peel the covers off the platters of gourmet munchies the caterers had brought to the house. She carried them to the dining room table, already covered with her grandmother's ivory lace tablecloth.

She heard the front door open. Lauren, Porter, and George came in.

"We'll settle you in the living room, Dad—what on earth happened here?"

Jilly took napkins out of the cupboard and set serving spoons and little forks on the dining room table. As she did, she listened to the conversation in the living room.

Pat was explaining Jilly's theory of how the wreckage came to happen.

"You'd better relieve yourself of that darned cat," snapped Lauren. "He's too much trouble."

"Get a dog," Porter said. "You can train a dog. You can't train a cat."

"I like this cat," said George stubbornly. "He's like life. You can't control the cat and you can't control life, but sometimes if you take a risk and do something new, it's worth it."

"Oh, man, Dad." Lauren sighed. "Don't start talking about your fabulous wipeout again."

Pat said calmly, "I've got most of it picked up. I need to run the vacuum quickly. Porter, perhaps you could help bring in some of the champagne and set it in the ice buckets?"

"Good idea," said Porter and went back to the kitchen.

Jilly and Porter worked efficiently, setting the champagne in the two silver ice buckets on the dining room table. Jilly set out champagne flutes and returned to the kitchen to make pink lemonade in a pretty pitcher for the children and for anyone who didn't drink alcohol. Pat made a quick pass over the living room rug with the vacuum and was returning it to the kitchen closet when the first guest knocked on the front door.

Jilly took a deep breath. She always enjoyed this special moment before a party began, when everything was in place, shining and complete. This occasion was different, she realized. This occasion marked a passage in her life. Her second daughter was now married. Jilly had made a good—and she had an intuition, a long-lasting—friend in Pat. She, Jilly, who had always been the one to help, organize, and criticize her daughters, had somehow become a woman who needed help with organizing and who had to face up to the criticism of one daughter, if not both, simply because she had acquired a cat.

She liked the cat. George liked the cat. A great rush of affection swept through her for her husband because he had championed Rex, and she realized that maybe this was a watershed moment for George, too. Not because of his daughter's wedding, but because he had done something challenging enough to cause him to wipe out.

"Mom," said Lauren, approaching her and giving her a little shake. "Why are you just standing here? People are coming in."

"I need to put the cake in the center of the table," Jilly murmured, reentering the present.

"Porter and I will do that for you. You go greet your guests."

"All right, dear." Jilly was happy to take orders as well as give them. Always before, when she gave a party, she was so busy refilling people's glasses or bringing out more hors d'oeuvres that she really didn't have a chance to enjoy herself. Today she decided to let Lauren and Porter take responsibility. Why not? They were both capable, not to mention bossy.

She walked forward to meet Nicole and Sebastian, Madeleine and Lloyd, Steven and David, Diane, Susan, and Laura and their husbands, and Father Sloan, with a smile.

## EPILOGUE

Two days after Christmas, Jilly made her last airport run, driving Pat to her plane to Boston and on to Miami. George, his wrist and ankle much recovered, came along using his cane, to see Archie's mother off. They checked her luggage, got a boarding pass, and waited in line with Pat for her flight to be called. Outside clouds gathered, sprinkling new snowflakes down.

"You promise you'll look for a spot on your calendar when you can come visit me this winter?" Pat asked. "I have a guest bedroom. My condo's on the edge of a golf course."

"I think sometime in February or March would be heavenly," Jilly told her.

"Maybe you and I can race golf carts," George told Pat with a grin.

"Don't even joke," Jilly told him.

The flight was announced. Jilly hugged Pat, surprised and pleased that they both had tears in their eyes. "We'll email often," she promised.

Pat nodded, hugged George, walked through the gentle snow to the plane, and then she was gone.

"The house is going to seem so empty," Jilly told George as they drove home.

The newlyweds had left after Christmas dinner on the twenty-sixth, promising to send iPhone pictures. Lauren and her tribe had left that morning, leaving behind several large boxes of gifts for the Gordons to send to their house in Boston. The Gordons were invited to a New Year's Eve dinner party and to a New Year's Day brunch, but until then, nothing social was on their calendar.

"Yes, it will be empty," George agreed, adding, "and thank heavens, it will be quiet."

Jilly pulled the car into the garage and helped George out. "I do have a few new books I've been longing to curl up with," she said.

"Yeah, me, too. I've got the new Jonathan Kellerman. I'm going to make a fire, pour myself a drink, and read."

"I'll read, too. Although I suppose I should think about dinner . . ."

"Don't worry about dinner. We have leftovers. A dressing sandwich and a piece of pumpkin pie with ice cream is what I plan."

"Hardly healthy," Jilly remarked as they hung up their coats.

"Hey," George said. "Every now and then we deserve to go wild."

"You know, George, that's an excellent idea."

The house was still. The rooms seemed enormous. Jilly hadn't dusted for days and bits of ribbon and wrapping paper littered the rooms. But there was always tomorrow. Today she was going to do exactly what *she* wanted.

She made herself a hot drink and set it on the end table between a sofa and the fire George was building. She kicked off her shoes, lay down on the sofa, and pulled up a Christmas quilt she'd bought at the craft fair. She put on her glasses and picked up her book.

Across from her, George settled into his favorite chair and began to read.

Small rustling noises came down the hall, stopped, and continued. A moment later, Rex jumped up on Jilly's lap, turned around three times, and curled up in a ball. He wrapped his tail around his nose and purred. His light body was warm against hers.

Outside the window, snowflakes drifted dreamily down. Jilly opened her book and picked up her drink, a fat mug of hot cocoa topped with whipped cream and a confetti-like sprinkling of crushed candy canes.